Back to You

A NOVEL

by Priscilla Glenn

ISBN: 1479103780
ISBN 13: 9781479103782

To my family, who has supported me in everything I've ever wanted, thank you.

To my test readers: Amanda Reina, Therese VonSteenburg, Daniella Leifer, Millie Morelli, Rachel Wilkins, Joanne McConnell, Kari Cieslak, Crystal Wilkins, Caryn Brogan, Grace Wilkins, Beth Poust, and Brett Sills—your feedback, advice, and encouragement have been invaluable, and I am extremely grateful for you all.

And to my husband, who cooked dinners and changed diapers whenever I would disappear with Lauren and Michael for a while, I love you. Thank you for your endless support and reassurance.

"It has been said that time heals all wounds. I do not agree. The wounds remain. In time the mind, protecting its sanity, covers them with scar tissue and the pain lessens. But it is never gone."

–Rose Kennedy

August 2011

S omething about this place made Lauren Monroe feel
nostalgic.

It didn't make sense. She'd never gone to day care as a child,
and never worked in a day care facility before, so she shouldn't have
been feeling reminiscent. But as she stood in the vestibule of Learn
and Grow Day Care, looking at the drawings of stick figures and rainbows and suns with smiley faces, she felt a faint ache in her chest,
almost like homesickness, that she couldn't explain.

Maybe it was just the wonder and innocence of being a kid again
that she was missing.

"Ms. Monroe?"

She turned to see a woman standing in the doorway of the office,
her blond hair pulled back into an efficient ponytail. Her outfit was
casual, jeans and a T-shirt with the day care's logo emblazoned across
the front, and Lauren guessed she was probably in her mid-forties

or so. But her smile made her seem almost childlike, and Lauren couldn't help but smile in return.

"Please, call me Lauren," she said, walking toward the woman as she extended her hand.

"Nice to meet you, Lauren. My name is Deborah Sayer. Come in and have a seat," she said, stepping to the side and gesturing for Lauren to enter after they had shaken hands.

The desk was all business: a desk calendar with meticulous handwriting, a computer, a phone, and a stack of manila folders a mile high. But the walls—the walls matched the woman she had just shaken hands with; they were a warm creamy blue, the backdrop for dozens of framed class photos. Image after image peppered the wall, pictures of children lined up as neatly as toddlers could be, smiling, laughing, holding hands, with a few proud teachers standing behind them. As the photos went on, the teachers changed and aged, and some came and went.

But Deborah Sayer was in every one.

"Amazing, isn't it?" she said, nodding toward the pictures as she walked behind her desk and took a seat. "It feels like I opened this place up yesterday, and yet there are kids on that wall that are in law school right now." She smiled fondly at the wall before she turned her attention back to Lauren.

"So, Lauren," she said, reaching over to the first manila folder on the pile and opening it. "You're from Bellefonte?"

"I've lived there for the past three years. I'm originally from Scranton."

"I have family in Scranton," Deborah smiled. "I was just there a few weeks ago." She looked down, eyeing the document in front of her, and from her place across the desk, Lauren could see it was her résumé. Deborah looked up, a smile lifting the corner of her mouth. "Penn State girl?"

"Through and through."

"Me too," Deborah said. "Class of eighty-seven."

"The professors there are amazing. I'm going back there now to get my master's."

Deborah nodded, the smile still playing at her lips as she looked back down at the résumé. "So, you taught kindergarten for the past three years at Unionville Primary. Tell me about your time there. What would you say your biggest accomplishments were?"

"Probably my biggest personal accomplishment was learning how to become a teacher," Lauren said with a laugh. "You take all these classes on best practices and teaching methods, but you don't really learn how to swim until you're thrown to the sharks." Deborah laughed, and Lauren added, "And as for professional accomplishments, while I was there I developed a literacy rubric that was adopted by the other kindergarten teachers in the district, and I also founded and headed a committee for increased parental involvement that was really successful."

She nodded. "I see you were heavily involved in the community. In fact," she said, looking up as she closed the folder, "from what I see here, I have to say, for only having worked there three years, you definitely left your mark on that school."

"Thank you."

"Which brings me to the million-dollar question."

"Why am I no longer working there?" Lauren said.

Deborah nodded once, a small smile on her lips.

"I know how it looks, leaving after my third year, but I can assure you I received tenure. I would have loved to stay. I left because of my master's degree."

Deborah tilted her head and Lauren continued. "I'm going for my master's in child psychology. I guess in a way I've always been drawn to that field, even when I was getting my bachelor's in primary education. But working full time as a teacher and going back to school for a master's degree," she trailed off, shaking her head.

"I always throw one hundred percent of myself into everything I do, and there was no way I could give one hundred percent to both of those things at the same time. I took some courses this summer, and the workload was…*intense,* to say the least." She exhaled a breathy laugh. "I knew I wouldn't be able to get this degree while planning lessons and grading and evaluating students and running committees and completing all the paperwork that comes with them. Not without sacrificing my sanity anyway."

Deborah laughed, a musical trill, and Lauren continued. "But I couldn't leave education, and I couldn't stand the thought of not working with children anymore. And so here I am.

"Don't get me wrong," Lauren added quickly. "I know this will be work. But it's different than a primary school. I can devote myself to my kids fully during the day, but I'll still be able to devote myself to my degree at night and on the weekends. I can give a hundred percent to both things."

Deborah looked down at the closed folder, and for a moment, the room was silent. Lauren began to wonder if perhaps she had said the wrong thing.

"You know," Deborah finally said, taking a deep breath. "When I received your résumé, I loved you on paper."

Lauren swallowed, her eyes on the woman, trying to read her. "And forgive me for saying this, because it might be unprofessional… but after meeting you, I absolutely adore you."

Lauren exhaled heavily, a relieved laugh escaping her lips. "Oh thank God," she said softly, and Deborah laughed.

"What do you say we put an end to this stuffy interview process? When can you start?"

"Really?" Lauren asked, her eyebrows in her hairline. "Just like that?"

"You're not that surprised, are you? I've already called your references. I think they wanted to put a hit out on me for stealing you."

Lauren laughed, blushing slightly, and Deborah continued. "You are so beyond qualified for this job, it's ridiculous. And I can sense your passion for kids, your passion for what you do. You'll be a perfect fit here."

"Wow, thank you so much," Lauren said. "I don't know what to say."

Deborah quirked her brow and Lauren added quickly, "No, no! I mean I know what to say. The answer is yes. Yes, I want the job."

"Wonderful," Deborah said as she pushed back her chair and stood. "Why don't you come back tomorrow? We'll walk you through some of our procedures in the morning, and then we'll just throw you to the sharks and see if you can swim," she added with a wink.

"That sounds perfect," Lauren said, standing and extending her hand. "Really Mrs. Sayer, thank you so much."

"Call me Deb," she said. "I look forward to having you on staff."

"*You got it?*" Lauren's mother squealed into the phone. "That's wonderful! Oh, honey, I'm so proud of you! When do you start?"

"Tomorrow," Lauren said, glancing in her rearview mirror before switching lanes to make the right turn onto East Bishop Street.

"Well, good luck, but you won't need it. Daddy and I will be sending you good vibes."

"Thanks Mom," Lauren laughed. "Okay, I gotta go. I'm pulling into the chiropractor's office."

"Is today your first appointment?"

"Yes," Lauren said, and she knew her mother would be able to detect the anxiety in her voice.

"You'll be fine, Laur. These doctors are trained professionals, and you said he got a good recommendation, right?"

"Yeah."

"You'll feel so much better afterward, you'll wonder why you didn't do this years ago."

"I'm sure you're right," Lauren said, cutting the engine.

"Call me later tonight, let me know how it goes, okay?"

"Alright. Love you, Mom. Talk soon."

"Love you too. Bye-bye."

Lauren ended the call and took a deep breath, tying her dark auburn hair back into a ponytail as she glanced out of the window at the office building.

She really, really didn't want to do this.

She'd had issues with her back ever since she was a teenager, but being a gymnast always came with injuries. It was never so bad that she couldn't perform or compete; it was just something she had to pay a little extra attention to every now and then. Occasionally it would spasm, but after a few days of rest and stretching, she'd be as good as new.

Lately, however, that wasn't the case. It took her longer to recover from the spasms, and it took less and less to set them off. Lauren had always been intimidated by chiropractors; the idea of letting someone move her spine around was very daunting, and up until now, she had avoided it. But she had read an article the other day about degenerative spinal disorders and how a common cause was untreated back injuries, and that was enough to scare her straight.

One of the girls in her class this summer had recommended her chiropractor, Dr. Adam Wells. She said he worked wonders and was friendly and comforting, and she promised he would put her at ease immediately.

If he can pull that off, Lauren thought, *it will be an impressive feat.*

She exited the car and walked into the office, giving the receptionist her name and her insurance card. In turn, she was given a packet of about twenty pages that she needed to fill out with her personal information.

When Lauren was just about done, one of the technicians came out to get her and led her back to the room where they'd be taking her x-rays.

"I'm going to need you to stand here, feet shoulder-width apart, arms out at your sides," the girl said monotonously, her face expressionless. Lauren did as she was told, thinking that if Dr. Wells was anything like this girl, she was going to hightail it out of there.

"Are you pregnant?" the girl asked suddenly.

Lauren's arms dropped back to her sides. "Excuse me?"

"Are you pregnant? We can't do this if you are." The girl cracked her gum, waiting for an answer.

"No, I'm not pregnant."

The girl nodded, giving her the once-over and said, "I'm going to ask one more time. It's important that you're honest. Are you pregnant?"

"And I'm going to give you the same answer I just gave you. I'm. Not. Pregnant," she said slowly, enunciating each word.

The girl snapped her gum. "Arms out," she said before she pressed a button on the machine and left the room.

After the x-rays, she came back in and brusquely informed Lauren that Dr. Wells would be with her in a minute and instructed her to go back to the waiting room.

And Lauren went back to the waiting room, grabbed her things, and headed toward the exit.

"Lauren Monroe?"

She had her hand on the doorknob, and she closed her eyes. *So close,* she thought before she righted her expression and turned to see a man standing there in dark blue scrubs. If he hadn't been wearing them, she would never have assumed he was the doctor. He looked more like a university soccer player with his tousled blond hair and beguiling grin.

"Yes," she said somewhat sheepishly.

"Dr. Wells," he said. "Were you about to stand me up?"

"No, no, I was just…" She stopped as his grin grew wider, and she dropped her shoulders in defeat. "I was about to stand you up."

He laughed. "I appreciate your honesty. Do you think you might give me a few minutes, though? If after that you still want to bail, you can have a friend call you with a fake emergency. Or excuse yourself to the bathroom and escape through the window."

Lauren tried not to smile. "It sounds like you've been stood up a lot."

"Who, me? No, that's just what I've heard happens."

Lauren laughed, and he stepped to the side, sweeping his hand toward the door behind him. "Nothing scary yet. We're just going to talk, okay?"

She nodded. "Okay," she said, taking a tentative step toward him.

He allowed her to go first, and when they entered the office, he pulled the chair out for her before he walked around his desk and sat down.

As he began flipping through the papers on the clipboard, reading her information, Lauren glanced around the office, looking at his medical certificates and awards.

"How long have you been a doctor?"

He looked up at her from under his lashes before he smiled. "There better not be a Doogie Howser comment coming." Lauren felt her cheeks turn red as he added, "I'm thirty, by the way."

"I didn't mean that to be insulting—"

"It's okay," he smiled before he turned his attention back to her packet. "I know I look young. It makes some people nervous, but I promise you, you're in good hands."

Lauren waited quietly for another minute before he closed the packet and looked up. "So, talk to me a little bit about your pain."

Lauren explained her issues, stemming back to her days as a gymnast, and he nodded and jotted notes down on her chart, sometimes asking for further clarification or stopping to explain a technical term to her. After a few minutes, he slid her packet into a file folder and pushed back from the desk.

"I'm pretty sure I know what your problem is, although I'd like to take a peek at your x-rays before we decide on a plan of action. Do you mind if we move to the exam table? I'm not going to adjust you; I just want to check your mobility."

Lauren was surprised to find she wasn't at all nervous to move to the table. Her friend had been right; something about him was very soothing, very reassuring.

Lauren laid on the table, and he moved her legs and arms into various positions, describing all the while what he was doing and why. In the midst of him testing her flexibility, the x-ray tech from earlier brought her film into his office with a grunt and promptly left.

Dr. Wells glanced down at Lauren. "She's here to scare off the scam artists who want to fake an injury to get out of work."

Lauren laughed as he reached out his hand, clasping hers and pulling her to a seated position on the table.

"You doing okay?" he asked, and she nodded. "Great. Let's take a look at these x-rays and figure out what we're going to do with you."

He turned toward the lighted board, but before he slid her x-ray onto it, he turned. "Do you need to take a call from your friend? Or perhaps use the bathroom?"

Lauren smiled. "No, I'm not going anywhere."

He grinned his college-boy grin before he turned and slid her film onto the board. "Yep," he said. "Right here." He ran his finger along the image of her spine. "See the curve of your lower back? Or lack thereof?" He turned and grabbed another film and put it up next to hers. "This is a typical healthy spine," he said. "See how your curve is less pronounced?"

"Yes. Why is it like that?" Lauren asked, leaning closer to the board to get a better look.

"The bones of the lumbar vertebrae, or the lower back, are more susceptible to injury in a developing adolescent. Now, take a strenuous sport or activity, like gymnastics. That puts a strain on the ligaments and muscles surrounding the spine. Since connective tissues don't grow at the same rate that bones do, the pressure placed on the ligaments and muscles ends up putting undue stress on the spine."

Lauren chewed her lower lip, glancing up at him, and he smiled.

"You're in great shape, and this is an easy fix. We just have to retrain your spine to sit the way your body needs it to, and then strengthen the muscles surrounding it to hold it in its proper place. That's what's happening when your back spasms, by the way. It's your body's way of trying to protect itself. Once we fix the problem, your muscles won't have to work so hard to rectify the problem."

"Okay," Lauren nodded. "That makes sense."

"And I'm thinking I'd also like to put you on a decompression machine."

Her eyes widened, and he held up his hand. "That's not as scary as it sounds. It's just a machine that stretches your back, focusing on designated areas of the spine. It increases the space between the vertebrae so nutrients and fluids can be absorbed into the discs more efficiently. Quickens the healing process."

Lauren tilted her head at him and smiled.

"What?" he asked.

"Nothing, I'm just…I'm impressed."

"What, that I know what I'm talking about? Were you still convinced I was some frat guy playing doctor?"

"No," Lauren said through her laughter. "I didn't mean it like that. I just didn't expect to be okay with any of this. But the way you describe things, I don't know. I'm not as freaked out as I thought I would be."

He smiled. "I'm glad you said that, because—if you're comfortable—I'd like to adjust you today. But only if you're comfortable."

Lauren inhaled a slow, deep breath before she blew it out in a rush. "Okay, let's do it."

"You sure?"

She nodded. "I think I trust you."

"Well then, I think I'm honored," he said with a laugh, motioning for her to lie back down on the table. He positioned her on her side and placed one hand on her shoulder and the other on her hip. "Deep breath in for me, okay?" Lauren inhaled. "And blow it out." As soon as she started to exhale, he applied quick pressure with his hands, and it sounded like someone had just stepped on bubble wrap.

She froze and he smiled down at her. "How was that?"

"Not bad." She wiggled a little bit. "Wow, that *does* feel different."

"Like magic, right? Shift onto your back, please."

She did as he asked, and he came to the head of the table, standing behind her. He slid his hands behind her ears, placing them on the sides of her neck.

She tensed instantly.

"Were you freaked out the first time you did this to someone?" she asked, just to be filling the silence so she didn't jump off the table.

"Um, yeah, I was. But that was only because I ended up killing the guy."

Lauren blinked up at him, and that roguish grin appeared. "Very funny," she deadpanned.

"Ready?"

Lauren closed her eyes and nodded, and just like the first time, with a quick flick of his wrists, it was over. She sat up slowly, rolling her neck.

"Feel good?"

She looked over at him. "You're so smug."

He tossed his head back and laughed, and Lauren smiled. "Thank you, Dr. Wells," she said.

"That's what I'm here for. And please, call me Adam." He helped her off the table and then opened the door. "Schedule your next few appointments with my receptionist and we'll get you started on your rehabilitation. I'd like to see you at least two times a week, if your schedule allows it."

And as Lauren shook his hand, she thought, *I'd like to see you at least two times a week too.*

The next morning, Lauren arrived at work an hour before her shift started so she could get herself acclimated to the new structure of Learn and Grow's program.

Deb walked her through the paperwork she'd be exposed to: registration forms, incident reports, and memos, before she introduced Lauren to Delia and Janet, the two women she'd be working with in the pre-K room. Delia was a Hispanic girl a few years older than Lauren with a head full of long dark curls and beautiful caramel-colored eyes. Janet was a special educator, slightly overweight with graying hair and the most inviting demeanor Lauren had ever encountered. She warmed to both of them instantly.

Delia showed Lauren the three different rooms—the infant room for children under the age of one, the tot room for the one and two-year-olds, and then Lauren's room, the pre-K room, for the three and four-year-olds.

Then both Delia and Janet sat with her, and they explained what a typical day in the pre-K room looked like.

"Do you have any questions?" Janet asked when they were done.

"No, not right now," Lauren said, "but I'm sure I will as the day progresses."

"That's what we're here for," said Delia as she patted her on the back. "You'll be great."

"Are you done hazing her yet?" Deb said from the doorway.

"We decided not to haze her, although the kids might not be as kind," Janet said with a wink in Lauren's direction.

Deb laughed. "I just need to borrow Lauren for a minute before the kids get here."

"We're all set," Delia said, walking over to the wall of books to choose a story for the morning reading circle.

"Great. Come with me," Deb said to Lauren. "I'm gonna walk you through the registration process. You picked a great day to start; we're registering three new kids today."

Lauren followed Deb behind the front desk and watched as she opened a file drawer. "These are all our registration forms, divided alphabetically by room. These forms are filled out and mailed in with tuition prior to the students coming here, but on their first day, what we do is take out the forms and go over them with the parents to ensure that none of the information has changed. And then, you have a brief sit-down with them to answer any last-minute questions. Parents of first-timers can be a little nervous." Deb made a face and Lauren laughed, remembering how anxious some of her kindergarten parents used to be.

"The most important thing is to make the child feel comfortable, because then the parent will feel comfortable."

"Right," Lauren said with a nod.

"In fact," Deb said, glancing up with a smile as the front door opened. "Here's our first one. Why don't you stay here and watch me do the first one, and then if you're comfortable, you can try the second?"

"Sounds good," Lauren said, smiling over at the young mother who was walking in with the most adorable little boy.

The first half hour was organized chaos, but it couldn't have run more smoothly. Lauren watched Deb go through the registration process with Micah, the two-year-old boy who looked like he walked straight out of a commercial, and then hurried back to the pre-K room as the other students began arriving. They were fascinated with her, as children usually are with new people, and spent the first part of the morning asking her questions and fighting over sitting next to her.

Lauren took to them with ease, and by the end of that first hour, she, Delia, and Janet had fallen into a routine that made it look as if they'd been working together for years.

"Hey, Lauren?"

She looked up to see Deb popping her head in the door of their classroom. "Our second registration is here. You want to give it a shot?"

"Sure," she said, looking over at Delia, who nodded and absorbed the two kids Lauren was working with.

"This one's coming to your room. Call me over if you need anything," Deb said before walking back into her office.

Lauren walked behind the desk to see a man with his back to her, holding a little girl and pointing to some of the drawings on the bulletin board.

"Hi," Lauren said sweetly. "Welcome to Learn and Grow."

He turned then, and Lauren felt her smile drop. For a second, her vision got sort of fuzzy, and she reached down and placed her hands on the desk to steady herself.

There was no way it could be him.

But even as her mind chanted that mantra, she knew that it was. She hadn't seen him in eight years, but his face was still the same.

In that instant, something in his eyes changed, and she realized he recognized her too.

She was too stunned to say the things she knew she was supposed to be saying, the things Deb had taught her that morning.

She was too stunned to even breathe.

And so she stood there, completely frozen and numb with shock, unable to feel what she expected herself to feel if she ever saw him again: confusion, disbelief, longing.

But most of all, anger.

November 2000

*L*auren held her notebook tightly to her chest as she darted through the hallway, weaving in and out of the bodies that still lingered there, seemingly unfazed by the bell that had just signaled the one-minute warning.

"Why the hell are you walking so fast?" Jenn asked, slightly winded as she scurried to keep up with her friend. "That was just the warning bell."

Lauren ignored her, glancing at the doors of the classrooms they were passing. It was the first day of the second quarter, which also meant the first day of new specialty classes. Basic Health was in room 228, and they had only just passed room 210; they were never going to make it in under a minute.

With that realization she broke into a jog, muttering her apologies as she squeezed in between and around other students.

"Lauren!" Jenn whined. "Slow down!" She caught up with her friend and grabbed the back of her shirt, but her pace was unbreakable, and Jenn ended up being towed behind her. "Everyone knows that teachers give freshmen a break for being late," she said, her voice choppy as she struggled to keep up. "Especially on the first day of new classes."

As they circumvented a group of students and came up on room 228, Lauren stopped abruptly, causing an oblivious Jenn to collide into her from behind. She flew forward, catapulted by the force, and crashed directly into the teacher who stood waiting outside the door.

"Oh God, sorry. I'm so sorry," Lauren said, taking a step backward and discreetly elbowing Jenn.

The man regained his balance just as the bell sounded overhead, and he smiled. "Your timing is impeccable. Your method of arrival, however, could use a little work. Go on in and have a seat, ladies."

"See," Lauren said over her shoulder as they walked into the room, "we wouldn't have made it if we didn't run."

Jenn rolled her eyes as she gestured toward the four students seated there. "And thank God! It would have been *so* humiliating if we walked in after the bell with the rest of the entire class."

Lauren smirked as she put her notebook down on a desk. "Well look on the bright side; now we get first choice in seating."

"Wonderful," Jenn deadpanned, placing her books down on the desk next to Lauren's. "So, will you come with me later?"

"Where?"

"To the drugstore."

"I guess," Lauren said. "Why do you need me to come?"

"I want to hold boxes of hair dye up to your head."

Lauren turned, looking blankly at her friend. "Are you serious?"

"That's the only way to guarantee it comes out just like yours," Jenn said, going through her purse and pulling out ChapStick.

"Nothing ever comes out looking like the box. You're better off just picking a color you like."

"But I like *your* color," she said as she applied the ChapStick. "So pretty but like, sexy at the same time, you know? It's like...deep auburn. Rich mahogany. Or...mmm, dark chocolate cherry."

Lauren shook her head as she looked through her bag for a pen. "You sound like you're auditioning for a commercial."

Jenn laughed as she capped her ChapStick and tossed it back into her purse. "Just come with me. It will take ten minutes, tops."

"Fine," Lauren sighed as she opened her notebook to the first clean page and wrote the date. "You're a total weirdo, you know that, right?"

"And you're my best friend, so what does that say about *you?*"

Lauren smiled. "Good point."

"I can't wait," Jenn squealed, clapping her hands quickly in front of her. "I am *so* ready to get rid of this mousy brown mop. You're so lucky it grows out of your head that way..."

As Jenn expounded on the wonders of changing her hair color, Lauren watched as the rest of the class filed into the room. The seating arrangement was set up in a large *U*, with the teacher's desk and the blackboard set in the opening at the top. She had heard through the grapevine that Mr. Mavis was notorious for making his students debate controversial issues, which she could only assume was the reason behind a seating plan that allowed chatty high school students to face one another during class.

As her eyes scanned the students seating themselves on the other side of the room, Lauren immediately recognized Keith Wagner in the back corner and sighed. She'd had a few classes with him in middle school, and every one was torture; he would spend the entire class period obnoxiously trying to outsmart the teacher, arguing every point, questioning every statement.

He was going to make this class unbearable.

The sound of a chair scraping the floor caught her attention, and she turned her eyes to the boy taking a seat at the desk directly across the room from hers. She didn't recognize him, but there were a lot of students she didn't recognize in this class. It wasn't uncommon for specialty classes to integrate different grade levels. In fact, as she took stock of the room once more, it seemed she, Jenn, Keith, and two others were the only freshmen in the class.

"Ladies and gentleman, your attention, please," Mr. Mavis said as he sat on top of his desk facing the room. "This is Basic Health, room 228, and I am Mr. Mavis. Please make sure you are in the right place before I pass around the sign-in sheet."

As the room rumbled with the slight murmur of students checking their schedules, Lauren's attention went back to the boy sitting across from her; his eyes were downcast, watching his fingers twirl a pen in dexterous, complicated patterns.

Mr. Mavis put the sign-in sheet down on Lauren's desk, and she wrote her name neatly on the top before passing it to Jenn, who nudged her and then gestured with her head in Keith Wagner's direction before rolling her eyes. Lauren nodded and rolled her eyes in agreement, and as Jenn looked down at the sign-in sheet, Lauren looked back to the boy across the room. She had no idea what it was about him that kept grabbing her attention; nothing in particular made him stand out. Broad-shouldered, dark-haired, and wearing some sort of nondescript gray T-shirt and a baseball hat turned backward, he looked just like any other boy.

He stared at the pen weaving in and out of his fingers, completely expressionless, and Lauren watched the movement of his hand for a moment before she raised her eyes back to his face. And in that instant, she suddenly realized what was so intriguing about him.

He wasn't expressionless at all.

His face was placid, almost indifferent, but there was something just behind his eyes that betrayed that cool composure. She was suddenly reminded of a class trip she'd taken in fifth grade; her teacher had brought them to a pond that was completely serene, as smooth and still as a sheet of glass, but when they inserted a tiny camera just beneath the surface, it revealed this unrestrained, tumultuous world of fish and plants and organisms whirling and crashing and spinning out of control, totally hidden beneath the deceptively unruffled exterior.

It was fascinating.

And there he sat, looking outwardly composed, and all she could think of was that pond. Because something about him, something in his eyes, divulged the secret; there was a whole world in there somewhere, thriving just below the surface where no one could see it.

"Alright everyone, good afternoon," Mr. Mavis finally said once the sign-in sheet was circulating. "As I said before, this is Basic Health, and in the next ten weeks we will be discussing both the positive and negative external influences that can affect the human body, from exercise to nutrition, from diseases to drugs and alcohol, to sexual intercourse and everything in between. This class is heavily rooted in discussion, but you will also be asked to take notes, so if you do not already have a notebook designated for this class, please get one by the end of the week."

At that moment, the boy with the backward hat lifted his gaze, making eye contact with Lauren, and her stomach lurched as she ripped her eyes from his. She could feel the heat blooming on her cheeks, and she hoped he wasn't still looking at her; getting caught staring was bad enough without her blush giving a voice to her humiliation.

As Mr. Mavis continued with his class overview, Lauren picked up her pen and began doodling on the page in front of her, determined not to look up at him again. She chewed on her lower lip, slowly etching the outline of a flower in the upper right-hand corner of the page, and after a minute she finally felt the warmth begin to leave her cheeks.

"Our first unit will be the alcohol unit, and later this week a few representatives from the SADD organization will be coming to give us a presentation on the dangers of driving while intoxicated."

"Mr. Mavis?"

Lauren closed her eyes and exhaled a breathy laugh. Keith Wagner. That didn't take long at all.

"Yes?"

"Do we have to do this every year? I mean, we've been getting drilled on the dangers of alcohol since middle school."

"While I appreciate the fact that your past educational experiences have resonated with you, I assure you that the information and stories you'll hear in this class are not only new, but relevant," Mr. Mavis responded. "Especially considering the fact that many of you are now of the age to be driving."

"Yes, but still," Keith went on, and Lauren occupied herself by imagining what Keith's face would look like if a teacher finally told him to shut the hell up for once. "We get it. We all know a person would have to be a complete idiot to get behind the wheel of a car while drunk. I don't think any of us are that stupid."

The sudden sound of a chair screeching against the floor followed by a deafening bang caused Lauren to jump nearly out of her seat, and she lifted her eyes quickly, immediately freezing as she took in the scene.

The boy with the backward hat was standing, and the desk in front of Keith was gone, overturned somewhere on the other side of the room.

Keith sat completely immobilized, gripping the sides of his chair as he stared up at the boy, looking terrified and utterly exposed. The boy with the hat loomed above him, his jaw clenched and his eyes murderous.

What had she missed?

She was vaguely aware that Mr. Mavis was saying something to the boy with the hat, but she couldn't make it out. Everything outside of the scene she was witnessing became fuzzy background noise; she was completely frozen, her eyes pinned on the boy, watching the way he trembled with his fists clenched at his sides. She couldn't be sure if it was a sign of restraint or impending explosion.

Mr. Mavis flew to the phone mounted on the wall by the door, and Lauren thought she heard him asking for Mr. Banks, although she knew that couldn't be right. Mr. Banks was the guidance counselor; it was Mr. DeCarlo, the assistant principal, who handled discipline. She remembered that from orientation.

Before she could even make sense of what was happening, the boy with the hat whirled around suddenly, and Lauren flinched as he stormed past her toward the door. In one fell swoop, he yanked it open and charged out, slamming it closed behind him so forcefully that she thought the glass would rattle out of its pane and crash to the floor.

And then the room was silent.

For a long moment no one moved, and Lauren exhaled a shaky breath as her shoulders slowly dropped away from her ears.

She looked across the room at Keith, who was trying to play it off like he was unfazed, but the faint traces of panic remained etched on his face. Out of the corner of her eye, she saw Mr. Mavis hurry over to his desk and frantically scribble something on a sheet of paper.

He stood quickly, folding it as he walked over to Lauren's desk, the closest one to the door. "Please take this to Mr. Banks' office immediately," he murmured as he placed the note in her hand, and Lauren nodded as she pushed her chair back and exited the room of students still stunned into silence.

She walked swiftly through the hall, her heart still pounding with leftover adrenalin, but when she glanced down at the paper in her hand, her pace instantly slowed. She licked her lips nervously as her eyes darted around the empty hallway, and then she looked back down at the note.

It would be wrong to do it. She knew that.

She pressed her lips together as she glanced around one more time, and then before she could talk herself out of it, she cut to the left and darted into the stairwell.

Lauren took a deep breath, internally scolding herself as she unfolded the note with shaking hands.

Michael Delaney was just triggered. He left class and is somewhere in the building.

"Triggered?" Lauren whispered, her brow pulled together.

She folded the note quickly, exiting the stairwell and continuing down the hall to Mr. Banks' office. His secretary smiled up at her sweetly as she approached.

"Can I help you?"

"Yes, this is a note from Mr. Mavis. It's urgent."

"Thank you. Mr. Banks is in a meeting right now, but I'll see that he gets it immediately," she said, taking the note and smiling up at her again.

"Oh, okay. Thanks," Lauren said uneasily, and she took two steps backward before she turned and exited the office.

So his name was Michael Delaney. She'd never heard of him before. What had she missed back there? She was hoping Jenn had been paying enough attention to figure out what had set him off like that.

For some reason, she felt like she needed to know.

As she turned the corner and started back down the hallway toward her class, Lauren's eyes landed on the glass doors at the end of the corridor that led out to the parking lot.

She could see someone out there, perched on the trunk of a car, and before her eyes could confirm it, her mind already knew who it was.

Lauren slowed, cautiously observing him as she neared the classroom. He was completely still, statuesque even, a far cry from what she had just witnessed moments ago. When she finally reached room 228, despite her better judgment, she continued on down the hall, slowly approaching the doors at the end of the corridor the way someone might approach an injured animal.

He was sitting on the trunk of a car, his feet propped up on the bumper and his hat dangling lifelessly from his fingers as he rested his elbows on his knees. His head was bowed so that all she could see was his hair, full and dark and slightly mussed from the hat.

Lauren watched him, the oddest feeling settling in her chest as he reached up and dragged his hand down his face before dropping his head back. His shoulders rose dramatically as he took a slow, deep breath, blinking up at the sky.

And for some unfathomable reason, in that moment, she felt like she should do something.

But what could she do? Go out there? That seemed like an incredibly foolish thing to do. He didn't even know her. And besides, if she did go out there, what would she even say?

Mr. Mavis had said he'd been triggered, but what did that mean? That he was dangerous? He'd certainly looked it back in the classroom; in fact, dangerous was an understatement.

But right now? Right now, he just looked broken.

He brought his head back down and closed his eyes, and as soon as he opened them, they fell on Lauren watching him through the doors.

She gasped audibly as she whirled around; any fear she should have felt at that moment was completely overshadowed by the embarrassment at being caught staring at him for the second time. She darted back to the Health room without looking back, but she didn't need to; she could still feel his eyes on her.

He never came back to class that day.

By the following period, it seemed everyone had heard about what happened. The story spread with alarming speed, along with a slew of other rumors about Michael Delaney.

Everyone seemed to know him as Del. He was a sophomore, one year older than her. He'd been suspended in his middle school more times than anyone could keep track of. The only reason he hadn't been expelled was because he was smart enough to manage good grades, despite the classes he missed due to detentions and suspensions. He didn't have a father. His mother hated him. His brother was dead.

And then came the ridiculous ones: *"I heard he pulled a knife on a teacher once." "I heard he's been in prison." "I heard he murdered his brother."*

Lauren had no idea what was fact or fiction, what was true and what was exaggerated or embellished, but by the end of that day, she was pretty sure she had come to two accurate conclusions: Michael Delaney had a very troubled life, and the general population was smart enough to stay away from him.

When Lauren walked into school the next day, she wasn't surprised to hear students still talking about Keith Wagner's near-death experience in Health class. She had expected that.

But what she didn't expect was to see Michael.

Lauren had thought for sure he would have been suspended for the outburst, and that Health that afternoon would be relatively uneventful.

But when she emerged from the stairwell that morning on her way to English class, she stopped in her tracks. There he was, leaning against the wall in front of the cafeteria, talking with two other boys.

She stood there for a second, expecting to feel fear surge through her body after everything she'd heard and witnessed the day before, but even as the thought crossed her mind, his lips parted as he laughed at something one of the other boys had said.

There was nothing frightening about him in that moment: the lighthearted laugh, his casual stance against the wall as he bounced a small blue rubber ball mindlessly on the floor, flicking his wrist and catching it effortlessly without ever removing his attention from the conversation.

Lauren stepped to the side, safely shielded by the mass of students in the hallway, and studied him, trying to see what she knew she was supposed to be seeing.

Trying to make the danger appear.

But for some reason, all she could conjure up was the image of him totally vulnerable on the trunk of the car the day before.

And when he laughed again, this time the hearty sound of it carried down the hall to her, and suddenly Lauren felt like the people who spewed those rumors yesterday must have accidentally confused him with someone else.

She had to find out.

Without even fully deciding to do it, she squatted down on the side of the hallway and pulled her Health notebook out of her backpack before tearing out the two pages of notes she'd taken the day before. She looked them over briefly before closing the notebook and shoving it back into her bag, tossing it over her shoulder as she stood.

And then Lauren walked toward the three boys standing outside the cafeteria.

As she closed the distance between them, there was a split-second when her resolve wavered and she thought about turning around, but then Michael looked at her, having noticed her approaching, and she knew she had to follow through.

"Hey," she said softly when she reached them, and the other two boys turned to look at her, saying nothing.

She glanced at the others before looking back at him, and she almost lost her nerve. His eyes were the darkest brown she'd ever seen, almost black, and his lips were full and pink, the kind of lips women would kill for. His face, like everything she knew about him, was purely contradictory. That cherubic mouth with those penetrating eyes: he was too lovely to be menacing, but too intense to be innocent.

The three boys stared at her, waiting.

She held out the pieces of loose-leaf she'd torn from her notebook. "These are the notes you missed yesterday."

Michael glanced down at them, unmoving.

"In Health," she clarified after a few seconds had passed.

He lifted his eyes back to hers, and out of the corner of her eye, she saw one of the boys nudge the other and nod in her direction, followed by muffled laughter; she lifted her chin slightly, her eyes still on Michael and her hand extended, offering him the papers.

Finally, he reached forward, taking them from her and glancing down at them.

"Thanks," he said absently, and then he shifted his body so he turned away from her to face his friends again.

And she knew the conversation was over.

Lauren stood there for a second before she turned and walked away, and she heard that same muffled laughter again. She had no idea if his friend was laughing at her or not, but it didn't matter. She realized she wasn't feeling embarrassed, or surprised, or disappointed by the turn of events, because she had gone into the situation without any expectations.

It was an experiment. She was just testing the outcome, not anticipating one.

While he had been civilized, he certainly hadn't been friendly. And that was fine. Now at least she had her own opinions of him, based on her own experiences, not some crazy rumors. He wasn't a monster per se. He just wasn't very nice.

At least she had made the effort.

She walked through the door of her English class, her head held high, feeling proud of herself.

In Health that afternoon, Lauren kept her eyes dutifully on Mr. Mavis or on her notebook, never allowing them to cross the room to him, although he remained in the periphery of both her vision and her mind for most of the period.

"Miss Monroe?"

Lauren glanced up from her mindless doodling, startled out of her musings.

"Can you name a common mistake most people make when attempting to sober up a friend?"

She sat up a little straighter, running her hand through her hair. "Um, well, you're not supposed to have an intoxicated person try to walk it off."

"Not true," a male voice interrupted, and she looked over to see one of the juniors in the class shaking his head. "The worst thing you can do is let a drunk person lie down. It allows their vital systems to slow down, which increases their chances of getting alcohol poisoning."

Lauren opened her mouth to respond just as another male voice said, "Actually, she was right."

Her eyes flitted across the room to where the voice came from. Michael was looking down, watching his fingers twirling his pen as he spoke. "Physical activity can't make your body metabolize alcohol any faster. Your liver works at the same pace, no matter what you're doing. And the last thing a drunk person should be doing is walking around. Or doing anything physical, for that matter. A drunk person will have impaired balance, impaired reflexes, and a wasted person won't have any. The chances of them hurting themselves are too great of a risk."

He lifted his eyes then, looking at the boy who had spoken, charging him with his stare. "So maybe you should check your facts before you try to make someone else look stupid. That way you won't end up looking like a moron yourself."

There were a few stifled gasps and giggles before Mr. Mavis chimed in. "Okay, Mr. Delaney, that's enough. But yes, you and Miss Monroe are right, an intoxicated person should never be asked to engage in any type of physical activity, even walking..."

As Mr. Mavis continued with his explanation, Lauren looked across the room at Michael. He was watching her, and when she made eye contact with him, he didn't turn away. Instead, the corner of his mouth lifted in the faintest hint of a smile before he straightened his expression and dropped his eyes, watching the pen weave between his fingers again.

Later that afternoon, when Lauren opened her locker to put her books away, two pieces of paper sailed out and fluttered to the ground. She recognized her own handwriting and realized they were the Health notes she had given Michael, but when she bent to pick them up, she saw something scrawled on the back in a jagged print that was unfamiliar to her.

She turned the paper over.

Hey Red—thanks for the notes. Del

And though she pressed her lips together, she couldn't suppress her smile.

August 2011

*L*auren left that day before he came back to pick up his daughter, so she didn't have to see him again.

But she was still reeling.

She hid it well, falling right back into the children, putting all of her energy into them. It was easy to get lost in a room full of eleven preschoolers.

But now that she was in the car on her way back home, all she had were her thoughts and the silence, and she didn't know what to do with either.

Lauren leaned over and grabbed her cell phone, holding down the speed dial for Jenn. Although Jenn was still back in Scranton, they made it a point to meet for dinner once a month ever since Lauren had moved to Bellefonte, and their record was nearly flawless. And while she'd be seeing Jenn that weekend for their monthly dinner, she knew there was no way she'd be able to wait that long.

"You better not be cancelling on me," Jenn said as her greeting.

Lauren smiled weakly. "I'm not. I just need to talk."

"You okay?" Jenn asked.

"I don't know yet."

"You're freaking me out here, Laur. What's going on?"

Lauren took a breath before she said, "I saw Michael today."

"Michael?"

"Del," she clarified.

"*What!*" Jenn shrieked. "Is this a joke?"

"No."

"Holy shit," she said. "Hold on." Lauren could hear the sounds of shuffling before the sound of a door closing, which meant she had just shut the door to her office. When she did that, she meant business. "What did you say?"

"I didn't say anything. I froze."

"Are you kidding me?" Jenn said, her voice equal parts disbelief and disappointment. "You didn't let him have it? We rehearsed what you would say! You used to dream about it!"

"Yes, we rehearsed what I would say—when we were *eighteen*. You realize that was eight years ago, right?"

"Eight years, eight days, it doesn't matter. He still deserves a piece of your mind."

"I was at work, Jenn!"

"So you didn't speak to him *at all?*"

"No, I did. But it was just really awkward."

"I still can't even wrap my head around this. Michael Delaney," Jenn said, her voice incredulous. "What exactly did you say?"

"Just stupid formalities. 'It's good to see you.' 'How've you been?' And then he registered his daughter and he left."

"What a jerk," Jenn said, her voice now full of disgust. "I can't believe you even talked to him. I can't believe you didn't spit in his face."

"Yeah, it would have been a great move on my part to spit in the face of a parent on my first day," Lauren said. "Besides, all that stuff was a long time ago. I'm an adult now. He's an adult. *With a child*, no less."

"Lauren," Jenn said in a warning tone.

"What?"

"Are you really going to sit there and make excuses for him?"

Lauren sat up a little straighter as she felt herself growing defensive. "I'm not making excuses for him. What happened *was* years ago. That's not an excuse, that's a fact. He came in to register his daughter, and I registered her. I don't see what the big deal is. Can you stop preaching at me, please?"

"I'm not preaching," Jenn said, her voice softening. "It's just that...you've always had selective amnesia when it comes to Del."

"Trust me, I remember everything that happened with Michael Delaney." And that time, when she said his name, she felt a twinge in her chest, the faintest echo of the pain that had nearly crippled her all those years ago. The corners of her mouth turned down slightly.

"Good. Keep it that way," Jenn said. "So, what's his daughter like?"

"Very sweet," Lauren said, regaining her composure. "Her name is Erin. She didn't say more than a few words today. Mostly kept to herself. Really polite."

"Well she must take after her mother then," Jenn said, the disdain back in her voice, and Lauren shook her head and rolled her eyes. "Know anything about her?"

"Who?"

"The mother."

"No, there was no information about a mother on her registration forms."

"So he abandoned the mother of his child? How out of character!" Jenn said in feigned shock, and Lauren sighed.

"We don't know if that's what happened."

"Sure we don't."

"Okay," Lauren said with a shake of her head. "I think I'm gonna go. I'll see you this weekend. And just so you know, holding grudges gives you premature wrinkles."

"Yeah, well, in this case, not holding them would make you a wrinkle-less fool," she retorted.

Lauren frowned, because as much as she didn't want to admit it, Jenn had a point.

When Lauren got to work the next morning, Erin was already there, and she exhaled a sigh of relief. She didn't think she could talk to him again. As childish as it was, she had already decided she would hide in the classroom so she wouldn't have to see him when he dropped Erin off; but now, it was a non-issue. Maybe she would be lucky and he'd drop her off early every day.

They started the day with the morning reading circle; for the first two weeks, they'd be working all together. After that they planned on dividing the class into three comprehension groups: the strongest, the average, and the struggling, so that they could individualize instruction.

As Janet read *Let's Go to the Zoo!* Lauren observed the children, their interest and attention levels and their comprehension. Her eyes fell on Erin, and again she felt the twinge in her chest, the same one she had felt the day before when she'd said Michael's name.

Lauren composed herself and shook it off; there was no way she was going to project her feelings about Michael onto his innocent child.

But God, she looked so much like him.

The eyes were exactly the same, eyes that were so dark they were almost black, except hers were large and round with childhood, ringed by a fringe of dark lashes.

She had the same full lips, the same dark hair, only hers fell in silky ringlets that brushed the tops of her shoulders.

She was gorgeous.

But more than that, she was different. Something about the way she carried herself; it was more than just being shy. She gave off this sense of maturity, like she was wise beyond her three-and-a-half years.

And even as Lauren sat assessing the other children, Erin remained in the corner of her mind.

After the morning reading circle, Lauren and Janet set up the arts and crafts table while Delia taught the kids a new song. The entire time, the children were watching Lauren and Janet like racers on the block. As soon as song time was over, the students darted to the end of the long table, battling for crayons, markers, and glitter.

Lauren stepped back with an amused laugh, watching to make sure everyone was being polite. As she circled the area and helped children gather as many crayons as their little hands could carry, she noticed Erin on the far end of the table by herself with one piece of paper and a single blue crayon.

The other kids settled themselves around the opposite end where the supplies were set up and began their pictures, but Erin remained on the far side by herself. She was carefully drawing a blue stick figure with her brow pulled together, deep in concentration.

After a moment of watching her, Lauren leaned over and grabbed a tin of crayons and a blank piece of paper before she pulled up a chair near where the rest of the students were coloring.

"Hey, Erin?" she called, and Erin's crayon stopped as she looked up at Lauren with big doe eyes.

"I'm trying to draw a rainbow, but I can't remember how to do it. Will you come and help me?"

Erin looked down at her own picture and bit her lip before she glanced back up at Lauren.

"You can bring your picture," she said, motioning to an empty seat across from her. "Come on over here with us."

Erin slowly pushed back from the table, taking her paper and crayon with her as she walked over to where Lauren was sitting.

"Thank you so much for helping me," Lauren said with a smile. "I used to be really good at making rainbows, but I think I forgot how. You look like you'd be good at it."

The corner of Erin's mouth lifted in a smile.

"Are you?" Lauren asked, and Erin's smile grew more prominent as she nodded.

"Awesome. Do you remember what color goes first?" Lauren asked, sliding the tin of crayons in between them.

Erin bit her lip, leaning over to study the crayons, her tiny fingers sifting delicately through the pile until she pulled out a red one and proudly handed it to Lauren.

"Hmm, I think you're right," Lauren said with a nod. "What color is this again?"

"Red," she said softly, and her voice was high and tinkling, like wind chimes.

"Ah, that's right, red," she said, tapping herself on the forehead with the crayon. "I always forget."

Erin smiled then, and Lauren winked before she began coloring a red arch on the top of the page.

"Daddy says you're his friend."

The crayon came to a halt on the paper as Lauren froze. It wasn't just the fact that Erin had spoken without having been asked a question, something she hadn't done at all the day before, but it was more what she had said that had thrown Lauren for a loop.

"Are you?" Erin asked, handing Lauren the orange crayon she had just dug out of the container.

"Am I what?" Lauren asked, trying to refocus her attention coloring the arch.

"Daddy's friend?"

She stopped then and looked up to see Erin watching her, her face the epitome of innocence, waiting for a response.

"Your daddy and I were friends a long time ago."

Her face turned thoughtful. "You mean like when you were babies?"

Lauren couldn't help but smile as she put the red crayon back and took the orange one Erin had laid out for her. "No, when we were teenagers."

"What's a teenager?" Erin asked, her eyes on her paper as she began working on her stick figure again.

"It's a big boy or girl. Bigger than a baby, but not as big as a daddy or a mommy." No sooner than the word left her mouth, Lauren felt like kicking herself. She glanced up quickly, waiting to see what kind of effect the mention of a mommy would have on Erin.

She didn't miss a beat.

"Daddy said you're nice."

Lauren's shoulders dropped. "He did?"

Erin nodded as she colored blue hair on top of her stick figure's head. "He said that if I got sad or scared, I should talk to you, because you're nice."

Lauren felt a lump rise in her throat, and she swallowed hard, forcing a smile. "You can always come talk to me, Erin. That's what I'm here for."

"Okay," she said casually.

"Can I use your crayon?" she heard a little voice ask, and Lauren looked up to see one of the boys from class standing next to Erin.

Erin nodded silently, handing it over.

"I'm Connor. Want to color with me?"

Erin glanced over at Lauren, who nodded reassuringly, and she turned back to the boy. "Okay," she said, and the boy pulled up a seat next to her.

Lauren smiled as she removed herself from the situation, putting a reassuring hand on Erin's shoulder before she crossed to the other side of the room to check on the other students.

At three thirty, Lauren said good-bye to Janet and Delia and the children that remained before she gathered her things and headed out to the vestibule.

Just as she placed her bag down on the counter to find her keys, the front door swung open, and Lauren looked up to see Michael walking through the doors.

She dropped her eyes again, sifting through her purse with more urgency.

"Hi."

She swallowed and gained her composure before she looked back up with a tiny smile. "Hi, how are you?"

Stupid contrived formalities. They felt so foreign on her tongue. Especially with Michael. But she didn't know how else to handle him.

"I'm okay," he answered, running a hand through his dark hair. "How'd she do today?"

And then it came to her. She'd handle him like any other parent. Friendly, but professional. All interactions based solely on the child in question.

"Good," Lauren said, and this time her smile was genuine as she thought of Erin's progress today. "She's coming out of her shell."

He shoved his hands in his pockets and exhaled in what seemed like relief. "That's good," he said. "She's smart, but she's *so* shy, and I don't want people to think she's not friendly, or that she's not listening, you know?"

"Oh, we know she's listening, even if she's not quick to talk about what she's learning."

This was good, Lauren thought. *Natural. Safe.*

But then Michael smiled, and she felt her poise waver. "God, that's so good to hear," he said. "We just moved to the area, so I'm hoping she'll be able to open up and make some friends here." He took his hands out of his pockets and leaned on the counter.

His proximity caught her off guard, and her stomach flipped as she instantly straightened, dropping her eyes to where his hands rested in front of her. Immediately he curled them in before gently sliding them out of view.

"Sorry," he said awkwardly. "I just came from work."

It took Lauren a second to realize he thought she was taken aback because his hands were dirty.

"No, no, I wasn't—" but she stopped short, because what could she say? *I wasn't looking at your hands because they were dirty; I was just trying to look anywhere but your face?*

"I work as a tin knocker," he said, shoving his hands back in his pockets. "I can't ever get them clean."

She had to get out of there.

"Well, Erin was great today," she said, tossing her bag over her shoulder and taking a step toward the door. "I'll keep you updated on her progress."

"Oh...okay," he said, stepping to the side to let her pass. "Um, okay, great. Thanks."

"Yep. Have a good afternoon," she said with a smile, rushing past him and out the door.

By the time she got to her car, her hands were shaking so badly that she struggled with starting it.

Her plan was to keep it about Erin, to speak to him like he was just another parent, but as he continued talking to her, she could feel the questions forming on the tip of her tongue. *What's a tin knocker? Do you like your job? Where have you been for the past eight years?*

None of that was about Erin.

And so she ran. She would not allow herself to speak to him on a personal level.

But as she pulled out of the parking lot, she couldn't help but ask herself if she was overreacting. Shouldn't it be okay to want to hear about someone who had once been important to her? After all, they had been inseparable throughout most of high school, albeit the most unlikely pair: the school badass and Little Miss Straight-laced, best friends. It was true things hadn't ended well, but that was years ago. It would be harmless to catch up with an old friend.

No. She had to remember who she was talking about.

Nothing about Michael Delaney was harmless. She had learned that the hard way.

"You get selective amnesia when it comes to Del," she could hear Jenn say.

But not this time.

It had been different in high school. She was a kid. But she was a grown woman now, and she knew better. Lauren realized it was quite possible that he had changed too, just as she had, that he would no longer make the same mistakes he did back then.

But she knew she would never risk herself long enough to find out.

As Michael Delaney tucked his daughter into bed, his mind was a million miles away.

"Good night, baby girl," he said against her forehead before he kissed her there, and she reached up and hugged him around the neck the way she always did.

"Daddy?"

"Hmm?"

"Are you sad tonight?"

She was so observant. He should have expected her to pick up on his behavior.

He pulled back and sat on the side of her bed. "No, I'm not sad," he said, brushing her hair out of her eyes and pulling her blanket up a bit higher. "I'm just tired."

"Me too," she said.

"Well then, we both better get some sleep," he said, standing from her bed.

"Okay. Connor asked me to color with him today and I said yes."

Michael stopped on the way out of her room, trying to remember that they were only three.

He turned in her doorway. "You know," he said, "if Connor wants to take you out on a date, he has to ask me first."

"*Daddy*," she said, rolling her eyes. "We're too little."

Michael grinned. "Sorry," he said, blowing her a kiss. "Night."

"Good night," she murmured, rolling over and pulling her stuffed cat against her.

He stood in her doorway for a minute, watching the rise and fall of her chest under the covers before he gently closed her door.

And then he went and sat at the kitchen table, clasping his hands in front of his mouth as he stared blankly off into space.

Lauren. He couldn't stop thinking of her.

She had always been pretty, but now there was a maturity, a confidence, a womanly quality to her that made her that much more beautiful.

She still had that dark red hair, those impossibly long eyelashes, and those eyes. Forest green. But they could turn dark with protectiveness, or desire.

Or pain.

He had caused all three in her.

Michael sat back in his chair as he ran his hand through his hair and exhaled, wondering if she'd forgiven him. It would be typical of her if she had.

But he didn't even know if he wanted her forgiveness.

She had been civil today, but not amiable.

Professional.

That openness, that innocence, the unfailing and unconditional acceptance she had always shown him, despite what he was, was gone.

She was the only one who had ever given him that, and he'd destroyed it. Consciously.

Michael closed his eyes as he dragged his hands down his face, because as much as he longed to have that back, even for a minute, he hoped she hadn't forgiven him.

He didn't deserve it.

December 2000

*D*el stood up against the lockers in the East Building, waiting for his friend Jay so they could cut fifth period and go down to the deli to grab something to eat.

The other students skirted past him, giving him a wide berth, and he watched them, the way they chattered mindlessly, the way some of the girls flirted pathetically, the way a few of them eyed him like they didn't know if they should acknowledge him or run.

And then she walked past, glancing over at him and smiling softly before she stopped at her locker a few feet ahead.

She had been doing that for a while now. Ever since he had defended her against that arrogant asshole in Health class a few weeks ago, anytime she saw him or passed him, she would smile.

Once, when she had been entering the building as he was leaving, he held the door for her, and her shoulder brushed his chest as she smiled up at him and thanked him.

And now she was at her locker, balancing her books in one arm as she worked the combination of her lock, blowing her breath out the side of her mouth every few seconds to get the veil of hair out of her eyes. He couldn't stop watching her.

She wasn't like any of the other girls.

It wasn't just because of the sweet way she acknowledged him. It was more than that. She didn't carry herself like a freshman. Or a teenager at all, for that matter. She dressed trendy, but managed to do it with class, while other girls wore things that were tight and low-cut and made them look trashy instead of sexy. She seemed sophisticated, but not arrogant. She was quiet, but not withdrawn. He could tell she watched everything; she took it all in, assessing everyone and everything around her.

And because of that, she shouldn't have been smiling at him the way she did. She should have been afraid of him.

Even that Jenn girl who was always with her gave him an uneasy look whenever he'd pass, or she would whisper vehemently in Lauren's ear in either disgust or horror when Lauren would acknowledge him.

Yet she still continued to do it.

Lauren opened her locker, jumping back suddenly as a book tumbled out, and as she struggled to catch it, the other books she was holding scattered to the floor.

Without thinking, he pushed off the lockers and walked toward her. She was crouched on the floor gathering her things, and he knelt down beside her, reaching out to grab the last of the books.

Advanced Biology.

"Here you go, Red," he said, handing her the textbook, and she glanced up at him and smiled.

"Thanks."

"You're in Advanced Bio?" he asked as he stood. "Aren't you a freshman?"

Lauren stood on her tiptoes as she placed some of the books back on the top shelf. "Yeah. I'm a year ahead in sciences. It's kind of my thing," she said with a shrug, brushing the hair out of her eyes before pulling a notebook off the shelf.

He leaned back against the locker next to hers, folding his arms. "Are you in Wendt's class?"

"Yep. Good ol' Wendt," she said with an eye roll, and he smiled. It was the first real conversation they'd had, and he found himself scrambling for a way to keep it going.

"You ready for that unit test next week?" he asked.

"I think so," she said. "You?"

Del laughed as he absently ran his fingertips over the vents on a nearby locker. "Me? No. I'm screwed."

She turned then, looking up at him with dark green eyes. It was the first time he noticed what color they were.

"Do you want me to help you?"

It took him a second to answer. "Do you *want* to help me?" he finally asked, genuinely confused.

"Sure," she said casually as she turned away for a moment to close her locker. When she turned back to face him, she pulled her books into her chest and looked up at him. "I can help you after school for a bit. I have practice at three, but if you're free before then, we could go over some stuff."

He straightened up as he ran a hand through his hair. He had no idea what to say to that.

She blinked up at him, waiting, and at the look in her eyes, he felt his shoulders soften. "Yeah, that's cool. We can meet up for a bit after school today if you want."

"Okay."

"Alright, see you then," he said, turning quickly as he walked way from her in a stupor.

"Wait, Michael?"

He froze as the oddest feeling settled over him. No one called him Michael. Ever. Not even his teachers called him by his real name. The only one who ever had was his grandmother. It should have bothered him that she didn't call him Del. Michael was too familiar.

But for some reason, he realized, Del wouldn't have seemed right on her lips.

He turned, and she was still standing at her locker, looking at him. "Where do you want to meet?"

She's actually serious about this, he thought before he finally said, "Um, you know where Palace Pizza is?"

"Yep," she said. "See you then." And then she smiled her quintessential smile before she turned and walked down the hall, leaving him staring after her.

By the time Del was walking up the sidewalk toward Palace Pizza, he had convinced himself she wouldn't be there. She had been put on the spot back at her locker and felt obligated to offer him help. But after she'd had time to think about it, she'd change her mind. It was one thing to smile at him in the halls; it was another to spend an afternoon alone with him.

She'd come to her senses by the end of the day, he assured himself.

But as he reached the glass door of the pizza parlor, there she was, sitting with her back to him in one of the booths and twirling a strand of hair as she read something in her notebook.

After a baffled second he walked in; Lauren turned when she heard the bell ding above the door, and when he hesitated, she waved him over.

"Hi," she said as he sat across from her.

"Hey," he said, still feeling caught off guard. "I didn't think you'd be here."

She pulled her brow together. "Why? Didn't we say we'd meet here?"

He looked at her then, and he saw that she genuinely didn't understand why he thought she wouldn't show up.

"Can I take your order?" the waitress asked as she approached their table with a pad in her hand. Del pulled his attention away from Lauren to look at the waitress as he gestured for Lauren to go first.

"Um, I'll just have a plain slice, thank you."

"Me too, but make it two," Del added.

"Three plain. Got it. Help yourselves to a drink," she said, motioning to the beverage refrigerator on the far wall as she walked back toward the kitchen.

Del slid out of the booth, walking over to the glass doors of the fridge. "What's your poison, Red?" he asked over his shoulder.

"Iced tea, please," she said, and he grabbed a can of iced tea and a can of root beer before he sat back down and placed it in front of her.

"Why do you keep calling me Red?"

He blinked at her for a second before he leaned over and took a strand of her hair in between his fingers and held it up in front of her face.

"Yes, I get that part," she said with an eye roll, and he couldn't help but grin as he let her hair fall from his fingers. "Do you not know my name?" she asked.

He felt his smile drop, and she quickly added, "It's no big deal. People don't really know me. And I mean, it's not like we're even friends or anything, so…" She trailed off, busying herself by digging in her backpack.

"Why do you call me Michael?" he countered, and she froze, glancing up at him.

"Isn't that your name?"

"No one calls me that. Everyone calls me Del. I don't think any-one even knows my real name is Michael, except for the principals here. How did you even know that?"

Lauren bit her bottom lip, and if he didn't know better, for a sec-ond she almost looked guilty. "I can't remember where I found out," she said, looking down and going through her backpack again. "Do you want me to stop?"

He spun the can of root beer in his hand and looked at her. "You don't need to ask anyone's permission for anything in this life. You can do whatever you want."

At that moment, the waitress brought over their slices, and Lauren glanced up and thanked her as she slid her notebook to the far side of the table to make room.

She opened her iced tea before looking up at Del, tilting her head as she watched him lift his slice and turn it around, taking a bite out of the crust first.

"The crust is the best part," he explained around his mouthful of food. "If they made an all-crust pizza, I'd be a pig in shit."

Lauren took a delicate bite of her own slice. "I'm pretty sure they do. It's called bread."

He stopped chewing as he looked at her, and a smirk lifted the corner of his mouth. *She's a wiseass,* he thought with equal parts amusement and appreciation, and she smiled to herself before she took another bite of her pizza.

"Okay," she said after she'd followed it with a sip of iced tea. "So, did you get the notes on the evolution of microbial life?"

She seemed so at ease with him. It didn't make sense. He found himself watching her face, her movements, constantly appraising her. If it was an act, he would have seen through it by now.

"I don't know what I got," he said, leaning down to grab his note-book from his bag. "I definitely don't have all of them, though. That man is a goddamn lunatic."

Del placed his notebook on the table between them and flipped it open, and she leaned across the table to get a better look, bringing herself closer to him in the process.

She didn't even flinch. Not the slightest hesitation.

The words were out of his mouth before he'd even decided to say them. "You're not afraid of me."

A beat of silence passed before she spoke. "Why would I be?" she asked, her eyes still on his notebook as she tried to decipher his notes.

"Most people are."

She didn't react to his words at all, and he found himself wondering if it was possible she hadn't heard about him, that she didn't know the rumors. But even if she didn't—and the chances were small—she should still have her own reasons for being uneasy.

"And I mean, after what I did on the first day of Health…"

She looked up at him, her expression smooth before she looked back down at his notes.

"You know why I did it?"

He watched her take a small breath as her tongue darted out to wet her lips, but her eyes remained on the paper in front of her. "No, I don't know why you did it. But I know you've had some bad things happen to you."

So she *had* heard the stories. She knew all about him: no father, dead brother, angry kid with a vendetta against the world. And God only knows what other embellishments. And yet she was still here with him, calm and casual.

He didn't understand.

People either kept their distance from him or grilled him for information about his ugly past, information he had no intentions of sharing with anyone. Avoidance or scrutiny, that's how people handled him.

But she did neither.

And he hadn't expected to like it as much as he did.

"Anyway," she said, her voice indicating she was changing the subject. "Wendt always adds more notes after the fact. He's totally unorganized. I swear, I think he plans his lessons at the stoplights on the way to school," she said with another one of those eye rolls that made him grin. Instead of looking annoyed, she looked adorable. An angry kitten.

"I just leave a few lines in between the notes as I take them," she went on. "This way when he starts skipping around, I can go back and fill them in where they actually belong. Otherwise, your notes end up as unorganized as he is."

She tilted her head, looking back down at Del's notes as she absently tore the crust off her pizza.

And then she reached across the table and handed it to him as if it were the most natural thing in the world.

He glanced down at the crust and then back at her; her eyes were still on his notebook as she flipped a page and began reading again, and he felt something settle in his chest. It was pathetic, but that was probably the nicest thing anyone had done for him in a long time.

"Here," she said, reaching to pull a pen out of her bag, "let's just rewrite these so they make sense before we start trying to figure out what you missed." She spun his notebook so it was facing her fully before she flipped to a clean page and began to write.

He watched her with a small smile of appreciation. "I like how you act around me."

She lifted her eyes, and when she looked up at him that way, he noticed her lashes were so long, they brushed just beneath her eyebrows. "How do I act around you?"

He shrugged. "Normal."

Lauren stared at him for a second before she smiled softly. "Hand me that textbook," she said, nodding toward the book sitting on the booth next to him.

As he placed it on the table, Lauren squinted at the page in front of her, pointing to his notes. "What's this?"

"What?" he asked, tilting his head to see what she was pointing at.

"Pair-a-ballis?" she asked, sounding it out slowly like a child learning to read.

He pressed his lips together, fighting a smile. "Parabasilids," he said. "I think pair-a balls is a different unit."

She looked up at him for a second before she cupped her hand to her mouth and laughed. He brought his can of soda to his lips, trying to mask his own laughter and failing miserably.

"God," she said, shaking her head as a slight blush lit her cheeks. "I think after we work on your note-taking skills, we might need to do something about your handwriting."

"You'll have your work cut out for you there," he said, and she continued laughing as she returned her attention to his notes.

A sudden raucous laughter combined with muffled voices from outside caught his attention, and he lifted his eyes and looked over Lauren's shoulder through the glass front of the pizzeria.

Instantly, he felt the heat build in his stomach as his teeth came together.

The guy outside was named David. He couldn't remember his last name, but he didn't give a shit what it was. What he *did* remember was what David had done to him when he had come back to school after missing a few days for his brother's funeral. He had said the most awful things, hurtful things about his brother that had made the other kids laugh. At the time, Michael had only been eight. David was two years older, and Michael was too sad to do anything about it and too young to know how to stop him even if he had it in him to try.

But now, things were different. Now, he knew how to hurt the people who hurt him.

By the time he had figured out how to do that, David was long gone, having transferred to the local Catholic school, and Del had forgotten all about him.

Until today.

He shifted in his seat, his knee bouncing furiously under the table and his eyes on David's profile outside.

Out of his peripheral vision, he could see Lauren was looking at him, having obviously noticed the change in his behavior. *This is it,* he thought. *This is the moment she's going to realize who she's with and run out of here.*

Lauren watched him, evaluating him for a second before she glanced behind her.

"Problem?" she asked, and although her face and posture were calm, her voice shook slightly, betraying her.

"That kid's a piece of shit," Michael answered, his jaw tight as he shifted again, bringing his hand to his mouth and chewing his thumbnail just to be doing something.

Lauren turned again, looking outside, and David held up his hand and waved to someone across the street before he began to cross.

"It doesn't look like he's coming in here," she said softly, turning back toward Del.

He shook his head slightly, knowing if he opened his mouth, no good would come of it. He wished David had come in there. He wanted to bash his fucking head in.

Would he have done that in front of her?

It only took a second for him to come to the conclusion that he would have. He wouldn't have been able to help it.

"Besides," Lauren said softly, pulling his attention back to the present, "even if he did come in here, you wouldn't have been able to turn this table over. It's nailed to the wall."

He stared at her, stunned, and she stared back at him, her expression completely innocent.

And then he broke, his grin quickly followed by the first genuine laughter he'd experienced in a while. He watched the corners of her mouth turn up as the slight tension left her shoulders.

Del sat back against the booth and folded his arms as he tilted his head at her. "You know, you keep your head down and your words soft, but shit, there's some fire in there too, huh?"

She shrugged, still fighting her smile as she picked up her pen and went back to writing in his notebook.

"I like that," he said. "In fact, I think I'm gonna bring that out of you more often. And you can help me keep my head." He picked up his soda and took a sip, appraising her one last time before he nodded. "You know something, Red?" he said after he had swallowed. "I think we got a good thing going on here."

She laughed softly before she glanced up at the clock, and her expression dropped.

"Shoot," she said. "I have to go. I'm sorry—"

"Don't be sorry," he cut her off. "I can rewrite these. Thanks for the tip."

"Okay," she said reluctantly, beginning to pack up her things. "If you want, we can meet to fill in the blanks before the test next week."

"Cool," Del said with a nod.

"Here," she said, reaching into her pocket before offering him money, and he waved his hand and shook his head. "My treat," he said. "Thanks for helping me."

"You don't have to do that—"

"Go. You're gonna be late for practice," he said, cutting her off.

She stood there for a second before she nodded and smiled. "Okay. See you soon. Thanks, Michael."

She swung her backpack over her shoulder and turned, shoving her money back in her pocket as she walked toward the door.

"Hey, Lauren?" he called, and she stopped so abruptly, her bag slid off her shoulder. She caught it at the last second and turned, her expression taken aback.

Del smirked. "Don't be so surprised that I know your name. You're not as invisible as you think you are."

She closed her mouth, looking at him.

"I'm not gonna stop calling you Red, though," he added casually, picking up the crust she had given him and taking a bite.

She smiled then. Not one of those timid, friendly smiles she'd been giving him for the past few weeks, but a wholehearted smile, one that lit her entire face, before she turned and walked out.

After she had rounded the corner and was out of sight, he looked down, pulling apart the crust she had given him as he replayed the afternoon with her. She was actually funny. And smart. And trusting.

And pretty without trying to be.

She was one of the most genuine people he'd ever met, and he knew at that moment that if he did nothing else in his life, he wanted to be friends with Lauren Monroe.

"*Del?* I can't believe you, Lauren! What were you thinking?"

Jenn and Lauren were warming up before gymnastics practice, helping each other stretch, but at that moment, Jenn's first priority had become reprimanding her.

"You know," she huffed as she grabbed Lauren's hands and began to pull her into a more thorough hamstring stretch, "I ignored it when you said hi to him, but to leave campus with him? He could have done anything to you!"

"Stop it," Lauren scolded. "He's nice."

"Yeah, I heard that's what he got suspended over a hundred times for. Being nice."

"It has *not* been over a hundred," Lauren said wearily.

"You know what I mean," Jenn said, letting Lauren out of the stretch. "He's crazy! Um, hello? Were you in Health that day? What if he flipped out on you? Or even next to you?"

A brief flash of Michael fighting to maintain his composure in the pizzeria flashed across Lauren's mind, but she quickly shook it off.

"Well, he didn't. It's really not a big deal," Lauren said, taking Jenn's hands as they switched her into the stretch.

After a minute of silence, Lauren released Jenn, and she sat up. "So are you like, friends with him now or something?"

"I don't know. I guess so," Lauren said, standing as she reached above her head to stretch out her arms.

Jenn shook her head. "You're out of your mind," she said under her breath as she stood and mirrored Lauren's pose.

As the two girls continued to stretch in silence, Lauren couldn't help but wonder if Michael would have to endure a similar conversation with *his* friends, if they would give him the same appalled reaction.

"You hung out with that girl? The freshman loser who gave you the notes?" she could hear them say. She could picture them laughing and saying her name like it was a four-letter word. *"Lauren Monroe?"*

As if on cue, Jenn sighed. "I mean, *Del?* I think you've officially lost it."

But then Lauren thought of his voice in the pizzeria: *"You know something, Red? I think we got a good thing going here."*

And she smiled, because regardless of what their friends said, she thought so too.

September 2011

"So, how's my favorite patient?"

Lauren glanced up from the magazine she was reading to see Adam wearing his trademark blue scrubs and boyish grin.

"You say that to all your patients," she said with a smile as she stood and put the magazine on the small table in the middle of the waiting room.

"Hmm, I might," Adam said, stepping to the side as he gestured for her to enter one of the exam rooms. "Health insurance companies don't cover what they used to, and a man's gotta make a living. But if it makes you feel any better, with you, I mean it."

Lauren laughed and shook her head as she walked through the door of the exam room and sat on the table facing him.

"So," he said, closing the door behind him as he approached her. "How are you feeling today?"

"Great," she responded, and she meant it. In fact, she was floored at the difference only a few weeks of chiropractic adjustments had made. It made her realize how ridiculous she had been for not doing it sooner.

"Excellent," he said, standing beside the table and holding her shoulder as he ran the palm of his other hand down the curve of her back. "Nice," he said with a nod, pressing into the muscle on either side of her lower back with his thumbs. "This tender?"

"Not really. The right side is a little worse."

He nodded as he stepped back and opened the door. "Okay then. Let's go."

"Go?"

He ran his hand through his tousled blond hair and smiled at her obvious anxiety.

"Where are we going?" Lauren asked hesitantly as she slid off the table.

"Out to the gym. The honeymoon's over. I'm putting you to work today," he said as he walked out of the room.

"Putting me to work?"

"Yep," he said over his shoulder before continuing down the hall.

"I should probably warn you," she said as she followed him, "I had a personal trainer once. He and I did not enjoy each other."

"Well then there must have been something wrong with him. Who wouldn't enjoy you?"

"Wow," Lauren laughed. "Laying it on thick now."

"Nonsense. This is part of your therapy," he said. "People work out more effectively when they're in a good mood. Something about endorphins. That's just medical verity."

"Well, I think we're gonna need a lot more endorphins," she said with a sigh as she came to a stop where Adam was standing next to a machine that looked like something used in medieval torture.

"Come on now," he said with that impish smile of his. "You were an athlete. You can't hate exercise this much."

"That's different. With gymnastics, I was doing something I loved and just happened to be getting exercise in the process. But just running in place on a hamster wheel, or sitting here staring aimlessly into space while I move parts of a machine? Are you really going to try to sell me on the fun of that?"

"I can hardly try now," he said with amusement, folding his arms as he leaned against the machine. "You seem pretty set in your ways."

"Well, it makes sense, doesn't it? I have no problems doing something physical, as long as I'm deriving some sort of pleasure from it."

The second the words left her mouth, she pressed her lips together in a hard line, and the last thing she saw before she closed her eyes was his smile morphing into a wide grin.

"You know what I meant," she said softly.

"I believe I do," he laughed.

She covered her face with her hands. "Okay, just show me the damn exercises. They can't be worse than this."

He laughed then, a jovial contagious laugh that made her chuckle behind her hands, and she finally uncovered her face, fanning herself until she felt the warmth of her blush dissipating.

"Alright, I'll cut you a deal," he said, walking away from the torture machine to a mat in the corner. "No machines. Just some floor work. Some stuff you can do anywhere."

"Deal," she said, walking over to the mat.

Lauren spent the next twenty minutes on the floor with Adam as he walked her through a few exercises that focused on strengthening her core, sometimes using his hands to align her body into the appropriate position and sometimes demonstrating them on the floor next to her.

As Lauren lay on her back with her feet flat on the floor and her pelvis lifted, she rolled her head to look over at Adam where he was lying next to her, mirroring her position. "Thank you," she said. "I'm sorry I was being such a brat."

"You're not a brat," he said. "You just know what you want, and you're not afraid to express that. It's admirable, not bratty." He lowered his pelvis to the floor and turned to look at her. "But I do want you to do these exercises, okay?" he said, his expression serious.

"I will. I promise," Lauren said, lowering her pelvis and pressing her palms against her stomach. "Whew, I can feel that already."

He smiled. "Good. A few weeks of this, and your back will be good as new. Then you can get back to all that pleasurable physical activity," he added with a wink before he patted her knee and hopped up off the mat.

"God," Lauren groaned, covering her face with her hands. "Are you ever going to let that go?"

"Eventually," he smiled. "Alright, up you go. Back to the exam room for a quick adjustment and then you're free to go."

"Thank God," she said as she stood, and Adam clutched his heart with stage-worthy skills.

"Ouch," he said, turning to walk back to the exam rooms. "Tough day with the kiddies?"

"Actually, today was surprisingly uneventful," Lauren said as she followed him back down the hall. "Although in saying that out loud, I've just thrown down a gauntlet with the universe, and tomorrow will probably be unspeakable."

Adam's hearty laugh carried back to her as he walked through the door of the exam room, and Lauren smiled. He had the best laugh: wholehearted and genuine and completely infectious.

"Alright my dear, if the universe is going to have its way with you tomorrow, then let's get you in fighting shape."

Lauren climbed up on to the table and laid on her side, and immediately Adam came up beside her, placing one hand on her hip and the other on her shoulder. But instead of aligning her the way he always did, his hand slid over her hip and came to rest on her lower back, just above the curve of her bottom. She lifted her eyes to his face.

It was strange, because these procedures were strictly medical. He was never inappropriate with her, never crossed any lines, and yet she couldn't deny how intimate it seemed: his hands on her body, moving her, manipulating her, speaking to her softly and making eye contact with her as he made her body yield to his will. She inhaled slowly as she watched him.

His brow was furrowed, his eyes downcast, and she felt his fingers curl against her lower back. Just as he applied slight pressure, she winced slightly.

"Mm-hm," he nodded. "After I adjust you, I want to work a little on that trigger point on the right side."

"Okay," she said softly, looking away from him, because he was her doctor, and he was touching her this way because it was his job, and she needed to pull it together.

Adam adjusted her with his usual efficiency and precision, and then he asked her to lie on her stomach.

"I'm going to put direct pressure on the trigger point and hold it there. It will break up the lactic acid and help release the muscle. This is going to be a little uncomfortable, but I don't want it to be excruciating, so tell me if it gets to be too much, okay?"

"Okay," she said again, and she felt his hand run over her back until he found the area he wanted and applied the pressure. She couldn't tell if he was using his thumb or his knuckle, but the pressure was instantly intense, and she curled her hands into fists at her sides.

"Too much?" he asked gently.

"No, it's okay," she said through bated breath.

"Alright. Hang in there, you're doing great. About ten more seconds," he said, rubbing her shoulder with his free hand.

When he released the pressure, the instant relief almost made her laugh, and then she felt Adam take the pad of his thumb and gently rub across the knot.

"Oh, that's already much better," he said softly, and she closed her eyes at the gentle pressure that now felt so good. "Ideally, you should do this three or four times in a row. Can you handle one more, do you think?"

She whimpered softly. "Fine, one more, but only if you do this again afterward."

She heard his quiet laugh before he soothingly laid his palm over the trigger point. "Okay, try to keep breathing this time," he said, and when she felt the firm, concentrated pressure again, she pulled her brow together and focused all her energy on taking slow deep breaths.

After what seemed like forever, he finally released his hold. "Okay, that's enough for today," he said in a soothing voice as he rubbed his thumb gently over the now-weakened knot, causing Lauren to sigh.

"That feels really good," she mumbled into the table.

"From this side too," he said. "It's almost completely broken up. You should keep doing this over the next couple of days. Have your boyfriend or your roommate do this for you."

"I don't have one," Lauren sighed into the table, and she felt his thumb stop on her back.

"What, a roommate? Or a boyfriend?"

Lauren pushed off the table slightly so that she could turn to look at him, fighting her smile when the hope she thought she heard in his voice was written all over his face.

"Either," she said before she lay back down on the table, burying her face like a child to hide her grin.

"Okay," he said, resuming his ministrations. "Well then I can just keep doing it for you for the next few visits."

"Okay then," she said through her smile.

"Okay then," he echoed.

And she could tell he was smiling too.

"So you're not gonna offer it up?" Jenn said, lifting her glass of Merlot and taking a sip, her eyes pinned on Lauren. "You're really going to make me ask?"

"Make you ask what?" she said casually as she perused the menu.

Jenn sighed in exasperation before she said, "Del. What's going on with you and Del?"

Lauren glanced up at Jenn, her expression unimpressed. "Are we going to do this at every dinner now?"

"Oh, stop it. I asked you last time because he'd just shown back up in your life like two days before that. And now, it's four weeks later. And you see him every day. You don't expect me to be curious about how that's panning out?"

"If something had happened, don't you think you would know? I talk to you on the phone all the time."

"Ah, yes, but I can't see your eyes then."

Lauren shook her head and laughed. "You're an idiot."

"An idiot who knows her best friend," she said, placing her glass down and leaning across the table. "So I repeat, what's going on with you and Del?"

Lauren sighed and placed the menu on the table, looking her friend in the eye as she answered, because she knew Jenn wouldn't be satisfied any other way. "Nothing."

"*Nothing?*"

"Sorry to disappoint," she said with a shrug.

"How is it that you haven't addressed anything with him yet? You talk to him everyday."

"Just like I talk to every other parent," Lauren said nonchalantly as she took a sip of her wine. "A quick update on their kid, answer any questions, and off they go."

Jenn sat back in her chair. "It doesn't matter what the topic of conversation is. You're not starting on square one with him."

Lauren shook her head, but Jenn continued anyway. "You guys have a ton of history. With people like that, no matter how long you've been apart, sometimes when you reconnect, it's just like hitting un-pause. A simple conversation, and *boom*," she said, snapping her fingers for emphasis, "you're in too deep."

"Well, there's no need to worry about me. I'm wading safely in the shallow end. Strictly professional."

Jenn tilted her head and made a face. "Laur, it's me. You don't have to put up a wall here. Why are you acting like you're totally unaffected?"

"I'm not acting," she said, opening her menu again. "What happened was a long time ago. We've obviously both moved on with our lives. What would be the point of dredging up something painful from when we were kids?"

"Because you deserve answers," Jenn said matter-of-factly.

"Well, maybe I deserve them, but I don't need them," Lauren said, deciding it was time for a subject change. "Besides, if you're looking for something juicy, you're asking the wrong questions."

Jenn quirked her brow, leaning forward again. "What should I be asking?"

Lauren smiled, knowing her friend was fully baited, and she took a slow sip of wine, drawing out the suspense. "Ask me about my chiropractor," she finally said.

"Your chiropractor?" Jenn echoed, confused.

Lauren waggled her eyebrows, and Jenn's jaw dropped.

"Are you screwing your doctor?" she asked, appalled.

"God, Jenn," Lauren scoffed before she closed her menu again. "No, I'm not. But I do have a major crush on him."

"Really? Your *chiropractor?*"

Lauren nodded, a small smile playing at her lips as she twirled the stem of her wine glass. "He's so smart and well-spoken, but at the same time, he's funny and completely down to earth. I feel like I'm hanging out with a friend when I'm with him."

Just then the waiter approached the table, and the girls were temporarily distracted as they placed their orders. As soon as he left, however, Jenn turned back to Lauren.

"But when I think chiropractor, I think graying hair and crow's feet and a little potbelly."

"Not even close," Lauren said.

"No? What's he look like?"

Lauren pursed her lips and looked up to the ceiling, thinking. "Kind of like Abercrombie and Fitch released a new line of medical scrubs."

"Shut up," Jenn said, her eyes lighting up, and Lauren nodded. "Well shit. That's got jackpot written all over it. Good for you, lady."

Lauren laughed as she moved her wine glass out of the way to make room for the salad the waiter was placing in front of her. "We'll see," she said, laying her napkin on her lap.

Jenn nodded, spearing a tomato and then pointing at her with the fork. "I'm so on to you, by the way."

"On to me?"

"Yep," Jenn said, popping the *p* before she ate the tomato. "This guy's your doctor, which comes with controversy. It's your MO."

"*What?*" Lauren said through a laugh. "What are you talking about?"

"Come on, Lauren. For starters, can we agree on the fact that you jump into relationships with guys, and as soon as things start to get good, you bail?"

"I do not!"

"Tyler Ramsey."

"He was my college roommate's brother. Things got weird. Try dating a guy when you live with one of his family members."

"Greg Harris."

"He was a substitute at my school!" Lauren said, exasperated. "He was always around. I didn't have a chance to miss him. Or breathe, for that matter. Besides, it's like a cardinal rule that you shouldn't date people you work with."

Jenn grinned. "Which brings me to my point. Guys with controversy. You know it going in, but you pick them anyway. It's like your insurance policy. It gives you a reason to get out before things get too serious."

"Please," Lauren said with an eye roll, taking another sip of wine.

"You can deny it," Jenn said with a shrug. "Doesn't make it any less true."

"Whatever," Lauren laughed. "All I know is that when I find the right guy, there won't be a reason for me to leave."

Jenn lifted her glass. "I can toast to that." And Lauren tapped her glass to Jenn's, her smile masking the fact that she couldn't help wondering if there would ever be a guy she wouldn't run from.

"What story do you want tonight?" Michael asked his daughter as she climbed into bed wearing her Disney Princess pajamas, her hair still damp and smelling of her shampoo.

"Can we look at the picture book?" she asked as she grabbed her stuffed cat and tucked it under the covers beside her.

"The picture book?" he asked, surprised. "You haven't asked for that in a long time."

Michael walked over to her bookshelf, squatting down in front of it as he looked for the small red photo album he'd put together the first year he moved to New York. There were only about eight pictures in it; for him, it had been a way to remember those things from his old life that he wanted to remember. And everything else, everything that wasn't in that little book, could just disappear.

It was a nice idea, but he should have known his demons would exist with or without photographic documentation.

Still, he kept the album, even though he'd only looked at it a handful of times in rare moments of wistfulness. And then one day, Erin found it when she had crawled under his bed while they were playing hide and seek. For months on end after that, she asked for "the picture book" as her bedtime story; Michael would sit with her and they'd look at the pictures, and he'd tell her the story behind each one. After a while, all he had to do was turn the pages, and she'd be the one reciting the stories to him.

But when they had moved to Bellefonte last month, their new neighbor, a kind, elderly lady named Mrs. Brigante, had given Erin a box of fairy-tale books as a welcome present, and she had become so entranced with them that she had forgotten about the album until tonight.

Michael grabbed the little red book and walked back to her bed, sitting beside her and lifting his arm. She immediately crawled into the nook of his body, snuggling against him with her stuffed cat, and Michael put his arm around her before he opened the album in front of them.

"Do you think you remember the stories, or should I tell them?" he asked.

"I remember," she said softly, pointing to the first picture. "That's you, Daddy, when you were a little boy and a baseball star."

Michael smiled, looking down at the faded picture. He was in his red and white peewee baseball uniform, his oversized hat nearly covering his eyes, which were squinted against the sun despite the giant visor. He was just shy of six years old; the team's coach had taken photos of each of the players that year and given the pictures to them in their end-of-the-season goodie bags. Michael had kept his in his drawer for months after that, with hopes that when he finally found out his father's new address, he could send him the picture and show him that he was a baseball player now, just like his dad wanted.

He hoped maybe that would be enough to bring him back.

"That's right," he said. "I played second base. Nobody ever got past me."

"Can I play second base?"

"You can do anything you want, baby girl. How about one of these days while it's still warm, we go outside and I'll show you how to throw and catch like me?"

"Okay," she murmured sleepily, reaching up to turn the page. "That's you and your Grandma Rose. You were sticky, Daddy," she said with a giggle. "'Cause you got in the jelly."

Michael smiled down at her, leaning over to kiss the top of her head. "That's some memory you got." He turned his attention to the picture of him sitting on his grandmother's lap, his hair wadded into sticky clumps and his face and hands covered in orange goop. "My Grandma Rose was the best cook ever. She made homemade jelly, and apricot was my favorite. And one day…" he trailed off, knowing Erin would continue.

"One day she made some and left it on the table and you ate it all up!" she squealed and burst into hysterics, the kind of youthful, genuine laughter that always made Michael respond in kind.

"I ate it all up," he repeated with a nod. "And I made a big mess, huh?"

"Yeah, you need a bath, Daddy." Michael smiled before she added, "My grandma lives far away."

His smile dropped. "Yes," he said, trying to keep his voice casual.

"When will she come to visit me and make me apricot jelly?"

He swallowed. "I don't know. It's a very far trip," he said, rubbing her hair, and he couldn't help but wonder, as he so often did, if he was doing the right thing by keeping his mother out of Erin's life. When he had called her against his better judgment to tell her he had gotten his girlfriend pregnant, she used the opportunity to point out all the lives he'd ruined, and how this would just be another one to add to the list. She ended the conversation with, "For God's sake, I hope you're going to abort that child."

And he hadn't spoken to her since.

But he wondered—if she were to meet Erin, if she got to see how smart and wonderful and kind she was, maybe she would be the kind of grandmother Erin deserved.

Or maybe she'd ruin her, the way she had him.

"What else did Grandma Rose cook?" Erin asked, pulling him back to the present, and he smiled, thankful for the reprieve.

"She made the best zucchini bread," Michael said, lifting his arm to accommodate her as she snuggled closer to him. "That's how she tricked me into eating my vegetables."

"*Daddy*," she sing-songed. "Begetables don't grow in bread!"

Michael laughed. "No, but you can bake them in bread. It tastes delicious. Almost like cake."

"Can we make zucchini bread?"

"We can try," he laughed. "I'm not as good as Grandma Rose, but we can certainly try," he added, turning the page.

"That's Daddy and his friend at bagruation," Erin said.

"Graduation," Michael corrected softly, his eyes on the picture.

"Hey!" Erin squealed, sitting up suddenly, pointing at the picture. "That's Miss Lauren!"

Michael stared at the picture, although he hardly needed to. He had looked at it so often after he first left Scranton that he could close his eyes and conjure it up with perfect clarity.

He stood several inches taller than her in his black graduation gown, his lips curved into a slight smile as he looked down at her. Lauren leaned into him with one arm extended, holding the camera away from them as she took the picture. Her head was resting against his chest, her dark red hair spilling over his gown as she smiled at the camera.

Her smile was always his favorite part.

She smiled straight up to her eyes, so happy to be next to him, so proud of him that day. She was the only one who had showed up for him, standing and clapping when his name was called, whistling loudly as he walked across the stage, and taking the one and only picture of him in his graduation attire because, as she had beamed, "Everyone needs to remember their graduation day."

"Miss Lauren dances with us," Erin said matter-of-factly as she laid back down.

"Oh yeah?" Michael answered, still lost in the picture.

"Yes. And if someone's sad, she hugs them. Once, Kayla was crying because she missed her mommy, and Miss Lauren taught her the Brave Song. And then she taught it to everyone. And she promised if we sing it when we're scared, we'll feel brave."

Michael smiled, pulling his eyes from the picture to look down at his daughter. "Didn't I tell you Miss Lauren was nice?"

"Yes," she said with a nod. "I think she's really a princess, but she just forgets to wear her crown."

"I think so too," Michael said, and his voice wasn't as upbeat as he intended; he dropped his eyes and swallowed before turning the page.

"That's Daddy and Uncle Aaron," Erin said. "That's how I got my name. Aaron, Erin. Erin, Aaron," she sang, moving her shoulders in a little dance beside him.

"That's right, baby," he said, forcing a smile. This probably wasn't the best night to do this; looking at Aaron's picture on the tail end of looking at Lauren's was a little more than he could handle just then.

"Uncle Aaron lives in heaven with your Grandma Rose, right Daddy?"

"Right," he said softly, closing the album, and Erin was too distracted to object.

"And his bed is a cloud and he plays games all day and he eats so much ice cream!" she expounded excitedly.

Michael laughed softly as he stood from the bed. "He has a nice life up in heaven. But he still watches over you. From all the way up there," he said, pointing up to the ceiling. "He protects you when I'm not around."

He leaned down and kissed her forehead before he ushered her under the covers and stood, turning on her night-light.

"Did he protect you when you were little too?"

Michael stopped and closed his eyes.

Always, he thought, but instead he said, "Yes, baby girl. Sweet dreams."

And then he walked out of her room, turning off the light and closing the door, thankful he was able to get out before she could see the look in his eyes.

March 1989

*M*ichael sat on his knees at the dinner table, pushing his green beans around on his plate with the hopes of making it look like he'd eaten some.

"Is it time for birthday cake yet?" he asked, thinking of the triple chocolate cake his mother had baked for him.

"Not until those green beans are gone," his mother called from the kitchen where she was loading the dishwasher.

"Come on buddy, a couple of bites," his father said from behind him, rubbing his hand over the back of Michael's head before he walked around the table and sat down next to Aaron.

"Are you excited for your party this weekend?" his brother asked, and Michael grinned and nodded. It was the first party he'd be having with his friends from school, and his mother had booked Jumpin' Beans gymnasium. It had been the talk of his class for the past few weeks.

"You should be. You're a big man now. Five years old is a whole hand." Aaron held up his hand, and Michael leaned forward to slap him high five. Aaron laughed, and Michael grinned proudly as he ate another one of his green beans. Nothing made him happier than when his brother thought he was cool.

"Okay, so what are you working on?" their father asked as he looked over Aaron's shoulder to see the homework assignment.

"Science, but I don't know if I'm doing this right."

"Well, I'll do my best, but seventh-grade science might be beyond my scope of memory," he said with a laugh, turning the notebook on the table so he could get a better look. "Oh, hey wait, I think I remember this stuff. Punting Squares, right?"

Aaron laughed. "*Punnett* Squares."

"Same difference," his dad said, playfully punching him on the shoulder, and Michael forced another green bean into his mouth as he watched them.

"We're doing eye color," Aaron said. "I have to figure out the possible offspring of two hybrids and two purebreds."

"Yeah, I remember this," his father said with a nod. "The dominant gene is represented by a capital letter, and the recessive is lowercase, right?"

"I think," Aaron said, squinting at his notebook.

"Here," his father said. "Let's do the purebred. We'll use two blue-eyed people. So put two lowercase *b*'s there, and two more over there," he added, pointing to the square on Aaron's page. "Right. Now cross them, and see what you get."

"Are you done with those green beans yet?" Michael's mother called from the kitchen.

"Almost," Michael lied, looking down as he pushed a few more around his plate.

"There, you did it," his dad said.

"Yeah, but that can't be right."

"Why not?"

"'Cause it says that two blue-eyed people can't have a brown-eyed baby."

"Right," his father said.

"But you and Mom have blue eyes, and look at Michael."

The sudden silence was what Michael remembered the most. It was so abrupt that he looked up from his plate, because to him it seemed like everyone in the room suddenly disappeared.

And then he saw his brother's face, and he was suddenly afraid without understanding why. It was the same face Aaron wore when he'd accidentally ridden his bike too close to their mother's new car in the driveway and scratched the side: a pathetic mixture of fear and guilt.

Michael only remembered bits and pieces after that, partly because he'd blocked it out, and partly because he didn't understand how the pieces fit together.

He remembered Aaron dragging him upstairs when the yelling started. The voices were so loud and strained that he didn't even recognize them as his parents'. He remembered hearing words he knew were bad even though he didn't know what some of them meant. And he remembered the shrill sound of his mother crying.

But above all, he remembered hearing his name over and over, interspersed with *sorry* and *please*. His mother kept saying, "He meant nothing," and Michael wondered if she was talking about him.

Did *he* mean nothing? Had he been bad? He tried to remember something that he could have done to cause this, but he couldn't think.

The yelling transitioned into the sound of things being thrown, and he cupped his hands over his ears.

He didn't understand any of this.

Aaron sat next to him on the floor of his bedroom, holding him and telling him that everything was okay, even though Michael could hear in his brother's voice that it wasn't. And that's how he fell asleep that night: curled against his brother's side as Aaron continued to talk to him in an attempt to drown out the sounds of what was happening below.

The next morning Michael woke up hoping everything would be okay. Everyone would say they were sorry, and maybe they could have his birthday cake for breakfast.

Instead, his mother was locked in her bedroom, and his father was standing in the living room with a bunch of suitcases. He wanted to ask him where he was going. He wanted to ask if he could come. But the words stuck in his throat, and he kept looking to his brother, wanting him to say the words that he couldn't.

But Aaron's head was bowed, his eyes sad, and that's when Michael knew that whatever this was, it was bad.

His father spoke to Aaron and promised him he would still see him, just not everyday.

And then he left without saying a word to Michael.

In the days that followed, he did come back. But only for Aaron, and only a few times. Each time he showed up, a screaming match would ensue between his parents that mirrored the first one, and eventually his father started calling Aaron instead of coming over.

And a month later, he moved away. Michael remembered asking his teacher where California was, and she said he'd have to take a plane to get there.

He knew better than to ask his mother about anything that happened that night, or anything pertaining to his father at all, for that matter. The one time he tried, his mother yelled at him and told him she didn't want to talk about Daddy anymore.

It was more than her just being angry with Michael. She was *mean* to him. She'd become mean in general after that night, but especially to him. And eventually he just found it easier and safer to keep his distance from her.

In a matter of a few weeks, he'd lost his father and managed to make his mother extremely mad, and he didn't understand how or why.

So Michael did the only thing that made sense; he clung to his big brother, the only sense of normalcy left for him, the only shred that remained of his former life.

For a long time, he didn't dare talk with his brother about what happened. Aaron never brought it up, and Michael was afraid to do so for fear of losing him, for fear of making Aaron angry the way he made his father and his mother angry.

But one night after Aaron got off the phone with their father, and Michael's hopes that his dad might ask to speak to him were once again crushed, he finally broke and asked his brother what he'd done wrong.

"You didn't do anything wrong," he said quietly, walking into his bedroom, and Michael followed.

"But Daddy's mad at me."

"No, he's not. He's mad at Mommy," Aaron said, walking over to his shelf and grabbing his Walkman.

"But why won't he talk to me anymore?" Michael asked, and his own voice sounded funny to him, like it was shaking.

Aaron looked up from his cassette tapes, his expression pained, but he didn't answer.

"Does he still love me?" Michael asked, and this time his voice squeaked, and his eyes felt hot.

"Yes," Aaron promised. "He still loves you. He just...he just forgot that he does," he added softly.

Michael didn't want to cry in front of his big brother. He wanted to be a big man. But he felt his face contort as a little sob escaped his lips, and he dropped his head, trying to hide.

Aaron was up in a second, putting his arm around Michael as he walked him over to the bed. "It's okay, Mike," he said. "You didn't do anything wrong. Mommy and Daddy are mad at each other. But they love you, and I love you."

"But what if you forget that you love me, like Daddy did?" Michael said through his tears, and Aaron shook his head.

"Never. I'll never forget."

"Even if you get mad?" he hiccupped.

"Even if I get mad. I promise, I won't ever forget that I love you."

And with that, Michael buried his face in his big brother's shirt and sobbed.

It was the last time he ever allowed himself to cry.

After that he ignored the pain and the confusion, the feelings of rejection from both his mother and his father. He had his big brother, and that was all that mattered.

That was all he needed.

Eventually, Michael got used to harboring questions he knew would never be answered. It just became a part of who he was, and he became very good at ignoring his feelings.

It wasn't until eight years later, sitting in the middle of Miss McCarthy's third-period science class, that he finally understood.

They were learning about Punnett Squares.

And suddenly he knew why the man he thought was his father left him when he was five, and why he never wanted to see Michael again. Just like that, after all the years spent wondering, it was suddenly crystal clear why his family had fallen apart.

It was all his fault.

October 2011

"Have a good day, baby girl," Michael said as he leaned over and kissed the top of Erin's head.

"Bye Daddy!" she beamed before she turned and ran through the door of her classroom, and Michael straightened with a sigh, torn between feeling relieved at her newfound independence and saddened that she no longer clung to him.

The director of the day care facility gave him a knowing smile, and he smiled sheepishly in return. Just as he turned to leave, he stopped suddenly, catching sight of Lauren through the classroom door. She was sitting on the floor, surrounded by five or six kids, clapping her hands and singing some type of song. After every few words, she would point to one of the children, and each time she did, they would throw their heads back in hysterics at whatever she had said.

He could see that she was laughing too, although he couldn't hear it, but he remembered so perfectly what her laugh sounded like that it didn't matter.

And then Erin came into view, dropping her backpack and sprinting over to the circle before throwing herself into Lauren's lap and hugging her tightly around the neck. Immediately Lauren wrapped her arms around Erin, rocking side to side, and when Erin pulled away, Lauren reached up and took her face in her hands, saying something to her with a smile. Erin nodded enthusiastically, and Lauren laughed, moving over to make room for her in the circle.

He turned quickly, ignoring the ache in his chest as he held the door for a woman entering with her two children before he crossed the parking lot to his car.

It was a short drive to West Linn Street, where his crew was working on the new medical offices that were going up. Michael parked his car in the designated off-site area and walked down a small hill to where two utility trucks were stationed.

"What's up?" Dean called from behind the truck as he slid a piece of sheet metal to the edge of the truck bed. Dean was tall and dark-skinned, a few years older than Michael, and they had become fast friends when Michael joined the crew a few months earlier. It was clear that Dean had a questionable past, and Dean seemed to recognize that Michael did too; it was one of those things that was understood between them but never discussed. He also had a daughter, six months old, and was in the middle of a nasty custody battle with his ex-girlfriend.

"Hey," Michael answered absently, and Dean stopped.

"You okay? Your girl have a hard time getting dropped off again?"

"Huh? Oh, no. She's good," Michael said, reaching into the truck and grabbing the measuring tape and an oversized black marker.

Dean looked at him for a second and nodded, never pushing. "Get the measurement of that union," he said, sliding the sheet metal off the truck and laying it on a wooden board on the floor.

Michael walked inside, weaving around the construction horses and wires, and he climbed up the small ladder with the tape in his hands.

The task was rote and monotonous; it kept his hands busy, but his mind was free to wander, which wasn't a great thing today.

It had been two months. Two months of seeing her almost every day. Two months of polite, pleasant formalities. And each day it became harder and harder to endure.

He missed her.

He'd spent the last eight years missing her, but this was different. It used to be that it just existed somewhere on the edge of his consciousness; it was always there, but it was like background noise. He had learned to ignore it, to function around it. But now, seeing her everyday, watching her with his daughter, she was in the forefront of his mind all the time. And no matter what he did, he couldn't function around it anymore.

Michael climbed down the ladder and out to Dean, giving him the numbers, and together they rolled the sheet metal into a long tube on the wooden platform. Dean held it in place while Michael walked down its length, measuring it with the tape, marking certain spots with the marker and jotting down lines to be used as points of reference.

He'd had enough of the torturous formalities, he realized. He wanted their friendship back.

And he was going to try.

If she wouldn't, if she refused, he would understand. But if she allowed him back into her life, despite everything that had happened, he would make sure he made things right.

He would never betray her again.

When Michael reached the end of the tube, he nodded at Dean and they unrolled the sheet. Michael knelt down on one side and Dean crossed to the other, taking a marker out of his back pocket, and together they began marking where the rivets would go.

"Hey, what's a nice restaurant around here?" Michael asked with the cap of the marker between his teeth as he marked the last rivet.

"Upscale? Or just good food?"

"Either."

"Gamble Mill Tavern over on Dunlap is good. Reasonable prices."

"Yeah?" Michael said, standing as he capped his marker and slid it into his back pocket before he turned to grab the nearby drill.

"But if you want to impress her, and you got the cash to do it, take her to Labella Trattoria," Dean said, glancing up with a knowing smirk before he slid a two-by-four under the sheet to reinforce it.

Michael laughed and shook his head as he grabbed a pair of protective goggles. "Think you're so fucking smart."

"Thinking and knowing are two different things," Dean said, placing his hands on either side of the markings to hold it steady while Michael lined up the drill. "On second thought, do the Trattoria," he added. "It seems like she's worth it."

Michael stopped. "What are you saying that for?"

Dean looked up. "Because of that right there," he said, nodding in Michael's direction. "That look on your face. As soon as I mentioned her," he added, looking down and gesturing for Michael to make the first rivet.

He stared at Dean for a second before he dropped his eyes and pulled the trigger, and the sound of grinding metal filled the space between them.

At four thirty, Michael sat in the front seat of his car, scrubbing his hands with an antibacterial wipe, but it was in vain.

"Oh, screw it," he huffed as he crumpled the wipe with his still-dirty hands and tossed it somewhere on the passenger side.

He exited the car, running his hand through his hair as he approached the entrance of Learn and Grow. He could see a few of the other parents waiting in the vestibule, and as he approached the glass doors, he noticed Lauren standing in the doorway of the pre-K room, calling those children whose parents were waiting and helping them on with their backpacks.

As Michael opened the door, she looked up at him and smiled, and he smiled back, shoving his hands in his pockets.

Lauren called the children one by one, and Michael waited patiently as the group of parents dwindled.

"See you tomorrow, Jack," she said, waving to the little boy who ran out to his mother, and then the vestibule was empty. Lauren turned to look at him.

"Hi," she said.

"Hey. How was she today?" he asked, playing into their usual routine.

"Perfect. I'm going to start her and another little boy on some kindergarten material. They're ready for it."

"Really? Wow," Michael said, his expression a cross between surprise and pride. "Thank you, for going above and beyond like that."

"Trust me, I'm doing very little to get her there. She's incredibly bright."

He nodded, running a hand through his hair. "So…is there anything I should be doing with her at home?"

"Um, I can get you some workbooks to do with her," she said, scooping her hair back into a makeshift ponytail, and when she let it fall, he caught the scent of her shampoo.

She turned then, motioning to someone inside, and he closed his eyes and exhaled.

Just do it, he thought.

"So, I was thinking," he said when she turned back around. "We never get to talk here. Do you want to maybe grab dinner with me? Catch up a little bit?"

Her face instantly dropped, and Michael's heart followed.

"Oh…I, um…I just…I don't…"

"Miss Lauren's coming to dinner? Yay!" Erin squealed from behind Lauren, and Michael closed his eyes and cringed.

He never would have asked had he known Erin was within earshot; he didn't want her to be disappointed, and he definitely didn't want Lauren to think he was using his daughter as a pawn. But as he opened his eyes, he saw Lauren looking down at her, and it was hard to regret his little slip-up.

Because he knew by the look on Lauren's face that she didn't want to disappoint her either.

She exhaled heavily, nibbling on her thumbnail before she glanced at Michael. "Um, okay, yeah. I guess we can do that."

"Yay!" Erin squeaked again, dancing in place.

"Go get your backpack, honey," Lauren said to her, and Erin darted back into the classroom.

"I'm so sorry," Michael said. "I didn't realize she was there."

"It's okay," Lauren said, but her eyes were uneasy.

"Where are we going?" Erin asked as she ran back to them, dragging her backpack.

"How about—"

"How about Chuck E. Cheese?" Lauren said, cutting Michael off.

"*Yeah!*" Erin cheered, jumping up and down, and Lauren squatted down to help her put her backpack on.

Michael smiled half-heartedly, running the back of his hand over his eyes. He had wanted to take her to one of the restaurants

Dean told him about. After all, Chuck E. Cheese wasn't the kind of place where they could sit down and have an uninterrupted conversation.

Although, maybe that was exactly what Lauren had in mind when she suggested it.

"Okay, so I'll just meet you over there?" Lauren said as she stood, looking at Michael.

"Sounds good," he said, forcing a smile. As Erin ran to him and hugged him around the leg, his smile turned genuine as he looked down at her and placed his hand on her head.

"Alright, I'm just gonna grab my things." She turned her attention to Erin and winked. "See you in a little bit."

As soon as she had disappeared back inside the classroom, Erin grabbed his hand and started towing him toward the door. "Come on, Daddy! Come on! We're going to have dinner with Miss Lauren!"

And he laughed as she dragged him toward the exit, because he was just as excited as she was.

Lauren and Michael sat at a booth with two substandard salads on the table between them, surrounded by the sounds of bells ringing and children yelling and laughing. Erin remained in Michael's line of sight, just as she promised, running around the Toddler Zone as she waited for her pizza to arrive.

"Sorry about this," Michael said, gesturing toward the salads. "We didn't have to come here."

"That's okay," she said before she turned to look at Erin. "She's having fun. She'll sleep great tonight," she added with a laugh, and Michael smiled.

"How long have you been teaching preschool?"

"About two months."

Michael raised his eyebrows, and she nodded. "Yeah. My first day was Erin's first day."

"No shit?" he said, immediately cupping his hand over his mouth as he looked around.

Lauren tried not to laugh, and Michael looked down at his salad and chuckled. "So what were you doing before that? Were you in school?"

"No, I was still teaching," Lauren said. "Except I taught kindergarten. I'm working at the day care now while I get my master's degree."

"Oh yeah? What are you going for?" Michael asked.

"Child psychology."

Michael looked up at her, and she glanced at him before she cleared her throat and rooted through her salad.

"So, what do you do?" she asked.

"I work construction."

"Oh, that's right. A bin knocker."

Michael smiled. "A tin knocker."

She glanced up at him with an embarrassed laugh. "Clearly, I have no idea what that is."

He flicked a piece of wilted lettuce with his fork as he laughed. "I fabricate and install ductwork in the heating and cooling systems of buildings."

"Oh," she said. "That sounds…difficult."

"Nah," he said with a dismissive shake of his head. "It pays the bills though, for now. I'm going back to school part time."

Lauren looked up at him and smiled, and he swallowed hard as his stomach flipped. It wasn't the strained, polite smile she'd been giving him for the past two months. It was his favorite smile.

The same proud smile she wore in the graduation picture.

"Good for you," she said. "What are you going for?"

"Mechanical engineering," he said, looking away and hoping she couldn't see how thrown he was by her reaction.

"Here you go," the waitress said as she brought the pizza to the table, and Erin came running out of the Toddler Zone when she saw it arrive.

"I'm hungry," she said, hopping up onto the bench next to Lauren, who scooted over with a smile.

"Hold on, honey, let's clean your hands first."

Michael watched as Lauren reached in her purse for a sanitizing wipe and gently cleaned Erin's hands.

The heavy ache settled in his chest again, and he distracted himself by handing out slices of pizza to everyone.

"Yummy!" Erin said as she chewed her first bite, and Michael looked down at the second-rate pizza on his plate, complete with goopy red sauce and orange cheese.

"Yeah, yummy," he deadpanned, and Lauren giggled to herself as she took a sip of her water.

Michael picked up his pizza and took a bite, and when he lifted his eyes, he froze. Lauren was watching him, and her eyes were glassy with what looked like unshed tears.

"You okay?" he asked.

"You still do that," she said with a sad smile.

Michael pulled his brow together and looked down at himself.

He was holding the slice backward, completely intact except for the large bite he had taken out of the crust.

He blinked before he looked back up at her, but she had already turned her attention to Erin.

"How's your pizza?"

"Good," Erin mumbled around a large mouthful of food, and Lauren laughed, sliding Erin's drink closer to her. She grabbed it with both hands, taking a long sip through the straw.

"Are you somebody's mommy?" she asked after she had swallowed.

"No, I'm not," Lauren answered.

"How come?"

"*Erin*," Michael said firmly.

"No, it's okay," said Lauren before she turned back to Erin. "Because I haven't met someone who would be a good daddy yet. When I find someone who I think will be a good daddy, then I'll be ready to be a mommy."

"My daddy's a good daddy," she said, and Michael choked on the sip of soda he'd just taken, covering his mouth to mask the coughing.

"Well you're a lucky girl," she answered without missing a beat.

"You'll be a good mommy," Erin stated matter-of-factly, and Lauren rubbed her hand over Erin's hair.

"Thank you."

"My mommy lives far away."

Michael looked up just in time to see Lauren's eyes flash to his, her expression startled.

"But she still loves me a lot. Daddy, can I go back and play some more?"

Michael cleared his throat. "Um...yeah. Go ahead, baby." Before he even finished his sentence, Erin was out of the booth and running back toward the Toddler Zone.

"God, I'm so sorry about that," Michael exhaled.

"It's fine," she said. "I've spent the past three years working with five-year-olds. Her line of questioning was mild by comparison."

Michael laughed softly, tossing his pizza to his plate. "God, this is awful."

"Yeah, I've had better," she said with a laugh before she turned to look at Erin. "Look at her," she smiled. "Have you thought about enrolling her in gymnastics?"

Michael looked over to where Erin was attempting cartwheels with another little girl in the play area.

"I haven't. I don't know of any places around here. And besides, she's a Delaney, so I didn't think gymnastics would be in the cards for her."

Lauren put her drink down abruptly, covering her mouth to avoid spitting all over the table, and Michael grinned. "You remember?" he asked.

"Of course I remember," she said through her laughter. "That was one of the funniest things I've ever seen. My God, you looked like an arachnid or something. Just legs and arms everywhere."

"Hey!" he said in mock offense. "I had never done anything remotely gymnastics related, and you expected me to be able to just do a backflip!"

"It wasn't a backflip," she scoffed. "It was a *back handspring*. Much easier. You get to use your hands for that."

"Still," he laughed. "And anyway, I think maybe I could have learned how to do it if my instructor hadn't been laughing and making fun of me the whole time."

Lauren laughed again, staring at her straw as she twirled it between her fingers. She inhaled deeply, and when she exhaled, her face changed; her smile dropped and she pulled her brow together.

No, Michael thought. *No, don't go backward.*

Lauren shifted in her seat and cleared her throat. "I'm gonna go to the ladies' room," she said, glancing up at him with the same contrived smile he had become so familiar with over the past two months. Before he could even respond, she was out of her seat and walking quickly toward the lobby.

Michael dropped his head against the back of the booth and closed his eyes.

In that moment, for just a split second, she had been the Lauren he left behind all those years ago. And although he had no right to expect that version of her, he still felt cheated when she retreated back to her guarded self.

When he watched her with Erin, he could see the real her: the kindness, the humor, the tenderness.

But the second she turned to look at him, the slight veil would shade her eyes, and the invisible wall would go up.

It could have been worse; he recognized that. She didn't have to be as nice as she was being to him. She could have berated him, castigated him, told him exactly what she thought of him and exactly where he could go.

Or worse, she could have refused to acknowledge him all together.

But she didn't. Instead, she tried to keep things amiable, and he should have been happy about that. He *tried* to be happy about that.

But it just wasn't enough.

Because as kind as she was trying to be, he could still so clearly remember the way she used to look at him.

March 2001

*L*auren sat on the wall near the faculty parking lot waiting for the late bus to arrive. A crowd of other students waited as well—laughing, talking, sitting on the ground trying to get some homework done—but Lauren sat by herself, her eyes downcast as she absently picked at the strap of her book bag.

"Jesus. Did someone kill your puppy?"

Lauren glanced up to see Michael walking toward her, a cigarette dangling from his mouth. He leaned over and bumped fists with his friend Jay, who walked off in the other direction as Michael continued toward her.

"No," she smiled half-heartedly. "I don't have a puppy."

"Ah. So is that why you got that mug on?" he asked as he reached the wall where she was sitting, nudging her leg with his shoulder.

"No," she said with a tiny laugh. "It's just been a bad day."

Michael stood with his back to the wall and reached up behind him; with a quick jump, he was up and sitting beside her. "Do I need to kick somebody's ass?"

She laughed to herself and shook her head, and then she reached up and fanned the air in front of her face, scrunching her nose at him. He rolled his eyes before he took the cigarette out of his mouth and flicked it over the wall behind them.

"So what's the problem?" he asked.

Lauren sighed. "It's just been a frustrating day. For starters, neither one of my parents are coming to my meet this weekend, and it's the biggest one of the season."

"Why aren't they coming?"

"My dad's gonna be away on business, and now my mom has to go help my grandma move because my aunt can't do it anymore."

"Okay," Michael nodded. "What's the other problem?"

Lauren shook her head and looked down. "It's stupid. I just found out I won't be able to run for student government next year."

"Why not?"

"Because it coincides too much with gymnastics."

Michael leaned back on his hands. "So fix it."

Lauren looked over, her brow pulled together.

"If you want to do both, then do both. Talk to your coach. See if you can work something out. Or talk to the student advisor. The whole point of being on student government is to bring about change, right? It's stupid that athletes can't participate. You should say something."

"I'm not good at confrontation."

"True," he said. "But you're good at being reasonable. It's a reasonable request. I mean, they might still say no, but shit, at least you'll know you tried."

Lauren nodded, looking down as she swung her feet.

"If you really want something, you shouldn't stop until you get it, no matter what you have to do. That's how I see it, anyway."

"Yeah," she sighed. "I guess that makes sense."

"As for the other thing," Michael said, looking off into the distance. "I mean…is it that important for you to have someone at your meet?"

Lauren looked down as she began picking at the straps of her backpack again.

"I'm not making fun of you," he added. "I genuinely want to know. I don't know about this kind of stuff. Does it really make a difference if someone is there?"

In that second, Lauren could have kicked herself. She felt so stupid and selfish, complaining that her parents would miss *one* meet, when Michael's parents had been missing out on things his entire life.

She shrugged nonchalantly, trying to belittle the situation. "It's not that big of a deal. I just feel like I do better when I know someone I care about is watching me. I guess it's like…motivation to make them proud or something."

She looked over at him and saw that his expression had turned thoughtful. "Yeah, I get that. But what about just doing it for you?"

She smiled. "You're right," she said, trying to look away before he could see it was forced.

She should have known he wouldn't buy it.

"Alright, that's it," he said, jumping down off the wall and turning toward her. "Let's go."

"Go?"

"Yep. Off the wall," he said as he turned and walked toward the parking lot.

"I have to catch the bus," she called after him, and he waved his hand behind him dismissively.

"I'll take care of it. Let's go," he said, not even turning to see if she was following him.

She watched him for a second before she rolled her eyes and jumped off the wall with a huff.

"Where are we going?" she asked when she finally caught up to him.

"For a ride," he said, waving his hand like a game show hostess in front of something that looked like it used to be a car a long, long time ago.

"Whose is this?" she asked, looking over the black hatchback that was missing two hubcaps and covered in scratches and rust spots of varying sizes and colors.

It looked like a Jackson Pollock.

"Mine," he said matter-of-factly, walking around to the driver's side.

"Since when?" she asked.

"Since now."

Lauren lifted her eyes to his. "Did you steal this?" she asked, and he tilted his head.

"Come on now, Red. Thanks for the vote of confidence."

"So you *paid* for this? That's actually worse than stealing it."

He laughed out loud, flipping her off over the top of the car. "Quit being such a bitch and just get in the car," he said through his smile, opening his door. "Wait," he said suddenly, holding his hand up to stop her. "You've had a tetanus shot, right?"

Lauren tried not to laugh as she pulled open the passenger door, cringing when it made a sound like a dying whale.

But it was nothing compared to the sound the car made when he started it.

As she put on her seatbelt, she flinched again. "That sounds like a broken blender," she yelled over the noise.

"It's great, isn't it? This guy down the road from me was gonna junk it. Sold it to me for a hundred bucks," he added before he switched gears, and Lauren cupped her hands over her ears and hoped it was a short drive to wherever they were going.

As they pulled out of the parking lot, she couldn't help but notice the stares they were getting from the other students. She told herself it was just the eyesore of a car and the deafening, metallic clanking it made as it chugged out of the lot, but the truth was, she knew they'd be getting that look even if they'd been merely walking together.

She didn't understand how people hadn't gotten over it by now.

They'd been friends for almost four months, and still people acted shocked when they were spotted talking in the halls, or sitting together at the pizzeria.

Or driving off campus together.

Fine. She could recognize the hint of controversy in that last one, but nevertheless, it didn't make sense that they were still fodder for gossip. Lauren Monroe had befriended Michael Delaney, and she hadn't ended up dead, or on drugs, or been arrested, or joined a cult. The whole thing should have been pretty boring, actually.

After about five minutes of driving, Michael finally pulled the car over and cut the engine, and the sudden silence made her ears ring.

"Here we are," he said as he exited the car, and Lauren got out, wiggling her finger in her ear.

"I feel like I just left a concert," she mumbled.

"God, you really got your panties in a bunch today," he said with an amused laugh as he opened the chain-link gate in front of them and gestured for her to go first.

It finally dawned on Lauren that they were at the community park.

"Why are we here?" she asked as she looked up at him. "I didn't even think this place was open in March."

"Well, apparently it is," he said, nodding toward the open gate. "Go."

She glanced at the empty park before looking back at him, and he stood there watching her, waiting.

"Okay," she sighed, walking into the park, and she heard the gate clang shut behind them as he followed her.

"To the slide," he said, and she walked around the swings to the left and stood beside it, turning to look at him. "Go ahead," he added, motioning for her to climb it.

She looked at him like he was crazy, but he was watching her, his expression even.

"Um, okay?" she said stoically before she climbed the ladder and sat down at the top of the slide. "Why am I doing this again?"

"Because I asked you to. Go ahead."

She shook her head before she pushed off the top and slid down to the bottom. As soon as her feet hit the floor, she looked up at him.

The corner of his mouth lifted in a smile. "No, that was horrible. Do it again."

"Michael," she said, annoyed. "I'm freezing. Can you just tell me what the point of this is?"

"Yes. As soon as you go down again."

Lauren pushed off the slide in a huff, and she heard him chuckle behind her as she climbed the slide again.

"Put your arms up this time. And say 'whee' when you come down."

"No," she said as she positioned herself at the top of the slide.

"Just humor me, please," he said, his smile gone. "This is serious."

She stared at him for a second before she nodded. "Fine," she said softly, and she pushed off the top and lifted her arms. "Wheee," she deadpanned pitifully, and as soon as her feet hit the sand below, he burst out laughing.

"My God, that was pathetic. Get over here," he said, grabbing her wrist and pulling her off the slide.

"Is the point of this to make me look like an idiot?" she said as he dragged her away.

"No, that's not the point, but it's definitely a plus," he said through his laughter, and she reached over and smacked him with her free hand.

"Here," he said, backing her into one of the swings, and she grabbed the metal chains on either side as he came up behind her, gripping the chains just above her hands. And then he took several steps backward until she was as far back as the chains would allow.

Michael leaned forward so that his chest was pressed against the length of her back, and her breath caught in her throat. "Ready?" he said in her ear, and before she could respond, he shoved her forward with such force that she lost her stomach; Lauren squeezed her eyes shut as she gripped the chains tighter and curled her knees up to her torso.

As she swung back, she felt his hands on her lower back, cushioning her descent and sending her right back up, even higher than before. The cold wind whipped her hair around her face, and as her stomach dropped again, she laughed.

She careened back toward Michael and this time he caught her by the hips, gripping them firmly as he ran forward and gave her a vigorous push as he darted underneath her. Lauren flew up higher than she'd ever been on a swing set, and she screamed, followed by unbridled laughter.

"There ya go," he said with a smile, walking back over to the swings and sitting on the one next to hers.

Lauren began pumping her legs, keeping herself going as her height gradually lessened, and she looked over at him and smiled.

"You feel better?" he asked.

"I do, actually."

Michael pushed off with his feet, rocking gently in the swing. "Whenever I'm pissed off about something, I always think to myself, 'What do I feel like doing right now?' And then I go and do it, whatever it is. Screw everyone else, ya know?" He looked over at her with a smirk. "And just now, I felt like coming here."

"Well, I guess that's better than kicking someone's ass."

"Hmm. That's debatable. It depends on whose ass I'm kicking."

Lauren laughed and shook her head as she pumped her legs, making the swing go a little faster.

"See, Red? When life hands you lemons, you know what you gotta do now."

"Wow," Lauren said. "Yes, Mr. Cliché, I know what I have to do. I make lemonade."

"No," he said. "You scream, *Fuck you, lemons!*"

Lauren whipped her head toward Michael, her eyes wide, and she quickly scanned the park, forgetting for the moment that it was the dead of winter and no one else was there.

"God," she said with a horrified laugh.

"And then you throw those goddamn lemons into oncoming traffic, and you go do what *you* want to do."

She tried not to laugh, but it was pointless, and as soon as she broke, he laughed along with her. She turned to look at him sitting on the swings next to her, rolling from the balls of his feet to the heels as he rocked himself in the swing.

Lauren wondered if she'd ever stop being floored by these moments. It was almost surreal. He'd been suspended three times in the four months they'd been friends, and two of those were for fighting on school grounds. She'd seen the way others looked at him, the way they avoided him, and she'd seen the way he carried himself around those people. The look in his eyes changed, his posture changed. It was like he was actually someone else.

And it was so strange, because the truth of it was, the infamous Del was just Michael to her, the boy who was quickly becoming her best friend in the world.

And that weekend, as Lauren stood at the edge of the mat chalking her hands, her eye was drawn to the stands, where one spectator stuck out like a sore thumb.

He sat on the highest bench, a sharp contrast to the adults sitting demurely in the rows before him, with his backward baseball hat, his overly casual posture, and his arm draped over the back of the bleachers as he absently drummed his fingers against the wood.

All her breath left her in a rush, and she shook her head slightly in disbelief.

His eyes were scanning the mats below, and when he finally made eye contact with her, she grinned up at him and waved.

And when he winked at her, she knew beyond a shadow of a doubt that from that moment on, she would do anything for him.

She turned then, walking to the other side of the mat as she got ready to make her run, her adrenalin racing because she knew he was watching.

And she couldn't help but smile at the irony of the fact that the baddest boy in school could somehow always make her feel like the world was good.

October 2011

*L*auren couldn't concentrate to save her life.

She sat in the back of her Psychological Defense Mechanisms class, her pen poised on her notebook as if she was getting ready to write, but her mind was a million miles away.

Actually, her mind was just a few miles away, back at Adam's office.

Earlier that afternoon, he had suggested a more aggressive stretching routine to counteract the core exercises she was now doing. Lauren had laid on her back as Adam took her leg and lifted it straight up, slowly but surely pushing it closer to her chest, all the while explaining to her how certain hamstring stretches actually release the lower back rather than the legs. As she grew more comfortable, he leaned over and pressed the front of his shoulder to the back of her leg, using some of his body weight to increase the intensity of the stretch.

And that was the moment Lauren's mind kept going back to: looking up at him as he leaned over her.

With her leg propped up on his shoulder.

"...Can be found in chapter six of your textbooks. These two are most commonly confused, and can often exist simultaneously in a person's psyche," Lauren heard her professor say as he gestured toward the screen behind him, and she blinked quickly, snapping out of it as she sat up a bit straighter in an attempt to regain her focus.

Two words were projected on the large screen in the front of the lecture hall: *repression* and *suppression*.

"Both are Freudian concepts concerned with removing unwanted or unpleasant memories from one's conscious, but the difference between the two is that suppression involves the cognizant desire to forget, whereas repression happens subconsciously."

Lauren made a shorthand notation of that on her page as the professor continued, "Now, either one of these methods in moderation can be considered healthy. It's only when they occur in extremes that they hinder a person's emotional development and impede their ability to heal from traumatic events."

She chewed on the corner of her lip, writing that down as her mind shifted away from Adam's office and back to the place it usually did as she sat in these classes.

Right back to him. Always to him.

"Now, believe it or not, most of the time, it's easier to work with someone who is suppressing painful thoughts rather than repressing them. Since repression is a subconscious method of protection, oftentimes the subject will not even be aware that the element being repressed even exists, which lends itself to denial. However, with suppression, the subject is well aware of the issue; he just chooses to avoid dealing with it."

Lauren sighed softly.

It was just so classically Michael.

She'd never admitted it out loud to anyone—in fact, she'd never even officially admitted it to herself—but it was Michael who made her want to go into child psychology. She couldn't help but feel like if he had been given the tools to deal with his emotional suffering when he was young, if he'd just had access to the necessary coping strategies, so much could have been different.

But instead, he fell back on what worked, on what was safest and easiest for him: he refused to deal with any of it. And it made an already miserable situation a hundred times worse. She hadn't even been aware of how severely it all affected him until the very end.

Lauren pressed her lips together, looking down as she rolled her pen between her fingers.

Because she realized then that she was guilty of the same exact thing.

As much as she denied still caring about everything that happened between them, as much as she insisted to Jenn that it was years ago and that it was all in the past, the truth was, she'd never gotten over it.

Lauren would have never admitted that if he hadn't come back into her life; she realized that. She would have gone about her business, choosing to pretend she was unaffected by her past, and if she'd never seen him again, she probably would have been able to believe her own lie. But his reappearance had given her past a voice again.

And as much as she wanted to, she couldn't pretend it didn't exist anymore.

Lauren put her pen down, not even attempting to take notes anymore as she thought of her dinner with him the other day. The whole time she sat across from him, she had to focus intently on maintaining her carefully cultivated façade. She could feel how effortless it would have been to fall right back into things with him, how simple it would have been to pretend there were no missed years in between, to pretend that nothing had ever gone wrong between them.

But she fought to stay guarded, because allowing herself to be vulnerable with him again would have been a very dangerous—and stupid—thing for her to do.

So she sat across from him, battling her instincts to let him back in, yet refusing to address what was preventing her from doing it in the first place.

Lauren sighed and shook her head: here she was, a future psychologist, blatantly guilty of suppression.

And just like that, it hit her.

She wasn't going to avoid it anymore.

She was doing the very thing that caused him so much additional suffering. She knew it wasn't healthy for him, so what made her think it would be healthy for her?

She needed to talk to him. *Really* talk to him. She knew that now.

The only thing she didn't know was why.

What did she hope to gain from talking it out with him? Did she want the answers Jenn claimed she was entitled to? Did she even need closure after all this time?

Or did she just want her friend back?

If it was about friendship, she knew she couldn't have the latter without the former. They could never truly be friends again without her understanding what had gone wrong between them.

So if she was going to let him back into her life, then she would need answers. They would have to talk about what happened, regardless of how awkward or unpleasant it would be, so that she could move on and not just pretend that she had.

Maybe they could *both* move on.

A small smile curved Lauren's lips at the realization that they could potentially rekindle their friendship.

She missed it.

She missed *him*.

Even when she was pretending she wasn't hurt, she never pretended not to miss him.

With newfound determination, Lauren picked up her pen and resumed taking notes off the front board.

She could just hear Jenn's reaction to the idea of forming a friendship with Michael Delaney again, and she couldn't help but smile.

Because if Jenn considered being an adult and moving on "selective amnesia," well, then that would be *her* problem.

"Lauren Monroe?"

Lauren looked up from her seat in the waiting room, her brow already furrowed. It wasn't the voice she'd been expecting.

"Hi, I'm Dr. Lawrence. I'll be taking care of you today," said an older gentleman with a polite smile. He wore light green scrubs, not Adam's usual dark blue, and his graying hair and little potbelly were the embodiment of what Jenn had pictured when Lauren first told her she had a crush on her chiropractor.

"Oh," Lauren said, clearly taken aback, and she hesitantly placed the magazine she'd been reading on the table in front of her as she stood.

"Right this way," he said, turning and walking into one of the exam rooms behind them.

Lauren felt the slight anxiety begin in her chest as she followed this new doctor into the room.

"Um, is Dr. Wells out sick?" she asked with strained casualness.

"No, he transferred you this morning. You'll be finishing up the remainder of your therapy with me."

Lauren froze, and Dr. Lawrence must have noticed the look on her face.

"He didn't mention this to you?"

She shook her head, silent.

"I apologize then. I thought he'd gone over the switch with you. Let me assure you though, I've thoroughly acquainted myself with your information and your therapy plan, and I'm well versed in all the procedures Dr. Wells has been using with you. I'm fully comfortable in going forward as long as you are."

Lauren swallowed and nodded, too focused on her own insecurities to even acknowledge her anxiety over having another doctor work on her.

Had she done something wrong? She honestly thought the flirting had been mutual. Things had never gotten inappropriate; it had all been so harmless.

At least, she *thought* it had been harmless.

She laid down on the table, her mind so lost in her own self-doubt that she forgot to panic as the new doctor adjusted her.

When Lauren left the office twenty minutes later, she was still in a fog of humiliation. She approached her car, mindlessly digging in her purse for her keys, and she found herself trying to come up with an excuse to discontinue her therapy there.

She didn't want to chance facing him again now that he was clearly trying to avoid her.

"Lauren?"

She froze with her hand in her purse, and she closed her eyes and swallowed before she turned.

He was leaned up against a silver car, dressed in a T-shirt and jeans. It was the first time she'd ever seen him outside of his scrubs.

"Hi," she said, forcing a smile, and he pushed off the car and walked toward her.

"Listen, I switched you over to Dr. Lawrence's care," he said as he shoved his hands in his pockets.

"Yeah, he told me," she said, the same contrived smile in place as she looked down and continued searching for her keys. She was so aware of herself, of her awkwardness as she tried to ensure that she wasn't flirting, but at the same time, wasn't showing her disappointment.

"He's wonderful," Adam said. "Taught me everything I know."

Lauren smiled politely, glancing up as she finally pulled her keys out of her purse.

"You're in good hands with him," he assured her. "You only have about two weeks of therapy left anyway, so you'll be fine."

Lauren nodded. "Okay, well, thanks for everything," she said before she turned and started walking toward her car.

Then she stopped.

No more avoiding unpleasant things, she reminded herself, and she turned to see him still standing where she'd left him.

"Can I ask you something?" she asked, straightening her posture.

"Of course."

"Why did you switch me?"

Adam took a deep breath, running his hand through his hair. "Well, I just thought it would be unprofessional if I asked out one of my patients."

Lauren blinked, her hand dropping to her side. "What?"

"I know. I could have waited the two weeks until you finished your therapy, but I've already waited seven, and it hasn't been easy."

She blinked at him again, unmoving, and he smiled his trade-mark grin.

"So, can I take you out? You basically have to say yes at this point, otherwise I've given away my favorite patient for nothing."

What he was saying finally registered, and Lauren tried not to smile. "So basically I have to go out with you now out of sympathy? Like a pity date?"

He laughed her favorite laugh. "You can call it whatever you want, as long as you let me take you out."

And when he looked up at her from under his eyelashes, she couldn't fight her smile any longer. "Well," she sighed, "I guess one pity date couldn't hurt. I can always have a friend call me with a fake emergency."

"Or excuse yourself to the bathroom and escape out the window."

"That's right," she laughed. "I always forget about that one."

"But Lauren?" he said, beginning to walk backward toward his car. "Yeah?"

"Give me a chance. I promise you won't want to escape."

She bit her lip. "I believe you."

Adam grinned. "I'll call you later. We'll make definite plans," he said, holding up his hand before he turned and walked back toward his car.

And Lauren watched him go, fighting the urge to jump up and down like a little girl.

Michael stood in the vestibule of Learn and Grow, disappointed to see it was the curly-haired woman who stood in the doorway of the pre-K room dismissing the children today.

He moved over to the bench along the wall, resigning himself to the fact that this was a sign he should leave well enough alone. But as soon as he sat, his new vantage point gave him a clear view of Lauren sitting on top of a table inside the classroom, writing on some type of clipboard.

He watched her chew the corner of her lip the way she always did when she was deep in thought, and he smiled.

She glanced up then, scanning the vestibule, and after a second her eyes landed on him. Before he'd even fully decided to do it, he motioned for her to come out, and she pointed to herself and raised her eyebrows as if to ask, *me?*

Michael laughed at her innocence and nodded, and she put down the clipboard as she hopped off the table and walked toward the entryway. He stood and circumvented a group of waiting parents as he met her at the door.

"Is everything okay?" she asked.

"Oh, yeah, everything's fine. I just wanted to run something by you."

"Okay, what's up?" she asked, smiling and waving at a little girl who ran past her and out to her mother.

"I wanted to know if you wanted to try that dinner thing again. A real restaurant this time. Someplace without games and kiddie rides."

"Oh. Um, I have class tonight."

"Not tonight. I was thinking this Saturday."

"I can't."

Whatever expression crossed his face, it must have been pathetic, because she immediately added, "It's not because I don't want to. I just…I already have plans."

"A date?" he asked, instantly embarrassed by his own brazenness. "Sorry," he added quickly. "That's none of my business."

"It's okay. But, um…maybe another time?" She smiled politely up at him, and he nodded.

"Sure. That sounds good," he said, and as soon as she turned and walked back into the classroom, he pulled his brow together and looked down.

"Erin Delaney," the curly-haired woman called, and seconds later Erin came bounding out of the room.

"Hi Daddy!" she beamed, hugging him around the leg, and he bent and scooped her up.

"Hi baby girl. Did you have a good day?"

"Yes! We played hide-and-seek and I won!"

Michael laughed. "Good job," he said, kissing her forehead before he put her down and took her hand. "Maybe we can play tonight after dinner."

"Okay, but you're gonna lose!" she sing-songed. "I'm really, really good."

As they walked out to the car, Michael tried to focus on what he'd make for dinner that night and where he would hide when Erin asked him to play later.

But instead, his mind kept going back to the fact that Lauren had a date this Saturday night.

He had been right when he said it was none of his business. It wasn't. Yet he couldn't help feeling irritated by the whole thing. It was ridiculous; he knew that. He was trying to reestablish a *friendship* with her, so why should he care if she was dating someone else?

He kept asking himself that question, although he damn well already knew the answer.

It would be hard enough trying to win back her trust, he reminded himself, hard enough trying to earn back her friendship. So he needed to put a lid on whatever possessive, jealous bullshit was fueling his thoughts. He needed to get a grip, and fast.

Because if he thought for one second he had a shot at anything else, he was out of his mind.

June 2001

*L*auren sat on Jenn's bed, reading aloud the questions to the latest *Cosmo* quiz titled, "Are You Good-Girl Hot or Bad-Girl Hot?" to Jenn at her insistence.

"Last question," Lauren said. "You spot a cute guy across the room at a party, and your interest is piqued. Do you: (a) Stroll right over and whisper, 'Need another drink?' breathily in his ear; (b) Stay put until he finally chats with a mutual friend and then make your move; or (c) 'Accidentally' brush up against him, smile, and introduce yourself?"

"Hmm," Jenn said as she put the cap back on her nail polish and gently blew on her freshly painted fingernails. "C."

Lauren smiled and shook her head, jotting that down as she totaled up Jenn's points. "Okay," she finally said. "According to the *Cosmo* gurus, you are a Badass Bombshell."

Jenn nodded proudly. "Damn straight. What else does it say?"

"It says you strike the right balance between being naughty and nice, and you lure guys in by being playfully provocative. You put just enough out there to keep guys guessing, and anticipation is sexy."

"Sounds about right," Jenn said with a smile, hopping up on the bed next to Lauren and holding her hands up with her fingers fanned out. "You like?"

"Very pretty," Lauren said, closing the magazine and tossing it to the floor as she flopped onto her stomach. "What do you want to do now?"

"Hmm. Oh, I know. Let's talk about how hopelessly in love you are with Del."

Lauren whipped her head toward her friend. "*What?* What the hell are you talking about?"

Jenn tilted her head. "Oh come on, Lauren."

She turned away from Jenn with a huff. "It's too bad there's not a quiz in there about how well you know your friends, because you'd fail it miserably."

"Would I?" Jenn asked, and Lauren ignored her, reaching for the remote and trying hard to focus on the television as she flipped quickly through the channels.

"I still don't know what you see in him," Jenn went on casually, checking out her nails. "I mean, I think he's a scary maniac. But he obviously acts different with you, so like, if you want him, and it will make you happy, then I say go for it."

A silence filled the space between them, and Lauren chewed on the corner of her lip.

"How?" she asked softly.

"*I knew it!*" Jenn yelled, hopping up onto her knees as she pointed at Lauren.

"Yes, you're a genius," Lauren deadpanned. "Are you going to help me or make fun of me?"

"Help you, of course," Jenn said, sitting back down on the bed and fanning her hands.

Lauren rolled onto her side, facing her friend. "I think you're going to have your work cut out for you. I mean, we've been friends for almost a year. He hasn't made a move at all."

Jenn blew on her thumbnail as she looked up at Lauren from under her lashes. "Have *you?*"

"No!"

"Have you even flirted with him?"

Lauren sighed. "I don't know. I mean, we laugh a lot. We always have fun. But I don't know that I've *intentionally* flirted. Besides," Lauren said, rolling onto her back and staring up at the ceiling, "he's not the kind of guy who holds back his feelings. If he liked me, I kind of think I'd know it by now. I'm like a sister to him."

"No," Jenn said, shaking her head. "I don't believe that."

"He calls me Red."

"So?"

"So that's like the equivalent of guys calling each other by their last names," Lauren said. "Guys don't call a girl they're interested in by her last name."

"It's not your last name. It's a pet name. It's adorable."

Lauren rolled her head to the side to face Jenn. "I thought you said he was a scary maniac."

"Oh, he is. He totally is. But you're, like, his kryptonite." Lauren laughed, and Jenn flopped down on the bed next to her. "I just think his head is so far up his ass with all of those sluts he hooks up with that he doesn't realize he wants to be with an actual good girl." She turned toward Lauren. "You, of course."

"Charming, Jenn."

"But," Jenn continued, not missing a beat, "there's a surefire way to get a guy to realize he wants you, and tonight's the perfect night to pull it off."

Lauren rolled back on to her side to face her friend, totally on Jenn's hook. "What do I have to do?"

"You have to hook up with someone else."

Lauren laughed, but Jenn looked at her straight-faced until her laughter gradually slowed. "You're serious?" she asked hesitantly.

"That junior Travis what's-his-name is having a party tonight. His parents are out of town, and there will be drinking there. No adults plus booze equals Del. So tonight, he'll go. We'll go. And you'll find a cute guy, and you'll hook up with him," Jenn said pragmatically.

Lauren threw her hands up in the air. "How in the *hell* would that be productive?"

"Because you're just so...*pure*. Which is a great thing," Jenn added quickly, holding her hand up. "But sometimes, guys need to be reminded that there's another side to girls like that. If he hears you hooked up with someone, it will make him think of you in a sexual situation. And once he does that, he won't be able to help thinking of *himself* with you in a sexual situation. And then he'll get jealous that it wasn't him, and you're golden," she said, as if she'd just explained the simplicity of two plus two equaling four.

Lauren bit her bottom lip, blinking up at the ceiling. In a twisted way, there was some logic behind what Jenn had just said.

"I don't know," Lauren said, but even she could hear the lack of conviction in her voice.

"Trust me, Laur," Jenn said. "If you want Del to want you, you have to make him think about what he's missing."

Lauren inhaled deeply, wringing her hands together. Maybe she should take Jenn's advice. She was popular with guys, and always seemed to get the attention of whomever she was interested in.

And after all, she *had* just been deemed a Badass Bombshell by one of the most popular women's magazines.

She closed her eyes and covered her face with her hands. "I can't believe I'm going to do this," she said, and she felt the bed bounce as Jenn jumped up beside her.

"That's my girl!" Jenn said, grabbing her wrist and pulling her off the bed. "Get in the shower. We've got a party to go to."

Okay, this is kind of nice, Lauren thought to herself as she felt Mark's lips find hers again in the darkness. They were in the den on the first floor of the party, and through the closed door, Lauren could still hear the muted sounds of everyone outside.

Jenn had picked Mark out for her not five minutes after they arrived at the party. Lauren had seen him around school a few times. He played lacrosse, and according to Jenn, he had helped her find her class once when she had gotten lost the semester before. "He's nice," she assured Lauren. "And single. Go for it."

So they had mingled a little bit as Lauren slowly sipped a beer, allowing her inhibitions to become slightly fuzzy, until eventually Jenn said it was time to make their move. They walked over to where Mark and a few of his friends were hanging out, and Jenn got the conversation going until Lauren and Mark were talking and laughing on their own.

At one point, Jenn leaned over and whispered in Lauren's ear that Del had just gotten there, although Lauren had yet to see him. "Ask Mark if he wants to go talk somewhere else. He'll get what you mean," Jenn said before taking a step back and continuing her conversation with one of his friends.

And as soon as Lauren asked him, he smiled and nodded as he took her hand and walked her to the den.

She had to admit, Jenn knew her stuff.

They had sat on the couch with the door slightly ajar, talking for another few minutes, and then Mark leaned in and kissed her. As soon as he realized she was willing to kiss him back, he had gotten up and locked the door.

And now they were lying on their sides, facing each other on a wide, comfortable couch in the darkness as he continued to kiss her.

She liked the way he kissed, how soft his lips seemed. He was playful, alternating between kissing her gently and kissing her passionately. It only took a few minutes of that before Lauren felt herself growing breathless.

But then they started to move past kissing. It wasn't that it was unpleasant; it was just...weird. Maybe it wouldn't have been if she hadn't been so nervous.

His hands on her breasts were kind of nice, but when his hand ended up between her legs, it was awkward and a little uncomfortable.

And when she put her hand on him, she tried to do what she thought would feel good, but it was the first time she'd ever touched a boy like that. Her movements were kind of clumsy, and he ended up putting his hand around hers and guiding her until it was over.

And then he got up, turned on the lamp, cleaned himself up, and asked if she was ready to go back to the party.

As soon as they opened the door, Lauren found herself squinting against the brightness of the light in the house. She reached up and ran her hand through her hair, realizing it was a tangled mess, and she began combing through it with her fingers.

She looked up at Mark, and he winked down at her before he turned and walked back toward the party.

Lauren stood there, blinking against the light as she tried to spot Jenn in the crowd, when suddenly someone grabbed the top of her arm and spun her around.

"Are you okay?" Michael demanded.

"Jesus, you scared the hell out of me," Lauren exhaled.

"Are you okay?" he repeated firmly, his hand still gripping her.

"I'm fine."

"Did he do something to you?" he asked, his eyes darting back and forth between hers.

"Yes."

In an instant, his eyes turned murderous as he straightened, releasing his grip on her as he turned to scan the party.

Lauren stuck out her chin. "But I wanted him to. I liked it." It wasn't *entirely* true, but for all intents and purposes, it seemed fitting.

His eyes flashed back to hers. "Lauren, what the *hell* did you do?"

Her stomach turned uneasily. He never called her Lauren. Ever.

And in that moment, she began to second-guess her decision to take Jenn's advice. She felt the bravado leave her body. "Not that. Not what you're thinking," she said meekly.

His eyes softened ever so slightly, but Lauren could tell by the set of his jaw that he was still fighting to keep calm. "Mark Valero?" he nearly hissed at her. "I don't get it. I've never seen you talk to him. You never even talk *about* him. Since when are you interested in this kid?"

Lauren shrugged. "Since tonight, I guess."

He studied her for a moment before he asked, "How much have you had to drink?"

"Not that much," she said, feeling more and more regretful as the seconds passed.

Michael shook his head before he turned to scan the party once more. Lauren followed his gaze to where Mark was standing with his friends. He bumped fists with one of them before another handed him a beer, and then a third came up behind him, clapping him on the back and saying something in his ear that made both boys laugh.

"And now he's done with you?" Michael said angrily, whipping back toward Lauren so suddenly that she flinched. "He's just gonna go back to the party? He can't even hang out with you for a little bit?"

Lauren bit her lip and looked down. When he put it that way, she couldn't help but feel kind of stupid.

"Good choice," he added, his voice livid. "Brilliant pick. He seems like a real fucking class act."

"There you are!" Jenn said cheerily as she came out of nowhere and grabbed Lauren's hand. "Excuse us." She smiled up at Michael before she dragged Lauren into the other room.

As soon as they were out of sight, she spun toward Lauren. "So, what happened?"

"With Mark?"

Jenn rolled her eyes. "I can figure out what happened with Mark," she said, purposely giving her the once-over, and Lauren felt her cheeks get hot as she started combing through her hair again. "I meant with Del."

"Nothing happened. He's really mad."

Jenn smiled. "Good."

"No, you don't understand," Lauren said, shaking her head. "I don't think this was a good idea. I think he's really mad at me."

"No. He's mad at himself for not being the one in the room with you."

Lauren glanced over her shoulder skeptically, but Michael was gone.

"Now," Jenn said, pulling her attention back. "We get another drink, and we let him come to you. Moth to a flame, baby," she said with a smile. "And he will."

Jenn dragged her back to the keg that was set up in the kitchen so they could get another drink, and then they sat on the coffee table in the living room, sipping their beers. Jenn made small talk with the people around them, and Lauren followed suit, but every few seconds, her eyes would scan the crowd, looking for Michael.

She couldn't see him anywhere.

After about a half hour with no sign of him, Lauren finally decided that he'd probably gone home.

She looked down, awkwardly playing with the lip of her plastic cup. This was bad. She had to fix this. She'd call him when she got home, she promised herself.

But what the hell was she going to say?

Lauren looked up again, scanning the kitchen one more time, and she found Mark standing in line for the keg with two of his friends.

Michael had been right. It *would* have been nice if he'd at least hung out with her for a little bit afterward.

She was an idiot.

And just as the thought crossed her mind, she saw a crowd of people part as someone entered the kitchen from the opposite side.

Her heart leapt into her throat when she realized it was Michael.

He moved quickly, passing everyone who was waiting in line for beer as he walked right up to the keg, cutting in front of Mark and grabbing the tap.

"Whoa, buddy," Mark said. "There's a line—"

Instantly Michael whirled, punching Mark in the face so hard that his feet came off the floor before he crashed back against the boy behind him and tumbled to the ground.

Lauren gasped loudly as she jumped up off the coffee table, her beer splashing to the floor. The sound—the sickening, cracking thud as his fist connected—carried all the way to the living room. She knew she'd never forget that sound.

Within seconds, people were scattering everywhere, most moving away from the scene as Mark's friends moved toward it, some of them trying to help him off the floor while the others tried pulling Michael away.

Lauren ran toward the kitchen, immediately noticing the blood on the floor as she entered. It was everywhere, looking like it was coming out of Mark's mouth or nose.

And then her eyes were pulled to the sudden, sharp movement of Michael ripping free from the boys who held him as he charged Mark again.

"Stop!" Lauren screamed, launching herself on top of the island counter that stood between her and the chaos, knocking over several bottles in the process. "Stop it!"

She tried to take his face in her hands, tried to get him to look at her, but his forward motion caused her to lose her balance. She flew backward, gripping the front of his shirt to steady herself as she landed on her backside on the countertop, sending a few more bottles shattering to the floor.

"Michael!" she screamed. For the first time since she'd known him, she felt a genuine flash of fear. He looked crazed, not even present.

"Michael, please!" she cried, feeling the tears building behind her voice.

He grabbed her wrist firmly, his eyes darting to hers, and once he realized who was gripping his shirt, she saw his eyes soften slightly. In that moment of hesitation, the boys that were behind him grabbed him again, yanking him out of her grip and restraining him long enough for the other boys to get Mark out of there.

Lauren sat on the counter surrounded by broken glass, her chest heaving and her eyes wide.

"Relax, bro! Relax!" one of the boys was yelling as a third ran to help them restrain Michael.

Lauren's eyes were locked on him as she watched him scan the scene, taking in the people backing away, the blood on the floor, the arms fighting to control him.

He jerked forward again, breaking free from the boys, but this time he moved toward Lauren.

"Let's get out of here," he said through labored breath, extending his hand to her.

Her body was shaking with adrenalin, her breath coming in gasps. She glanced over at Jenn, who was standing on the threshold of the kitchen, both hands clamped over her mouth and her eyes wide.

For a moment, it looked like she regretted the advice she'd given Lauren.

But then Michael grabbed Lauren's hand and pulled her off the counter, towing her out of the room, and as he dragged her past Jenn, she dropped her hands and smiled. "This is it. Call me," she whispered quickly as Lauren passed her.

As soon as they were outside, Michael released her hand as he tore down the driveway, and Lauren walked double-time to keep up.

When they reached his car a few feet down the road, he yanked open the passenger door before he stormed around the front of the car to his side.

"Are you okay to drive?" she asked softly.

He got in and slammed the door, and the next sound was the thunderous sound of the car starting. She stood there, hesitating for a moment as she took a shaky breath.

"Please just get in," she heard him say roughly from inside the car, and she swallowed before she slid into the seat and closed the door, buckling her seatbelt.

He took off like a shot, peeling rubber as they turned down the street, and Lauren leaned forward and grabbed the dash.

"Michael, please!" she said, and instantly, he took his foot off the gas and the car slowed to a reasonable speed.

She exhaled heavily, sitting back in her seat as she glanced over at him. He was looking straight ahead, his expression unreadable.

Maybe this *was* it. Maybe Jenn was right, and this would be the moment he'd confess his feelings. *I want you. I don't want you to be with anyone else. I want you to be mine, only mine.*

But there was nothing.

They drove the entire way to her house in silence. He didn't even turn the radio on.

When Michael finally pulled into the top of her driveway and cut the engine, they sat there for a few silent moments before Lauren finally sighed. "That really wasn't necessary," she said. "You could have gotten arrested."

"That kid mouthed off to me!" he snapped.

Lauren turned toward him, her expression unimpressed. "He said 'whoa, buddy' because you cut him in line."

"He's got a big fucking mouth!" Michael yelled, cutting her off. "And you had no business getting involved. You could have gotten hurt!"

Lauren closed her eyes and shook her head. She knew better than to try to have a conversation with him when he was like this. She took a small breath and turned to get out of the car.

He reached out and grabbed her arm, gently this time.

"You're not hurt, are you?"

His voice had softened significantly, although she knew him well enough to know that he was still annoyed.

"No, I'm fine," she said softly.

Michael released her arm and exhaled heavily. "I'm sorry if I scared you."

"You didn't scare me," she lied. "I just...I wish you would try to keep your head next time, okay?"

"And *I* wish you would use better judgment when it comes to guys next time, okay?"

Lauren looked at him for a second before she nodded silently.

"Good night, Red," he said, leaning over to kiss her forehead before he reached across her and opened the car door.

She got out and walked down her driveway in a stupor, knowing Michael wouldn't leave until she was safely inside her house.

No sooner than she opened her front door, she heard the phone in her bedroom ringing, and she ran upstairs, although she already knew who it would be.

"Yeah?" Lauren said as she sat on the edge of her bed.

"You're killing me. What happened?"

"Nothing," Lauren said, half-heartedly kicking off her shoes.

"*Nothing?*" Jenn asked. "What do you mean, nothing? Guys don't beat up other guys over girls they don't want."

"He went after him because he mouthed off to him at the keg," Lauren said.

"Oh, come on, Laur, you don't really buy that, do you? Even Del's not *that* crazy."

Lauren sighed as she flopped back onto her bed. "Either way. Remember when Tommy Greene beat up that guy who slept with his sister?"

There was only silence on the other end of the line, and Lauren knew she had Jenn cornered. "I'm telling you, I'm like his little sister. He told me to use better judgment with the next guy. That's hardly claiming me for his own."

There was another silence before she heard Jenn sigh on the other line. "So that's it, then?"

Lauren closed her eyes, because she didn't know what other choice she had. The bottom line was Michael Delaney never held back from what he wanted, and if it was her, she would know.

"Well, this sucks," Jenn said. "Because after what Mark Valero went through tonight, you're gonna have a hell of a time getting another guy to hook up with you."

November 2011

*L*auren sat in the passenger seat of Adam's car, alternating between glancing at his profile and looking out the window, trying to figure out where they were going.

When he had called her a few days ago to finalize their plans, he'd only told her to dress casually. Lauren had pressed him for more information, but he was deliberately vague. It didn't bother her then—in fact, she found it kind of endearing—but now that they were in his car driving to some unknown destination, it was driving her crazy.

When she looked back at him for what must have been the tenth time, she saw a smug smile curving the corners of his lips.

"You enjoying yourself over there?" she asked, her brow quirked.

"Am I enjoying watching you squirm? Of course not."

"Doesn't look like it from where I'm sitting," Lauren said, folding her arms and fighting her own smile as she glanced out the passenger window again.

"We're almost there," he said, his voice breaking on the chuckle he could no longer contain, and Lauren shook her head.

"That settles it. I'm definitely escaping through the bathroom window once we get there," she said, earning her a full-blown laugh as Adam slowed the car and turned up what Lauren thought was a side road, but ended up being a wide driveway.

Through the dusk, she saw the flash of the sign at the bottom of the drive: "South Hills School of Business and Technology."

She turned toward him, her brow lifted. "You're taking me to school?"

"Sort of," he said, pulling into a parking space in front of one of the buildings.

Before she could ask anything else, Adam was out of the car and walking around to her side, opening the door for her. He extended his hand to help her out, closing the door behind her, and Lauren had to bite her lip to hide her smile when he intertwined their fingers rather than letting her hand go as they began walking toward the glass doors at the front of the building.

They walked down the corridor in silence, stealing little peeks at each other as they went. His playful glances—along with the feel of his hand clasping hers—lit a warmth in her belly that reminded her of being a teenager again.

Lauren couldn't deny how good he looked tonight: a pair of nice jeans and a black button-down shirt, his blond hair looking somewhat unkempt and yet still impeccable at the same time.

And he smelled amazing.

"Here we are," he said, gesturing with his head toward the large sign on the door they had stopped in front of.

Couple's Cooking Class: Saturday Evenings, 6:30 p.m.

As Lauren read it, a slow smile broke over her face.

"I figured any guy could take you out to dinner, but how many guys can cook you a gourmet meal?"

"Impressive," she said, looking up at him. "I didn't know you could cook."

"Oh...well, I can't, actually," he said, rubbing the back of his neck with his free hand and shrugging. "Hence this class." Lauren laughed as he added, "But it still counts, right?"

He reached for the door and released her hand, placing his on the small of her back as she walked into the large room. There were about ten cooking stations, complete with stoves, appliances, measuring cups and spoons, and some ingredients already lined up on the counter space.

"Welcome!" beamed a middle-aged woman from the front of the room. "Have you signed up in advance for this evening's class?"

"Yes," Adam said. "Adam Wells."

The woman looked down through the glasses balanced precariously on the tip of her nose, scanning a clipboard. "Ah yes, here you are. Excellent! Help yourselves to any open station," she said, gesturing grandly toward the room.

There were five other couples already scattered at various stations, and they all smiled and nodded in greeting as Adam and Lauren made their way to the empty station on the far right of the room.

"This was a great idea," Lauren said as they settled in. "Thank you."

"A thank you before the date even begins? Does this mean I no longer have to fear a bathroom exodus?"

Lauren smiled as she went up on her toes to plant a kiss on his cheek. "I'm not going anywhere."

And when she pulled back, the look in his normally playful eyes was now something else all together, and it turned the warmth in her belly into a full-blown inferno.

"Okay ladies and gents," the woman called from the front of the room, breaking the spell. "I think we have everyone for tonight, so let's get started." With a quick clap of her hands, she added, "If you'll please head to the bin in the back of the room and grab yourselves an apron."

They walked to the back amid the other couples, each grabbing an apron out of a large container. Lauren slid hers over her head as she walked back toward their station, tying it behind her back as she went. She looked down as she smoothed her hands over the front of it, noticing the white letters scrawled over the red fabric: *Kiss the Cook.*

"Can you give me a hand?" she heard Adam ask, and she looked over to see him with his back to her, his normally dexterous hands fumbling with the flimsy strings.

"A chiropractor with inept hands?" she sighed, clucking her tongue and shaking her head. "I guess I should be thanking my lucky stars you transferred me to someone competent." She pulled the strings out of his struggling fingers and began tying.

Adam turned to look at her over his shoulder. "You think my hands are inept?" he asked, and Lauren shrugged, fighting a smile, her knuckles grazing the firm muscles of his back as she tied the apron.

"That's good," he said with a nod, turning away from her again. "That might work in my favor."

"Oh? How is that?" she asked, finishing up the bow, and he turned toward her; the mischief in his eyes belied his innocent expression.

"Because proving you wrong could be kind of fun."

Lauren's stomach twirled with something she couldn't quite place as she looked up at him, but before she could respond, her eyes dropped to his chest. She burst out laughing, cupping both her hands to her mouth in an attempt to muffle the sound.

He pulled his brow together and looked down. "Ah, crap," he said through a groan, shaking his head as his laughter combined with hers.

On the front of his white apron was the outline of a cartoon woman's body, her obscenely large breasts bursting out of a tiny bikini top and her thighs swelling out of an equally skimpy bottom. Adam looked up sheepishly as he held his hands over his cartoon breasts, attempting to hide them, which only made Lauren laugh harder.

"Switch with me," he said.

"Not on your life," Lauren said through her laughter. "Besides, it looks good on you. Who would have thought you were so voluptuous under those scrubs?"

Adam lifted his eyebrows. "How long have you been thinking about what's under my scrubs?" he challenged.

"Okay, ladies and gentlemen, now that we are all properly attired, let's begin!" the teacher said. "If you'll have a look at the folder on the right side of your station…" Adam leaned around Lauren to grab the folder, bringing his chest flush with her back.

"Saved by the bell," he whispered in her ear, and she felt a faint shiver run down her spine that was as pleasant as it was unexpected.

She should have known better by now; no matter how many times she thought she had him trumped, he always seemed to end up with the upper hand.

And she liked it. A lot.

Adam opened the folder and took out the papers inside, spreading them out on the counter and following along as the teacher went over the menu for the evening. Or rather, their assignment. Smoked salmon and crème fraiche bruschetta for an appetizer, filet mignon with a red wine mushroom sauce over sautéed spinach and baby carrots for the main course, and a cinnamon peach crumble with vanilla ice cream for dessert.

"Jesus," he mumbled, his eyes scanning the paper in front of him.

"A little out of your element?" Lauren asked, feeling a bit nervous herself as she scanned the recipe.

"There's a pizza place right down the road," he said, putting the paper down and looking up at the teacher. "If this takes a turn for the worse, we hit it up on the way home."

"Deal," Lauren laughed, turning to look at the teacher as she held up a knife and explained the proper way to dice a tomato.

About an hour and a half later, they were seated in the adjacent room, which was set up to look like a makeshift restaurant, complete with linens and good silverware and candlelight. The couples all sat, waiting to be served the meals they had just prepared for themselves.

"I'm telling you, you've found your calling," Lauren said as Adam poured them each a glass of wine.

"Don't get smart," he said, glancing up at her with a smirk as he placed the bottle back on the table.

"I'm not! I thought you were great in there. Well, except for the whole carrot thing."

Adam laughed, shaking his head. He had started to chop them, not realizing the recipe called for them to be served whole, and each time he brought the knife down on the raw carrots, tiny pieces would shoot off the cutting board in different directions, like rogue missiles, hitting Lauren and at times the couple in front of them. Finally, the teacher came over and laid a placating hand on his wrist, telling him it was unnecessary for the recipe, and Lauren had to focus extremely hard on sautéing the spinach to keep from laughing.

"Oh, and the onion thing," Lauren added, smirking before she took a delicate sip of wine.

"You know, a lesser man's ego would be bruised by all these backhanded compliments."

"Good thing you're not a lesser man, then."

Adam smiled, lifting his glass to hers, and she clinked it softly. "And besides," he said, "you were the one who assigned me the onions to chop. You could have mentioned it's a step below getting maced."

Lauren laughed. "Why do you think I passed the job to you?"

Adam narrowed his eyes at her. "Cruel."

"I'm sorry. I'll make it up to you."

He raised his brow before he smiled. "Fair enough," he said as a server brought their appetizers to the table.

"Well," Lauren said once the plates were in front of them. "Ready?"

"If you are," Adam said, lifting his fork.

Lauren nodded, and they both cut a small piece of the smoked salmon and crème fraiche bruschetta, bringing it to their lips. After chewing in silence for a second, Adam brought the back of his hand to his mouth. "Wow," he said around his mouthful of food. "That's…"

"Incredible," Lauren finished for him, taking another forkful. "Do you think this is actually the one we made, or are they taking pity on us and serving us the real deal?"

"If this is them taking pity on us, I'll gladly accept it. Damn," he added after taking another bite. "We're good. We're actually good. I'm impressed with us."

"Agreed," she laughed, dabbing her mouth with the napkin.

Adam took a sip of wine. "So," he finally said. "Can I ask what made you want to be a child psychologist?"

Lauren lifted her wine, taking a sip, which gave her a few extra seconds to formulate her answer. She went with partial truth.

"I don't know. I guess I've just seen a lot of kids who don't have the coping strategies for issues they're encountering at young ages, whether it's emotional or developmental. And I know that having those strategies, having an outlet, makes all the difference. In how they turn out, I mean. And I just…I want to do more than be a teacher for kids like that." She looked up to find him watching her intently. "I know…that sounds so…"

"Admirable? Humane? Commendable?"

Lauren felt her cheeks get hot. "I was going to say clichéd."

Adam shook his head. "Not at all," he said softly.

She smiled then, dropping her eyes for a moment. "What about you?" she asked, lifting her fork again. "What made you want to be a chiropractor?"

He shrugged. "I broke my neck."

Lauren froze with her fork halfway to her mouth, her eyes growing wide. "You broke your neck?"

He nodded, taking the last bite of his appetizer before he wiped his mouth.

"Oh my God," Lauren said. "When? How?"

"My senior year of high school. I had just landed a baseball scholarship to the University of Texas the week before it happened. We were playing the last game of our season. I was on second, and the guy up at bat hit a hard grounder down the left side. The third baseman squatted down to field it just as I slid headfirst into third, and *boom*." He crashed his two fists together in front of him. "My head, his knee."

Lauren cringed, shaking her head. "Jesus."

"Oh, it sucked."

"How are you...How can you...?"

"I got lucky. Really, really lucky. And on top of that, the rehab facility I was in was amazing. And that's when I knew it was what I wanted to do."

"Wow," Lauren said. "So, how long were you in rehab?"

The server who had just arrived to bring them the main course cast a look between them before he awkwardly cleared his throat and excused himself, and Adam laughed.

"Great. When they come and confiscate our wine, it's going to be your fault."

Lauren covered her face with her hands and laughed, and Adam leaned over the table, removing her hands. "A month," he said, running his thumb over her knuckles and lighting the warmth in her belly again. "And then another three months as an outpatient," he said, finally releasing her hand to lift his utensils. "Ready?"

She looked him in the eyes and nodded. "I think so," she said softly, and whether he realized it or not, she was referencing more than tasting the meal.

The main course was fantastic, and the dessert made Lauren moan, much to her embarrassment and Adam's amusement. Their conversation was effortless, and interesting, and funny, and Lauren couldn't remember the last time she'd had so much fun. The entire date couldn't have gone more perfectly.

But despite that, as Adam walked her up to her door, she felt the familiar trepidation building low in her stomach, creeping its way into her chest.

They stopped before her door, and Lauren turned to him, smiling softly. "Thank you so much. I had an amazing time."

"I'm glad," he said, looking down at her, and she could tell by the way his eyes flickered back and forth between hers that he was assessing her.

Lauren glanced down, biting her lower lip before she looked back up at him. She wanted to kiss him, she did. She just wished—

He leaned down then, stopping her thoughts as he pressed his lips to hers, and she gasped against his mouth. He immediately stilled, giving her the option to pull away, but after a stunned second she sighed, leaning into him as she deepened the kiss, temporarily forgetting her anxiety and even her name as their lips began moving together.

His mouth was amazing; tender, soft, and playful, sending little bolts of electricity to all the right places in her body.

She had no idea how long they'd been kissing—it could have been minutes or days, she was so lost in the feeling he was giving her—before she finally came back to reality. Her body was completely flush with his; one of his hands was in her hair, the other on her hip, and she had both of her hands fisted in the front of his shirt.

She pulled back slightly, releasing a trembling breath, and he dropped his forehead to hers and closed his eyes, smiling.

"Adam," she breathed.

"Mm?"

She exhaled shakily. "I'm not going to invite you upstairs."

He kept his forehead pressed against hers, but he smiled softly. "I wouldn't have come up even if you did," he whispered, his lips ghosting hers on every word.

Her mouth parted softly, and she found herself lifting her chin, trying to increase the pressure of his lips on her own, but he pulled back slightly, brushing the hair away from her face. "You're something different, Lauren. I'm not gonna rush this."

He leaned down again, pressing his lips to hers one more time before he took a step back. "I'll call you tomorrow?" he said.

Lauren nodded, unable to speak, and he smiled his trademark grin. "Good night," he said, kissing her hand before he turned to walk down the pathway toward his car.

Lauren watched him go for a second before she turned toward her door and unlocked it in a complete stupor.

She undressed, put on her pajamas, brushed her teeth, and crawled into bed, completely on autopilot.

But as soon as she was lying in the comfort of her bed, all her faculties returned to her at once, and she couldn't help but replay the entire night in her mind over and over. She smiled to herself, curling the blanket into her chest when it tingled with the memory of the way he made her laugh, the way he looked at her.

The way his mouth felt on hers.

There were only a handful of memories Lauren had done this with; committing it to her mind, playing it on repeat like a favorite movie, pulling it from her subconscious whenever she needed to smile, or laugh, or sigh.

And before this night, all those memories had belonged to Michael.

December 2001

*M*iserable did not even come close to describing how Lauren was feeling. She laid in her bed, her comforter and an extra quilt tucked up around her chin and a tissue crammed in each nostril. A sudden flash of heat overcame her, and she sat up and kicked off her covers with an angry huff, which quickly turned into a violent coughing fit.

"God," she groaned, her voice gravelly as she scooped her matted hair into a makeshift ponytail just to get it off her neck.

"Damn, Red. You look like shit."

Lauren's eyes flashed to her bedroom doorway; through her coughing, she hadn't even heard anyone come up the stairs.

"Gee thanks," she said, pulling the tissues out of her nose as discreetly as she could. She was lucid enough to realize she should have been humiliated at being seen in this condition, especially by

Michael, but truth be told, she was too sick to even pretend to care. "Why are you here?" she croaked. "You should be at the dance."

"I already told you, I don't do school dances," he said, taking off his jacket and throwing it haphazardly over the papasan chair in the corner of her room. "Besides, I can't go. Anyone who's been suspended out of school more than three times this year isn't allowed."

Lauren used a crumpled tissue to wipe her nose. "So is that why you behave the way you do? So you won't have to attend school functions?"

Michael smiled. "Yeah, you got me. Every move I make comes down to avoiding some cheesy-ass school dance."

Lauren shook her head. "Idiot," she laughed under her breath as she tossed the crumpled tissue into the trash bin near her bed.

"You sound like a phone sex operator with your voice like that."

"God, shut up," Lauren groaned, covering her face with her hands and dropping back onto her pillows.

"I'm serious," Michael said, leaning against her dresser and folding his arms. "You should try to make a couple of extra bucks for yourself while it lasts. Might as well, since you're stuck here in bed anyway. If you'll give me a cut, I'll give you the numbers of some guys that would stay on the phone for *hours*. We'll bleed them dry."

"Please just shut up," she said through her hands.

"Mmm. Just like that, baby. Keep talking," Michael said throatily, and Lauren pressed her lips together, fighting a laugh but failing.

"Honey?"

Lauren dropped her hands from her face and turned toward her bedroom doorway. "Hi Dad."

"You doing okay?" he asked, sending a quick glance in Michael's direction.

"I'm hanging in there," she said as she sat up.

Her father nodded, lingering in the doorway for a second. "Do you need more tissues?"

"No, I'm good, Dad, thanks."

He nodded again, looking around the room, his eyes landing on Michael one last time before he turned. When they finally heard the muffled sounds of him trudging down the stairs, Michael turned to look at her. His eyes dropped to the bed, taking in the three boxes of tissues that surrounded Lauren.

"More tissues?" Michael deadpanned, lifting his eyes to Lauren's face.

Lauren shrugged, fluffing her pillow up against the headboard before she leaned back against it. "That was just him making sure the door was open."

"Well shit, the man should give me a little credit, don't you think? You're a walking science experiment right now. As if I'd actually touch you."

Lauren grabbed the pillow next to her and threw it half-heartedly at him, missing by several feet. "Did you come here to make me more miserable than I already am?"

Michael laughed, walking toward his jacket on the other side of the room. "Relax. It's just the flu. You'll feel better soon."

"It's not just that," Lauren mumbled through a pout as she grabbed a fresh tissue from one of the boxes.

Michael stopped, giving her an amused look. "Oh come on. Did you really want to go to some winter formal?"

Lauren glanced up at him before blowing her nose. The truth was, she did.

But all her visions were of being at the formal with *him.*

And if he wasn't going, she really didn't care about going either way. But there was no way she was giving that as her answer.

"Not really, I guess," she said with a pathetic shrug.

"Good," he said, continuing toward his jacket, and he half-lifted it off the chair, digging in one of the pockets. "I got you something," he said, turning and tossing a plastic bag on the bed.

Lauren leaned over to grab the bag from the foot of the bed. As soon as she pulled out what was inside, she gasped, holding it to her chest.

It was a DVD of the movie *Dirty Dancing*.

"Oh my God, you remembered!" she squealed, although it came out more like a grating rasp. Jenn had borrowed her copy of the movie last summer and lost it, and Lauren had complained about it to Michael one day when she'd been in the mood to watch it.

"I only remembered because I didn't understand how someone so smart could love something so stupid."

She dropped her hands to the bed, still clasping the DVD, her expression defensive. "Have you ever even seen it?"

"I don't need to see it to know that it's crap."

"Yes, you do. It's a classic. It's practically a rite of passage!" Lauren expounded, and he smirked, shaking his head. "Here, put it in," she added, holding the DVD out to him.

"No way."

"Come on," she said, thrusting the movie at him again.

"You've lost your goddamn mind if you think I'm watching that."

Lauren dropped her hand to the bed, tilting her head at him. "Please?" she said softly, and for a brief second, something that resembled sympathy flickered behind the contempt in his expression. "It will make me feel better. Just stay and watch it with me for a little while. You don't have to watch the whole thing."

Michael stared at her for a second. "Did you practice that whole pathetic thing in the mirror before I got here?"

The corners of Lauren's mouth twitched, and he exhaled heavily. "Fine," he said, pushing off the dresser and extending his hand.

Lauren handed it to him, not allowing herself to fully gloat until his back was to her and he was putting the movie into the machine.

He hit play and walked back to the foot of the bed, sitting down and folding his arms.

The lyrics to "Be My Baby" filled the room as the opening credits played in front of black and white slow-motion clips of Kellerman's dance instructors dirty dancing in the clubhouse.

"Well shit," Michael said after a minute. He turned toward her, quirking his brow. "Whatcha got me watching here, Red?"

Lauren shook her head as he added, "You know, if our school dances looked like *this*, I might go."

She was attempting to ignore him, her eyes pinned on the screen over his shoulder, but as soon as he realized she wasn't going to give him a reaction, he got up.

Against her will, Lauren's eyes drifted from the television to where Michael now stood, both hands clasped behind his head as he gyrated his hips, biting his lower lip.

Lauren pressed her lips together, trying her hardest not to react, but then he bent his knees, dropping a bit lower as his gyrations grew more pronounced, and one of the hands that was behind his head dropped to spank the air in front of him.

"Lauren?"

She nearly jumped out of her skin at the same time that Michael straightened abruptly, his arms dropping to his sides as he whipped around to face her door.

Her father stood in the doorway, his arms folded. "Do you want some tea?"

Lauren knew the question was directed at her, even though her father's eyes were pinned on Michael.

"No, I'm okay Dad. If I need anything, I'll call down, okay?"

He looked at his daughter and nodded with a smile, turning to shoot daggers at Michael before he pushed the door open a little farther and walked back down the hall.

As soon as she heard his footsteps on the stairs, Lauren burst out laughing, falling back onto her pillows. But within seconds, her laughter transformed into a nasty, hacking cough.

When she was finally able to catch her breath, she glanced up to see Michael standing next to her bed, holding out the glass of water from her nightstand.

"I don't even feel sorry for you right now," he mumbled, and Lauren laughed again, sitting up and taking the water.

"Oh come on," she said, taking a small sip. "That was hilarious."

"How many more times is he gonna come up here?" Michael asked, sitting on the edge of the bed. "Now I remember why we always hang out at my house. Who cares if my mom is always drunk? At least she leaves us alone."

"Stop," Lauren said, leaning over to smack his shoulder. "You know that was hilarious.

"I know your parents hate me."

Her smile dropped. "No they don't."

Michael looked at her, clearly unconvinced, and she added, "My dad just gets nervous with me spending so much time with a boy."

"You mean spending so much time with *this* boy. It's okay. I get it."

Lauren sighed, leaning over to place the glass of water back on her nightstand.

"Cheer up, Red. At least your mom does her best to tolerate me."

She exhaled heavily. "My mom just kind of agrees with whatever my dad says, even if she secretly disagrees."

Michael looked down, nodding silently.

"My little brother loves you," Lauren offered.

"Yeah, well," he glanced up at her with a crooked smile. "He's too young to realize I'm an asshole."

"Stop it," Lauren said, her voice no longer playful. "You're not an asshole."

"Yes I am," he said dismissively. "Are we gonna watch this movie, or not?"

Lauren looked at him for a second, knowing it would be a waste of time to try and argue with him. She sighed again, scooting over on the bed, and Michael slid a bit farther on, sitting back against the headboard.

They watched in silence for a few minutes, and every so often, Lauren would steal a glance at him. His eyes were on the screen, but his expression was blank. She had no way of knowing if he was actually watching or if he was lost in his own thoughts, until he finally said, "This d-bag waiter. The college kid. What's his name?"

"Robbie."

"Yeah, Robbie. Is Patrick Swayze gonna kick his ass at some point?"

Lauren smiled, her eyes going back to the TV. "Yes."

"Thank God," he said, looking back at the screen. "Soon?"

Lauren laughed. "Just watch."

As he shifted on the bed, facing the screen again, Lauren glanced at him and smiled. "Why can't you show everyone this side of you?"

He didn't look at her, but she saw his brow pull together. "What side?"

Lauren licked her lips and looked down. She didn't know how to answer that. She didn't even know why she said it in the first place.

"I don't know," she finally said. "The side that clearly has a crush on Patrick Swayze?"

Without even looking in her direction, Michael shot his hand out and shoved her to the other side of the bed. He didn't even need the element of surprise; she was so pathetically weak that she would have gone flying anyway, and she grabbed at air, nearly falling off the other side.

Michael leaned over at the last second, gripping the back of her shirt and yanking her back onto the bed.

Completely disoriented, she flew back toward him and collided into his side, her head landing on his chest and her hand splayed across his stomach to stop her fall. She froze there for a second, getting her bearings, and just as she was about to push away from him, she felt his arm come around her, holding her against his side.

Her breathing momentarily stopped, and when he pulled her a bit closer, her body began to relax against him without her mind's permission.

His eyes were still on the television; she knew that from the way his chin rested on the top of her head. His body seemed totally at ease, totally content.

She turned her eyes to the television, trying to refocus on the movie, but she was not digesting a single word. She was too focused on the heat of him, which she could distinctly feel through his thin T-shirt, and the gentle thud of his heartbeat under her cheek. The smell of his soap or his detergent filled her nose, making her light-headed in a way that had nothing to do with the flu.

"You're gonna get sick," Lauren said softly.

"It's cool," he said, his eyes still on the screen as he began absently twirling the end of her ponytail. "It would be nice to miss school for something other than a suspension."

Lauren smiled then, the last of the tension leaving her body as she fully rested against his chest with a sigh.

"You know what the best part of this is?" he asked.

"Hmm?"

"Your dad's gonna shit a kitten if he comes up here."

Lauren laughed, and she felt him tighten his arm around her for a second, hugging her into his side.

"See?" he said. "Isn't this better than being at some stupid school dance?" And Lauren nodded silently against his chest.

It was definitely better.

Because she was with him.

November 2011

*M*ichael closed his daughter's door softly as he left her room, careful not to wake her. She was so exhausted that she'd fallen asleep halfway through her bedtime story, something she hadn't done since she was a baby.

He smiled sadly at the thought. He could remember those days with perfect clarity, as if it were just last night he was putting a cooing, writhing bundle down to sleep instead of a beautiful, intelligent little girl.

It was going too fast. He had the horrifying image of her declining a bedtime story one day, followed by one of her not being home at all for bedtime, spending the evening out with her friends, or worse, some boy.

He sat down with a sigh at the kitchen table, reaching toward the cell phone he'd left there earlier and spinning it absently on the smooth wood. As it slowed, he flattened his hand over it, stopping it completely before dragging it back toward himself.

Michael stared down at the phone, contemplating what he suddenly had the urge to do. He hadn't felt the need or the desire to call her for years, and he was pretty sure it was the image of Erin as a teenager that brought on the urge now; he didn't know what he'd do with a teenage girl, but he knew it would be so important for her to have a female figure in her life. Someone she could talk to.

He licked his lips as he lifted the phone, hitting a button to wake it. His head screamed at him not to make the call. She wasn't even a decent human being, so what would make him think she would ever be a suitable source of guidance and support for Erin?

The problem was he never knew if he was doing the right thing by keeping his mother out of Erin's life. In his mind, it made perfect sense for him to do it, but throughout his life, he had screwed up so many things, on so many occasions, that he wasn't sure he could trust his own judgment anymore. Granted, some of those times he purposefully made the wrong decision, chose a path he knew would be destructive. But then there were those times that he actually believed he had been doing the right thing, making the smart choice, and it still blew up in his face.

He couldn't be sure which category this particular circumstance would fall into.

He swallowed slowly as he lifted the phone and scrolled through his contacts, choosing her number and hitting send before he could talk himself out of it. As the phone began to ring in his ear, he felt his heart speed in his chest, and he closed his eyes and clenched his jaw.

"Yeah?" a voice rasped into the phone after the third ring, and Michael opened his eyes.

"*Hello?*" the woman said after another second, her voice growing a bit louder with irritation.

He opened his mouth, but no words would come.

"*Hello!*" she nearly shouted. "Who the hell is this?"

Michael's eyes fell closed again as the familiar slur rang out in that last sentence. Without opening them, he moved his thumb and hit the button to end the call.

He sat there for a second, staring at the table before he exhaled heavily and tossed the phone onto it with a soft thud. He pushed his chair back and stood, running a hand through his hair as he walked toward the sink to load the dinner dishes into the dishwasher.

When he was through, he wiped down all the counters. He straightened the living room. He put away Erin's toys. Then he went into the bathroom and wiped it down with cleaner. And when that was done, and he had nothing else to clean or neaten, he found himself walking aimlessly around the house.

The feeling of restlessness in him was unsettling, and after a few minutes he finally willed himself to go sit on the couch and calm down. He didn't understand why he felt so antsy. Sure, it was only nine o'clock on a Saturday night, but he could hardly attribute it to that; Michael hadn't been out on a Saturday night in years.

And suddenly, like a smack to the face, he understood why he was so edgy.

Lauren was out on her date tonight. It was the reason she had turned down his second dinner invitation.

He inhaled slowly through his nose as he lay back on the couch and closed his eyes, running both hands down his face.

As soon as he closed his eyes, he was assaulted with a memory of her, one that made him smile but at the same time caused his heart to clench.

It had been his junior year of high school; he was sitting in his living room, watching a football game, when there was a timid knock on his door.

He opened it, and the first thing he saw was her red nose, followed by her bloodshot eyes, and finally her tear-streaked face. He could remember the dichotomy of his emotions in that moment: the desire to pull her protectively into his arms battling against his innate desire to murder someone.

"What happened?" he asked, trying to remain composed for her.

"I need your help," she said, her voice quivering slightly, and she held out her hand.

He took it without hesitation, his jaw tightening with rage as she guided him down the driveway to where her car was parked. The entire time, he ran his thumb soothingly over the back of her hand as he envisioned making whoever did this to her bleed.

As they reached her car, Lauren had let go of his hand and opened the passenger door, and as Michael bent to get into the car, he froze.

He blinked a few times before leaning closer to the car, not sure what he was seeing.

"What..." he asked, looking over to where she stood, fighting tears. "What the *hell* is that?"

"Triple chocolate cake," she said softly. He closed his eyes and shook his head, trying to make sense of what was going on.

"For your birthday," she added, her voice so small it sounded like a child's, and his expression softened as he looked back at her. "I made it for you, and when I was driving it over here, this cat," she gestured wildly at nothing, her voice breaking on the last word, "bolted out in front of me...and I tried to swerve, but it darted back and forth, and I slammed on the brakes, and then..."

She motioned pathetically at the car, and Michael looked back inside, at the brown goop and chunks that were smeared and splattered all over the interior of the vehicle.

He pressed his lips together as he raised his eyes back to her, and she sniffled and hiccupped as she wiped her nose on her sleeve. He had been so overcome with relief in that moment that she was okay, and she had looked so adorably pathetic, that he burst out laughing.

When she heard him, she dropped her face into her hands as her shoulders shook with silent sobs, and he immediately straightened and wrapped his arms around her, pulling her into his chest.

"Come on, Red," he said through a smile. "Let's go get some rags and a bucket."

They spent the next two hours cleaning and scraping what had once been chocolate cake out of her car, and every so often, Michael would look over at her to find her eyes shining with tears again.

"Would you cut it out?" he said with a laugh. "This will all come out. You can have it detailed."

"I don't care about the stupid car," she mumbled as she dunked her chocolate-soaked rag into the bucket.

"Then why are you crying?"

"Because your cake is ruined," she said through a barely contained sob. She took a steadying breath to calm herself before she added, "I know this used to be your favorite thing about your birthday, and I really wanted you to have it again." Her chin trembled pathetically when she spoke, and Michael watched as two large tears welled along her lash line and spilled over her cheeks as she scrubbed the mat in front of her.

He stopped cleaning, the rag he was using dropping slowly to his side as he stared at her. He hadn't even remembered telling her that—the tradition of his mother making him a triple chocolate cake for his birthday—but obviously he must have.

And she had remembered. She had tried to recreate it.

It was one of the few times he remembered feeling like something happened to his heart, almost as if he could feel it swelling in his chest as he looked at her.

With a sigh, Michael shook the memory from his head as he sat up on the couch, looking around the room.

What he really wanted was a drink.

He had done that often when he was younger, drink until he felt like he had stepped out of his life for a while, but the older he got, the less he relied on it. And as soon as Erin had come into his life, he had nearly stopped drinking altogether. He had seen too much of what using alcohol as a coping mechanism did for people in his own house, and he'd be damned if he became his mother, if Erin had to watch.

He wished he had some other, safer vice. Ice cream. Reading. Playing video games. Anything he could use to escape the feeling he had tonight.

Michael inhaled slowly, pushing off his knees as he stood and walked to Erin's door. He cracked it open slightly, watching the rise and fall of her chest under the blanket. Just as he was about to close the door, he noticed the little red photo album on the foot of her bed.

He gently pushed the door open and walked over to her, sliding the book off her bed before exiting the room just as quietly as he'd entered.

He returned to his spot on the couch, opening the book and flipping ahead a few pages to the one he wanted.

His graduation photo.

He stared at the smiling, beautiful girl by his side, and he couldn't help but ask himself the question he'd been asking himself for the past eight years: if he could go back and do it all differently, would he? In all the time the question tortured him, he had never been able to come up with a definite answer.

But that was before she had come back into his life. And seeing her again, being near her again, he knew beyond a shadow of a doubt that if he could go back, if he knew then what he knew now, he'd never have made the decision he did. He'd do it all differently.

Michael ran his finger down the edge of the photo, and it lifted slightly, revealing the image on the next page. He turned it slowly, staring down at the picture of his brother, and at that moment, he realized just how bad of a fuck-up he truly was.

Because there were so many things he should have done differently.

May 1992

Michael tiptoed out of the strange bedroom, his pillow and his stuffed turtle clutched to his chest. The old lady was sitting in the chair in front of the TV, her head lolled to the side and her eyes closed. He froze for a moment, waiting, and the slow, rasping sound of her breath was enough to convince him that she was fully asleep.

He shuffled slowly into the kitchen, glancing over his shoulder every few seconds, careful not to wake the strange woman. She seemed nice enough when his mother brought him there earlier, but he didn't know her. He didn't know if she could be mean, if she would yell.

If she would do worse if he made her mad.

He didn't want to be in this strange place anymore. He just wanted his own bed. He just wanted his own house. He just wanted his brother.

Michael placed his pillow and turtle on the kitchen table, slowly and quietly dragging one of the chairs over to where a phone was mounted on the wall. At one point he stumbled, and the chair screeched against the linoleum; he froze, cringing as he turned toward the door. When a few moments passed, and he could hear nothing but the low murmur of the television and the soft breathing in the other room, he pulled the chair the rest of the way over and climbed on top of it.

He dialed the number, the one his brother made him memorize if he ever needed to speak to him when he wasn't home. It was Aaron's girlfriend's house, the place he spent basically all of his time if he wasn't spending it with Michael.

After a few rings, it sounded as if someone picked up the phone, but all Michael could hear was laughing and music. There were a couple of shouts in the background, but he couldn't understand what anyone was saying.

"Hello?" Michael said softly into the phone.

"Yo, who's this?" a strange voice said.

"Hi. My name is Michael. I'm looking for my brother Aaron." He glanced at the kitchen doorway every few seconds, trying to keep his voice down.

There was a clatter, like someone dropped the phone, and then he heard a deep voice call, "Yo! Delaney! Phone!"

There were a few more yells and laughter, and then the music changed to something that thumped so loud, Michael couldn't hear the voices anymore. Just before he was about to hang up and try again, he heard shuffling on the other end of the phone, and then finally, his brother's voice.

"Yeah?"

"Aaron," he said, his heart filling with relief. "I need you to get me."

"Mike? Where are you?"

"I don't know. The blue house across from the grocery store."

"What?" Aaron said, sounding confused. "Why are you there?"

"Mommy made me come here. She said she had things to do and I couldn't stay home tonight. I need you to come get me. I don't want to be here."

"Oh, buddy," Aaron said, his voice sounding strange. "I can't."

"Please?" Michael said, trying to keep his voice calm as he glanced toward the kitchen doorway.

"Mike, I'm with my friends...I can't..."

"Please?" he said again, and this time his voice cracked, much to his embarrassment. "I don't like it here. I'm scared. I want to sleep in your bed."

In the three years since his father had left, sometimes he would sleep with his brother when he felt scared, or sad, or when his mother was on the rampage. And even though Aaron was sixteen now, he never objected.

"Mike," Aaron said, his voice almost pleading, and then he took a breath. "Shit. Okay. Shit...alright. I'll be there in a little bit." Aaron exhaled heavily and mumbled another curse.

"Thank you," Michael said, blinking back tears. "I'm sorry."

"Hey, don't you be sorry. Don't you be sorry," he said, his voice taking on that strange quality again. "Love you, Mike. I'm coming." And then he hung up.

Michael hung up quickly and slid down off the chair, struggling to bring it back to the table without making noise. As soon as he did, he grabbed a napkin off the counter and wrote a note to the old woman, telling her he went home. And then he grabbed his pillow and his turtle and tiptoed through the living room to the front door.

He turned the knob slowly, his eyes on the sleeping woman the entire time, and gently squeezed out onto the porch, shutting the door softly behind him.

He wasn't sure how long he stood there on the porch in the dark, hugging his pillow and stuffed animal, but eventually he saw a pair of headlights coming down the road, and he smiled widely, walking down the steps and onto the sidewalk. As soon as he reached the bottom step, his smile fell slightly. The car had stopped a few houses down, and Michael realized with dismay that maybe it wasn't Aaron. Just before he could step back up onto the porch, the car lurched forward, coming to a sudden stop again, and then it swerved slightly to one side before righting itself and continuing slowly up the street.

Michael stood there, his hand clutching the banister, the fear growing in his stomach. He should have waited inside the house.

Just as he was about to turn back, the car passed below a street-light, and he recognized it as Aaron's. Michael grinned and ran down the walkway just as Aaron's car pulled slowly up against the curb and the passenger door opened from the inside.

Michael climbed in hurriedly, smiling over at his brother.

"Hey buddy," Aaron said, his voice still sounding strange, and Michael stopped smiling.

"Are you mad at me?"

"'Course not!" Aaron said a little too loudly, waving his hand at him dismissively.

Michael looked down at the stick shift in between them. "You're acting different."

"Nah," Aaron said. "Just don't feel good. I need some sleep," he added, leaning over to help Michael with his seatbelt.

Michael leaned back slightly, away from the strange smell that seemed to be coming off of his brother.

"Are you sick?"

Aaron laughed softly. "Yeah, I'm a little sick. It's all good though."

That should have made Michael feel better, that there was a reason for his brother's strange behavior, but it didn't. He hugged his pillow into his chest.

"Sorry I made you come get me when you were sick," he murmured.

"No need for sorrys, Mike. You know you can always count on me."

Michael looked down and chewed on his bottom lip. The more his brother spoke, the more unsettled he became. Something about his voice wasn't right. Maybe he should call the doctor?

"Hey," his brother said suddenly, leaning over to turn Michael's face toward him. His expression was serious. "I'd do anything for you. You know that, right?"

Michael nodded slowly, and Aaron smiled, letting go of his face as he turned toward the road. His brother had uttered those words to him hundreds of times, but tonight, they sounded so wrong on his lips.

"Okay," Aaron said to no one in particular, shaking his head quickly, and he shifted the car into drive and stepped on the gas. They lurched forward slightly, the right wheel going up on the curb before he righted the car. Michael flinched as a few branches slapped against the passenger window.

"Whoops," Aaron said. "Sorry." He blinked a few times and widened his eyes, gripping the wheel and leaning toward the windshield. "Just...be quiet, okay? I have to think."

"Okay," Michael said softly, squeezing his pillow against his chest and closing his eyes. He just wanted to be back in his house, where his brother could lie down and take some medicine and feel better.

Michael kept his eyes closed, aware that the ride seemed exceptionally bumpy, that they stopped more often than they should have.

Then suddenly, too suddenly, it felt like they picked up speed. "Shit. *Shit!*" he heard his brother shout, and Michael whipped his head up and opened his eyes just as Aaron cut the wheel sharply to the left.

Michael felt himself fly across the seat toward his brother, and instinctively his hands reached out for something to grab onto, something to steady himself. He clutched frantically, his hands finding no purchase. Things were flying by the windows, colors and lights, and then he heard a horrible sound, like metal crunching.

"Aaron!" he yelled, but a loud screech drowned out the word, followed by the sound of glass shattering. Michael barely registered the feeling of little pinpricks dancing across his cheeks and his hands before there was a thunderous bang and the car jerked violently to the other side, ripping him away from his brother and throwing him back toward the passenger door.

His right side slammed against something hard. It felt like someone had punched him, and he knew he must have cried out, although he didn't hear it. The pain in his side was excruciating, the intensity of it doubling and tripling until he was sure he was being ripped in half. He opened his mouth to scream, and then miraculously, as suddenly as the pain began, it stopped. Just like that. Like someone had hit a switch and turned it off.

As soon as the pain ceased, so did the sounds around him. It was deathly quiet, although they were still moving. He could see that. He could see the world outside the window in blurs and flashes, and he was vaguely aware that it shouldn't be as quiet as it was. He should have been thankful—the silence was such a relief from the horrible sounds that filled his ears before—but instead, it terrified him.

They were going one way, and then another, before there was another violent jerk. His head slammed against something hard, bringing little fuzzy stars into his vision.

And then the movement stopped.

Slowly the silence was replaced with an empty, buzzing sound. His eyes were wet, he didn't know with what, and the more he blinked and swiped at them, the worse his vision got until finally he didn't know if his eyes were opened or closed.

He knew his mouth was moving. He knew he was saying his brother's name over and over, although he still couldn't hear anything but a soft humming.

And then everything went black.

Eventually, the blackness was broken up here and there with random things, flashes of images and sounds. Everything seemed blurry and unfocused: a white room. A soft beeping sound. Unfamiliar faces. Some of them looked sad. Some of them were smiling softly, saying words he couldn't hear. Sometimes there was agonizing pain, and other times there was a peaceful dizziness that felt like floating. He didn't know what was a dream or what was real, and he was just too tired to try to figure it out.

The first time he consciously opened his eyes, the first time he recognized that he was awake and what he was seeing was real and tangible, it was four days later.

There was a woman in his room, dressed in Daffy Duck scrubs. She smiled warmly at him, told him her name was Renee, and that she would take good care of him.

She gave him some water, rubbed his hair, and answered the questions he was too weak to ask; she told him that he was hurt, but he was going to get better. She explained that he had two broken ribs and a bruised lung. He had broken his arm, but the doctors fixed it by putting pins in it. She told him he was just like a robot now, and Michael was pretty sure he smiled at that. The brace around his neck was because he had severely pulled muscles in his neck and back. The bandage on his head was protecting his stitches. She told him he had a concussion, and she assured him that was just a fancy word for banging your head really hard and that a little rest would make it all better.

And then another nurse came in and put a needle into the IV in his arm, and he went back to sleep.

Over the next few days, he started waking up more often, and staying awake for longer. It seemed like the world inside that room was the only one he knew at first, and so he didn't ask any further questions. The women were so kind to him, bringing him coloring books even though he couldn't color very well with his left hand, helping him find his favorite cartoons to watch on TV, and some of them even brought him flowers and toys.

But as the days passed, and the pain meds decreased, his mind became more aware, until finally he asked for his brother.

It was the kind nurse who told him, the one who had spoken to him when he woke up that first time. She held his hand, she stroked his face, and when Michael cried, she cried too, holding him softly against her chest.

The first time he saw his mother was a week later, when he was finally cleared to go home. She had not come to see him once, at least not while he was conscious. As she stood there, signing the discharge papers, she looked old. Her face was drawn, her eyes were bloodshot and rimmed with dark circles, and her hair was a matted mess.

She didn't speak to him the entire drive home, but Michael was used to her silence. He didn't want to speak either. He was afraid if he opened his mouth, he would start screaming, and he didn't think he'd be able to stop.

They pulled into the driveway of his house, and both of them sat there, staring out of the front window, until finally his mother turned toward him.

For a second, for one stupid second, Michael turned toward her, almost hopeful. But then she spoke the words that he himself had already known on some level all along.

"It's your fault your father is gone," she said, her voice shaking. "And now you took your brother too."

With that she turned and exited the car, slamming the door forcefully behind her.

And Michael sat there in the car for hours, drowning in the silence and the awful truth that his mother had just bestowed on him.

November 2011

*L*auren sat in the vestibule of Learn and Grow, a wastebasket at her feet and Erin's head on her lap. She stroked her hair softly.

"Is he here yet?" Erin mumbled weakly.

Lauren turned slightly over her shoulder to look out the front window. "Not yet, sweetheart. Soon. Do you need the basket again?"

Erin shook her head imperceptibly against Lauren's thigh, and Lauren continued to stroke her hair, looking up as Deb poked her head out of the office.

"How's she doing?" she asked quietly.

Lauren lifted her hand, tilting it from side to side. "Her dad's on his way."

Deb nodded, giving Erin a sympathetic look before she turned back into her office.

Lauren looked down at Erin; her face was pale and her eyes were closed. She was breathing softly through her open mouth, and Lauren gently stroked her cheek with the backs of her fingers. She watched as Erin's brow smoothed slightly at the gesture.

A few minutes later, some movement outside caught Lauren's attention and she turned again to look over her shoulder; Michael was walking quickly toward the entrance, his phone to his ear and his brow pulled together. He stopped just outside the door, pacing for a minute. She heard his muffled, "*Shit!*" before he took the phone down and ended the call, running a hand through his hair before he opened the door.

When he saw them waiting in the vestibule, the look in his eyes went from irritated to heartbroken.

Lauren held her finger up to her lips. "I think she's sleeping," she whispered.

He nodded, walking over to them and kneeling down in front of Lauren. She moved her hand away from Erin's hair, and Michael immediately replaced it with his own. His eyes were gentle as he looked down at her, and then he glanced down at the cell phone in his other hand.

"Is everything okay?" Lauren whispered, and Michael looked up to see her gesture toward the phone with her head.

"Yeah," he said, looking down as he hit a button on the phone and put it away. "I'm just trying to get a hold of my professor." He looked back up at her. "I have a test tonight, and this guy's notorious for being an asshole about makeups. Something about modern technology and cheating," he said, shaking his head with annoyance. "I was hoping if he understood my situation, he might cut me a break, but I can't get a hold of him..." His voice trailed off, the annoyance leaving his expression as he looked back down at Erin, stroking her hair as gently as Lauren had.

"Is it a big test?"

"Half our grade," he said softly, sweeping the hair away from Erin's forehead.

Lauren bit her bottom lip before she said, "Well, if he won't let you make it up, what then?"

Michael shrugged. "I take the course again next semester." He looked up at Lauren. "Thank you for taking care of her." He reached forward, about to scoop Erin out of Lauren's arms, but Lauren laid a hand on his bicep.

He froze, looking up at her.

"Go. Take your test. I can bring her home and stay with her until you get back."

Michael shook his head. "No. I can't let you do that, that's ridic—"

She cut him off. "No, what's ridiculous is you having to repeat a class over one stupid test." He looked at Lauren, and she said again, "I'll stay with her."

"I couldn't ask you to do that."

"You didn't. I offered."

He smiled slightly, but Lauren could see he was about to argue again. "She's sleeping now," she added. "There's a good chance she might not even wake up again tonight."

He bit his lip and looked down, his brow furrowed, and Lauren knew she had made headway.

"I wouldn't want you to have to leave work because of us," he said.

"My shift ends in less than an hour. Deb won't care if I head out a bit early today. Really, Michael. It's fine."

He was quiet for a minute before he said, "Are you sure?"

"Absolutely. Go. Take your test."

He exhaled heavily before lifting his eyes back up to her face; the look in them caused a tightening in her chest, and she felt her breath stop. He stared at her that way for what seemed like forever before he spoke. "Thank you."

Lauren swallowed. "You're welcome," she said, finally finding her voice.

For a moment, he just looked at her, and then he blinked quickly, snapping out of it as he started rummaging in his pocket. "Here," he said, pulling what looked like a crumpled receipt out of it. "Take my cell phone number." He reached over and grabbed a pen off the front desk and scribbled quickly on the scrap of paper before he pulled a key off his key ring, handing them both to her. "Call me if anything changes, if you need anything."

"I will," she said, taking them from him and closing her hand around them.

"Okay," he said, standing and taking a reluctant step backward. "Okay...so..."

Lauren smiled. "So...good luck," she said, motioning with her head toward the door.

The corner of his mouth lifted in a half-hearted smile. "Thank you. I'll be home right after. Around seven-ish."

"We'll be there."

He took another step backward, looking down at Erin one more time before he lifted his eyes to Lauren.

She smiled reassuringly. "Go," she said again, nodding toward the door, and he nodded once and turned, walking back out of the door and toward his car.

Lauren watched him leave through the window before she turned to look back down at Erin, sound asleep on her lap.

"Hey Deb?" she called softly, and a second later Deb poked her head back out of the office. "Could you grab the spare car seat from the back room? I'm gonna take her home."

Lauren stood at the bathroom sink, letting the water run until it turned warm. Once it reached the right temperature, she grabbed a washcloth from a pile of folded towels in the corner and held it under the faucet, gently wringing it out before she turned off the water and walked back out to the living room.

Erin was sitting up on the couch, her eyes half closed, and Lauren knelt in front of her, wiping her mouth with the warm cloth. She felt Erin lean into her touch.

"Better, sweetheart?" she asked, and Erin nodded.

The poor thing had nothing left to throw up. Lauren had to pull over once during the drive to Michael's, but Erin had just retched out the door, producing nothing. Then again, once they'd gotten home, Lauren had rushed to bring her the trash can, only to have her heave over it to no avail. Lauren was giving her tiny sips of water, but she dared not risk anything more than that.

"I'm sleepy," Erin mumbled, and Lauren wiped her cheeks and forehead with the rag.

"I know. How about we try to lie down?"

"'Kay," Erin sighed, falling over the side, and Lauren grabbed a pillow and placed it under her head just in time.

"The trash can is right here, okay?" she said, moving it close to the couch.

"Are you leaving?" Erin asked, a touch of panic in her voice.

"Of course not," Lauren said, sitting on the couch beside her and placing her hand on Erin's leg. "I'll be right here with you until Daddy comes home."

"'Kay," she said again, her eyes falling closed, and Lauren sat back on the couch, gently rubbing her hand over Erin's calf.

"Do you have a crown?" Erin asked softly.

"A crown?" Lauren asked. "No, I don't think I do. Do you?"

Erin shook her head.

"Well then I guess we'll just have to get you one," Lauren said.

The tiniest smile curved Erin's lips and she nodded, her eyes still closed. "Are you a princess?" she nearly sighed.

Lauren smiled. "No, I'm not a princess."

"Oh," Erin said, her voice soft and far away. "Daddy thought you were."

Lauren's hand stopped on Erin's leg for a moment as she looked down at her, but she could tell by her deep breathing that she was right on the border of sleep. She felt an ache in her chest at Erin's words, and she swallowed before resuming her ministrations, rubbing Erin's calf softly.

In a matter of minutes, Erin's breathing was deep and regular, and Lauren knew she was finally asleep. Careful not to jostle her, she stood from the couch and walked down the tiny hall to the room that was Erin's, grabbing the blanket that was strewn across the bottom of her bed. As she turned to leave, something that had been tangled inside fell to the floor with a muted thud, and she looked down to see a small red photo album at her feet.

She bent to pick it up, taking it with her as she walked back out to the living room and gently laid the blanket over Erin.

Lauren sat beside her, opening the album, and immediately she brought her hand to her mouth, masking a tiny laugh.

The first picture was of Michael in a little league uniform, wearing a baseball hat that looked much too big for his tiny head as he squinted up at the camera.

"Oh my God," she said softly, shaking her head with a smile before she turned the page. The next one was of Michael sitting on an older woman's lap, covered in something that looked like jam. She smiled softly, running the tip of her index finger over the image of his face. He had been the most adorable child; big brown eyes and messy black hair with those little Cupid's bow lips. She could so clearly see the Michael she knew in those tiny features, but Erin was distinctly there too.

Lauren smiled, turning the page, and instantly her smile dropped. Her hand came to her mouth again, but this time, she merely pressed her fingertips to her lips as her eyes began to sting.

It was the picture she had given him. The one of the two of them at his graduation.

She couldn't believe he still had it, that he had saved it after all this time.

Lauren inhaled slowly, shaking her head. It just didn't make sense. Why would he keep it? Especially after...

Blinking quickly against the tears she felt rising, she studied the picture. Michael wore a tiny smile on his lips, looking down at her with something like admiration in his eyes, despite the fact that *he* was the one who had just graduated. And there she was, looking at the camera, leaning her head on his chest and smiling widely.

Completely unaware that in a few short weeks, her world would be ripped out from underneath her.

She closed her eyes and the book simultaneously, dropping her head back onto the couch.

"Damn it," she said to no one in particular, breathing deeply to regain her composure.

When she felt like she had a handle on herself, she stood and took the album back to Erin's room, placing it at the foot of her bed. She stood in the doorway for a moment, staring back at the book before she turned and headed out to the kitchen.

Lauren glanced at the clock on the microwave. It was just after six. Michael would be finishing up his test any minute. She walked over to her purse and grabbed her cell phone and the scrap of paper with his number on it, sending him a quick text.

Hey, it's Lauren. Everything's fine. Erin's sleeping. You might want to pick up some Pedialyte at the grocery store on your way home.

She tossed her phone back into her purse and walked back over to the couch, grabbing the remote and sitting down next to Erin. She turned the television on, lowering the volume, and quickly found a sitcom rerun.

And she sat there, staring at the screen, but she couldn't make her eyes see anything but the image of her and Michael, forever immortalized and happy in that photo.

True to his word, Michael arrived home shortly before seven, carrying a bag from the grocery store.

Lauren glanced over at him as the door opened, and he smiled softly, taking off his jacket.

"Hey," she said, standing from the couch and stretching.

"Hi," he answered softly, tossing his jacket over a chair as he walked toward her. He placed the grocery bag on the table and glanced past her into the living room. "How is she?"

"She's okay. She's been sleeping for a while now."

Michael nodded, running his hand through his hair as he exhaled. "Thank you again. I'm sorry you had to give up your evening."

"It's fine," Lauren assured him with a shake of her head.

He nodded, walking past her into the living room. For a second he stood there, looking down at Erin, and then he exhaled a heavy breath, sitting down on the recliner beside the couch and dropping his head into his hands. "You can't imagine what this does to me," he mumbled.

"She'll be okay, Michael. It's just a virus. It's almost over," Lauren said, following him into the living room.

He shook his head, still looking at the floor. "That's not what I meant."

He looked totally dejected, and Lauren stood there, watching him but not pressing him further. Instead, she battled the innate reaction she had to cross the room to him, to kneel in front of him and wrap her arms around him, anything to take that look off his face.

"The only reason I'm even going back to school is for her," he finally said, glancing up at Lauren. "But it means I have to leave her when I could be spending time with her. It means I can't take care of her when she needs me."

He shook his head and looked over to where Erin lay sleeping on the couch. "Her mom's not around. *I'm* hardly around…" He trailed off before looking back at Lauren. "It's just, like, am I doing the right thing? Is it worth it? I just…I just wish I knew, ya know?"

Michael sat back against the seat and closed his eyes, sighing heavily.

"Hey," Lauren said softly, walking toward him. "You're doing the right thing. You're building a future for her. Most parents are away from their children during the day. It's the whole reason I have a job," she added with a tiny laugh, hoping he would smile in return.

His eyes remained closed, but the corner of his mouth twitched slightly, and Lauren smiled, closing the distance between them and kneeling on the floor next to the chair. "It's the time that you *do* spend with her that counts," she added. "And you're doing an amazing job."

Michael laughed humorlessly. "You're still the same," he said with a shake of his head.

"But you are," she insisted. "She's smart, she's motivated, she's so kind to everyone, Michael. She's a perfect little person. And she *adores* you."

Michael opened his eyes fully then, looking at Lauren with such intense emotion that she felt her legs falter under her weight, and she dropped gently from her kneeling position to sit on her calves, her eyes falling to the arm of the chair in between them.

After a minute of silence, she heard him shift in the chair. "You know something?" he said softly, and when Lauren looked up, she saw he was sitting up now, closer to her, his eyes intently on hers.

"That first day I dropped her off…the first time I had to leave her…the only thing that kept me from running back in to get her was that I knew she'd be with you."

Lauren's breath left her in a soft rush, her eyes locked on his, and he smiled gently. "It's true," he added.

"Miss Lauren?" Erin's tiny voice called, and both of them whipped their head in her direction.

"Hey baby," Michael breathed, sliding off the chair and kneeling beside his daughter. Lauren could only watch him, still stunned into silence. "I'm here now. You okay?"

"I don't feel good, Daddy," she said with a tiny whimper, and he brushed the hair away from her face and pressed his lips to her forehead.

"I know. You'll feel better soon."

Erin pulled her knees up into her chest, lying on her side, and Lauren wondered if her stomach was hurting her again. "Is Miss Lauren gone?"

"No, I'm right here," Lauren said, finally finding her voice again.

"Can you stay with us tonight?" Erin asked softly, closing her eyes.

Michael glanced back at Lauren, his expression startled, before he turned back toward his daughter. "Honey, Miss Lauren can't stay here. She has to go home."

"No," Erin said, pulling her brow together. "I don't want her to leave."

"Erin," Michael began, but Lauren cut him off.

"I'll stay, sweetheart."

Michael turned toward her, and Lauren quickly mouthed, *"Just until she falls asleep."*

He nodded, bringing his attention back to Erin, and Lauren crawled over to them, sitting on the floor by Erin's feet. Michael stroked her hair for a minute before he turned, sitting up against the couch by his daughter's head.

Lauren turned to look at him; he was so close now, the small trash can being the only thing that separated the two of them. Just as he turned his head to look at her, a loud, grumbling sound filled the space between them, and she raised her eyebrows, glancing down at his stomach.

He laughed softly, pressing his palm to his stomach, and Lauren asked, "Have you eaten anything?"

Michael shook his head. "No, I came right home."

"You must be starving," she said, standing from her spot on the floor. "Let me make you something."

"No, you've done enough already," he said, making a move to stand up, and Lauren held out her hand.

"No, stay with her. I'll throw something simple together," she said, walking out of the living room before he could protest further, and she heard him sigh in acquiescence as he leaned back against the couch.

Lauren opened his fridge, and after scanning it for a minute, she pulled out what she'd need to make him a sandwich. When she was finished, she grabbed a bottle of water from the door of the fridge and brought both out to him.

He was still sitting with his back up against the couch, but his head was resting against the cushion and his eyes were closed. She stopped, wondering if he had fallen asleep, but then he rolled his head to the side and opened his eyes.

"Hey," he said softly, shifting to sit up, and she walked over to him, handing him the plate and the water before she sat back down on the floor in front of Erin's feet.

"Thank you," he said as he picked up the sandwich and took an enormous bite, making a contented sound in the back of his throat.

Michael sighed around his mouthful of food, chewing slowly before he swallowed. "Sorry. I didn't realize how hungry I was until you brought this in here," he said, taking another bite and putting the plate down between them to open his water. He looked back at Lauren and lifted his brow, motioning toward the sandwich, and she shook her head.

"No, thanks. I'm fine."

He nodded, taking a sip of water and swallowing the bite he had just taken. "Damn, that's good. What's in this?"

Lauren laughed. "Whatever was in your fridge. I just used what you had."

He picked up the sandwich and turned it slowly, his brow furrowed like he was studying an ancient artifact, and then he shrugged before he took another bite. "It never tastes this good when I make one for myself."

"You're just hungry. It's all relative," she said with a laugh, leaning back against the couch and bringing her eyes to the television.

After a few minutes of silence, broken here and there by the sounds of appreciation Michael uttered as he finished his sandwich, Lauren said, "So, how was your test?"

Michael ran the back of his hand across his mouth, swallowing the sip of water he'd just taken. "It seemed fair," he said. "I probably did okay."

Lauren smiled and rolled her eyes. "Which means you aced it."

He laughed at her annoyance, his expression confused. "Why are you saying that?"

She lazily rolled her head to the side, looking at him. "You always used to do that. You'd always belittle how you thought you did on a test, and you'd end up blowing it out of the water."

"*That*," he said, pointing at her with his bottle of water, "is absolutely not true."

"Sure it is. The ones you failed, you blew off on purpose. But when you actually cared about a class?" She moved her hand through the air smoothly. "Straight A's. Just like that."

He shook his head, a small smile on his lips. "Apparently, your memory of me is a little warped."

Lauren felt her smile drop. "No, I don't think it is," she said softly, looking away from him.

Out of the corner of her eye, she could see him looking at her, although she couldn't make out his expression. Eventually, he turned his head, slowly spinning the cap back on his water bottle. She heard him take a small breath before he cleared his throat.

"So," he said tentatively, "do you like living in Bellefonte? Or do you miss home?"

Lauren inhaled deeply, trying to shake off the awkwardness of that last moment between them. "I like it here. I mean, of course I miss home, but I see my parents whenever I want, and I have dinner with Jenn once a month, so," she said with a shrug.

"*Jenn?*" Michael said, his brow lifted. "Jenn Powell? You guys are still friends?"

Lauren laughed softly, remembering their tumultuous relationship. "Yes."

"Holy shit. Jenn Powell," he said slowly. He shook his head and leaned against the couch. "Is she still the same?"

"You'd probably think so, yes."

He smirked. "So is that who you were with last weekend?"

Lauren bit her lip, the corners of her mouth going up. "No, I was out with a friend."

Michael looked at her for a second before he nodded. "Ah," he said in understanding. "Well…did you have a good time?" There was a forced casualness to his tone now, like he knew it was the appropriate question to ask, even though he had no desire to hear the answer.

She looked down, a tiny smile on her lips as she thought back to the previous weekend. "Yeah, I did. It was…nice," she said, her smile growing a bit more pronounced.

She felt Michael shift beside her. "Did you meet this guy at school?"

This time, Lauren pressed her lips together, but they twisted up in spite of her attempt. "No, he was my doctor. My chiropractor, actually."

There was a beat of silence before she heard a grunted, "Hmmph."

She turned her head toward him. "What?" she asked, trying not to sound defensive.

He looked at her, his expression derisive. "Must be a good guy."

She shifted toward him fully now, folding her arms as her brow knitted together. "And what is that supposed to mean?"

"Oh come on," he said, his expression matching his condescending tone. "Aren't there rules against that kind of thing? Aren't there lines doctors aren't supposed to cross with their patients? I don't know. The kind of guy that would take advantage of something like that just doesn't earn himself any points in my book."

Lauren could feel the need to justify herself—to justify Adam—swelling in her chest, battling with the overwhelming desire to tell him to mind his own business. She felt her teeth come together, and she took a steadying breath, trying to keep herself calm. Was he really going to have the audacity to sit there and question Adam's morality? After what *he'd* done to her?

"I'm sorry, do you even know him?" she snapped. "And I'm pretty sure it's not *your* book he needs to be earning himself points in anyway." Despite her best efforts, the bitterness was dripping from her tone.

Michael was looking at the water bottle as he rolled it slowly in his hands, his expression unreadable.

"And what about you?" she asked, turning roughly back toward the TV. "Still dating the winners?"

For a minute, there was nothing but the quiet murmur of the television between them, and Lauren thought he might not answer her. But then he spoke, his voice so soft that she almost had to strain to hear it.

"No. I don't date anymore."

Instantly Lauren felt the anger drain from her body at his tone. She hated that his vulnerability still had that effect on her. She inhaled slowly and blew her breath out in a huff, ridding herself of the last bit of animosity she had been feeling toward him. Wasn't she supposed to be over those feelings anyway? Hadn't she promised Jenn she'd left that all behind her?

"Yeah, I guess you don't have the time, huh," she said softly.

"No, I could make the time if I wanted to. But...I won't do that to her."

Lauren turned toward him. "To who?"

"Her," he said, motioning behind him to Erin. "I'm not gonna go out there and play the field, date around. She gets very attached to people. And I'm not gonna..."

He looked down, pulling his brow together, and Lauren watched his shoulders rise before he lifted his eyes back to hers. "I would never allow someone into this house unless I knew they were worthy of her."

Lauren's breath caught in her throat. There was no mistaking the meaning behind his words, behind the look in his eyes. There was no ignoring the fact that she was in his home right now, caring for his daughter. Lauren stared at him, unmoving, and as her breathing finally picked back up, so did her heart rate.

She knew at that moment that coming to Michael's house was a bad idea. Between Erin's earlier comment, the photo album, and now this, she could feel emotions brewing inside her that were supposed to be long gone.

It suddenly felt like there was a magnet in her chest, like some unseen force was pulling her toward him. Lauren pressed her hands into the carpet, trying to stop the imperceptible forward motion of her body.

What did her body even want her to do? Hug him? Kiss him? Rest her head on his shoulder in comfortable silence, the way she had so many times before?

His gaze was implacable, and as much as she tried, as much as she knew she needed to, she couldn't look away from him.

Her heart leapt into her throat when finally, he moved toward her. It was the tiniest movement, but she noticed it nonetheless.

"Lauren," he said, his voice gentle, and suddenly it was like someone dumped a bucket of water over her head. She jerked back slightly, her eyes widening.

"I think she's asleep," she said, looking everywhere but him as she fumbled to stand up. "I...I, um...should probably go."

She stood quickly, her movements uncoordinated, and he moved back to his original position, his eyes on the floor.

"Yeah, you should go," he said, running a hand through his hair and nodding, like he had just convinced himself that what he was saying was true.

Lauren hurried into the kitchen and grabbed her purse, concentrating on slowing her breath. She needed to get the hell out of there. Quickly.

No sooner than she had her purse in her hands, she heard the soft cry. "*I don't feel good. I need the bucket!*"

Lauren rushed back to the living room just in time to see Michael jump up and grab the bucket. He held it in front of Erin as she retched over it, missing the bucket slightly and getting some on Michael's hands and the floor.

She put her purse down and turned toward the kitchen, gathering some paper towels and wetting some. By the time she came back into the living room, it was over, and Michael was speaking in soft, reassuring tones to Erin as she laid back down on the couch.

Lauren knelt beside him, using the wet paper towels to wipe his hands, and he glanced over at her. "Thank you," he said softly, and she nodded, looking away from him to start wiping the floor.

Once everything was cleaned, Lauren went into the kitchen to dispose of the dirtied towels while Michael went to the bathroom to wash out the pail. When they both returned, Erin was sitting up on the couch. She looked exhausted, but marginally better. "I'm thirsty," she said, her tiny voice raspy, and Michael looked over at Lauren.

"Pedialyte?" he asked, and Lauren nodded.

She walked with him into the kitchen, grabbing a cup while he took the bottle out of the bag and read the directions on the back.

"Put that in the fridge after you open it," Lauren said. "And only a little at a time, or it will just come right back up."

He nodded, screwing the cap off and pouring about an inch into the cup that Lauren held out. As she brought it out to Erin, she heard the sounds of him putting the bottle in the fridge.

"Here you go sweetheart," Lauren said, sitting on the couch beside her. "Little sips, okay?"

Erin nodded, holding the cup in two shaky hands as she brought it to her lips, taking bird-like sips, and Lauren ran her hand soothingly over Erin's hair.

Michael entered the living room, kneeling on the floor in front of his daughter. "How's that?" he asked gently.

"Good," she said, resting the cup on her thigh. "Daddy?"

"Hmm?" he hummed, tucking her hair behind her ear.

"Can we watch the pony movie?"

He smiled. "Sure," he said, standing from his spot and turning toward the television, and just as Lauren went to stand, Erin reached over and clasped her hand.

"You can be the pink pony, and I'll be the purple one," she said.

Lauren smiled softly at her before she glanced over at the front door, at her salvation. With a resigned sigh, she sat back against the couch, rubbing the back of Erin's hand with her thumb.

After hitting play, Michael returned to the couch, sitting on the other side of Erin, and she laid down across them, putting her head in her father's lap and her legs across the top of Lauren's thighs. Michael glanced down at her and smiled before he looked over at Lauren.

"*I'm sorry,*" he mouthed.

She had no idea if he was referring to the fact that she was forced to stay and watch the movie, or what had just transpired between them, but she nodded.

"*It's okay,*" she mouthed back, and he smiled softly before turning his attention back to the movie.

For the next hour, they watched the pony movie, and eventually Lauren found herself starting to nod. The first few times, her eyes would snap open, and she'd shift on the couch, trying to refocus on the cartoon movie about magical flying horses. But at some point, that method must have stopped working, because the next thing she knew, she felt something softly brushing against her cheek.

She opened her eyes slowly, blinking against her blurred vision. The television was off, and the room was almost completely dark now.

"Hey," Michael whispered, brushing his hand against her cheek.

"Michael?" she rasped, sitting up slightly. She could just make out his features in the darkness as her eyes finally adjusted; he was leaning over her, his face mere inches from hers. "What time is it?"

"Midnight," he said, his hand resting on her cheek. "We all fell asleep."

"Erin?" she asked.

"She's in her bed. I think it's over," he said softly, his thumb brushing the side of her face as he spoke.

Lauren nodded, her eyes falling closed for a second before she opened them again.

She felt his breath against her face as he spoke. "Take my bed tonight. I'll sleep in Erin's room with her."

Lauren shook her head gently. "I'll be awake in a second."

"Please," he said softly. "I don't want you driving like this. It's the least I could do."

Lauren knew she should protest. She knew she had no business staying in this house. But she was so tired, and the idea of driving home right now seemed so daunting, and his bed was so close, just a few feet away…

With a sigh, she felt herself nod, and she could just make out the smile on Michael's lips.

"Thank you again. For everything."

Before she could even register what he was doing, Michael leaned toward her, pressing his lips against her cheek. The corner of his mouth touched the corner of hers, and Lauren closed her eyes, her body feeling heavy with sleep and surrender.

His lips left her skin slowly, but he made no move to pull away from her; their faces were so close now that Lauren could no longer decipher his features in the dimness.

And then, against her will, she turned slightly, closing her eyes and pressing her cheek against his.

His hand was still on her face, and she felt his fingers twitch ever so slightly as he exhaled a slow, shaky breath, the heat of it dancing over her ear and down her neck.

With one last stroke of his thumb against her cheek, he pulled back suddenly. "Good night, Lauren," he said, his voice somewhat strained, and he turned and walked down the hall toward Erin's room.

Lauren sat on the couch for a minute after he'd left her, her eyes closed and her breathing slow, but this time, it had nothing to do with being tired. When she finally regained her composure, she stood and walked down the hall to Michael's bedroom.

By the time she climbed into his bed, she was wide awake, and she lay there in the darkness, blinking up at his ceiling. There was a strange twinge low in her chest, and she wondered briefly if perhaps she'd caught Erin's virus.

With a sigh, she rolled onto her side and buried her face into his pillow.

It smelled like his bed in high school.

Lauren closed her eyes, remembering all the afternoons she'd spent lying in his bed, doing homework, talking, watching movies, the time he spent the entire afternoon trying to teach her how to play video games, to no avail. She remembered the night she had too much to drink at a party, and Michael had taken her home with him so she wouldn't get in trouble, tucking her into his bed and sleeping next to her above the covers.

The twinge in her chest surfaced again, and she knew it had nothing to do with Erin's virus. It was her body telling her what she had known on some level all along, despite the weeks of insistence otherwise.

She still had feelings for Michael. After all these years, after everything he'd done, she still had feelings for him.

Admitting that to herself instantly filled her with equal parts pain and relief, and she turned her face further into his pillow, inhaling deeply.

And then she forced herself to remember the night she wouldn't allow herself to think about for a long time afterward, and almost immediately, she felt the pillow grow damp beneath her cheek.

She pressed her lips together as all the emotions she expected to feel when she first saw him came crashing down on her with a vengeance: the humiliation, the betrayal, the confusion, the mind-numbing pain.

And yet all she wanted at that moment was for Michael to be in that bed with her, comforting her, reassuring her, wiping the memory of what had happened out of her mind.

She pulled one of his pillows into her body and stifled a sob, wishing more than anything that it was him she was holding. The need pushed against her chest so forcefully that it bordered on painful.

She needed the anger to come soon, the bitterness that briefly surged in her earlier that evening. She wanted to feel it again; it was the only thing that could prevent her from doing something stupid.

But the resentment never came. Or if it did, it didn't have a chance of winning out over the other things she was feeling for him at that moment.

And so she laid there, completely wrapped in the memories and the scent of him, in the intimacy of being in his bed, until finally by some miracle, she fell into the merciful refuge of sleep.

The next morning Lauren awoke with a strange feeling. It was some combination of foreboding and acceptance, like she knew something bad had just happened, but she also knew getting upset over it wouldn't change anything.

She walked out to the living room to see Erin sitting on the couch, watching some show about a talking blue dog. She smiled and waved at Lauren before she said, "Shh, Daddy's sleeping."

Lauren smiled and mouthed okay to her as she made a big production of tiptoeing into the living room, and Erin giggled.

"You hungry yet?" she asked, and Erin nodded.

"Okay, be right back," she said.

She went back into Michael's kitchen and made Erin some toast with a thin layer of jelly, and she brought it out to her with another small cup of Pedialyte.

"Little bites and little sips, okay? Just until your belly is back to normal."

Erin nodded and thanked her, turning her eyes back to the television show as she took a small bite of the toast.

"I'm gonna get my stuff and head back home now. But Daddy's here, and I'll see you on Monday."

"Okay," she said around her mouthful of toast, her eyes still on the TV, and Lauren leaned over and kissed the top of her head before she turned back toward Michael's room.

After grabbing her things, she stopped in the doorway to Erin's bedroom. Michael was sprawled out across the floor, lying on a pink comforter half the size of his body and covered with another that left the majority of his legs exposed. She pressed her lips together when she recognized the ponies on his blanket as the ones from the movie last night.

Her eyes moved to his face, his expression completely serene in slumber. His dark lashes fanned out beneath his eyes, and there was a shadow of stubble on his jaw, contrasting the full, pink lips that were slightly parted with his soft breathing.

Lauren walked carefully into the room, pulling the blanket off of Erin's bed and covering his legs. And then she closed her eyes and took a long, steadying breath before she turned to walk out of the room.

She said good-bye to Erin and got in her car, not even bothering to turn the radio on as she made her way back home.

Crossing lines. It had been what started their friendship in the first place all those years ago, and then what propelled it into something substantial. What built it up and made it strong.

And finally, what ended up destroying it.

Lauren knew she had just done it again. Her original plan had been to remain strictly professional with him, at least until they could talk about everything that had happened. But yesterday, when she had offered to go to his house and care for his sick child, that plan had gone out the window.

It shouldn't have been that big of a deal, crossing back into a friendship with him. But Jenn, damn her, had been right. She wasn't starting on square one with Michael. Lauren had let herself go an inch last night, and suddenly she was right back where she knew she couldn't be.

She needed to get back.

The "keeping it professional" ship had sailed; she recognized that. Instead, she needed to focus all her efforts on holding the line now, on keeping it strictly friendship. She couldn't allow herself to slip beyond that again, the way she had last night.

"You can do this. You can totally do this. Just...get back on the other side of the line and stay there," she told herself as she turned onto the interstate.

But Lauren had been crossing lines with Michael for as long as she could remember.

And she knew from experience that once she did, it was virtually impossible to go back.

August 2002

"I feel like we're in that movie *Dazed and Confused*," Jenn said. "Party at the Moon Tower," she added in her best attempt at a Southern drawl, and Lauren laughed and shook her head.

"First of all, that's the worst impression of Matthew McConaughey I've ever heard." She dodged Jenn's slap as she continued, "Second of all, there's no Moon Tower to be seen. Or water tower. Or even a lonely power line. We are just standing around in the middle of the woods, drinking like a bunch of idiots."

Jenn shrugged, taking a sip from her blue plastic cup. "Well, this is what happens when nobody's parents will let them throw an 'End of the Summer' party at their house. They force us into the wilderness to do our celebrating. Kinda stupid if you ask me. At least if we were in someone's house, they could supervise us."

Lauren looked around before taking a sip from her own cup. "There's got to be like eighty drunk teenagers here, Jenn. Nobody was gonna be able to supervise this, house or not."

"Oh well," Jenn said, plopping down on an old tree trunk as she finished her drink. "At least the cops won't be breaking it up out here. It's a perfect night to be outside anyway." She tilted her head back and sighed. "I love summer nights."

"Aaand, now we're in the movie *Grease*," Lauren said as she sat down next to her, and Jenn laughed, nudging her with her shoulder.

"Ah, there's my two favorite girls!"

Lauren and Jenn both turned to see Michael hopping over the fallen tree they were sitting on, reaching over to muss Jenn's hair in the process, and she pulled away from him, casting an irritated look in his direction.

"Idiot," she muttered, bringing her hand up to straighten her hair, and Michael smirked, his eyes on her as he took a sip from his cup.

"So, Jenn," he said once he had swallowed, sitting on the other side of Lauren. "You think you might ever get over your deal with me?"

"That depends," she said. "You think you might ever stop being a complete asshole?"

"*Guys,*" Lauren scolded firmly, rolling her eyes. Few things entertained Michael more than getting a rise out of Jenn, and no matter how many times Lauren asked her to ignore him, she would always take the bait. Every time. Lauren had grown extremely tired of their little routine after two years.

"You know what your problem is?" Michael said, ignoring Lauren's reprimand and leaning toward Jenn. "You need to loosen up. Learn how to have a little fun."

"Please," Jenn said, her expression disinterested as she looked away from him. "Like I need lessons from *you* on how to have a good time."

Lauren watched the smirk lift Michael's mouth, and she knew this conversation was going nowhere good.

"Okay then," Michael said, motioning with his head toward a group of boys standing around just a few feet away. "In that case, I think you should go up to Dennis Kinley and make out with him."

"Michael," Lauren said reproachfully just as Jenn shook her head.

"You're such a child," she sighed, and Michael laughed.

"Hey, you said you didn't need lessons on how to have fun, right? It's a party. Dennis seems like a cool kid. It's just a kiss after all. No big deal."

Jenn turned toward Michael, her brow quirked. "Yeah? Well then in that case, I think you should kiss Lauren."

Instantly Lauren whipped her head toward her friend, her expression incredulous.

She could have killed her.

Despite the fact that Michael and Lauren had been friends for almost two years, and he had never even come close to making a move on her, Jenn was insistent there was more to their friendship than what the two of them were acknowledging.

But none of her attempts to prove it had ever been as blatant as this.

Lauren turned toward Michael, ready to tell him to ignore Jenn, but before she could speak, Michael silenced her, leaning down with ease as he brought his mouth to hers.

Instantly she froze, her lips pressed tightly together, too stunned to react or respond in any way to what was happening.

But then his lips parted gently and he leaned into her, taking her bottom lip between his with a tenderness even Lauren would never have given him credit for. Instinctively, she felt the tension melt away from her mouth as she tentatively kissed him back.

His mouth opened one more time, and hers responded automatically, their lips brushing against each other's. Again, he captured her lip between his, holding it for a second before gently releasing it. He lifted his chin, brushing his full bottom lip over her top one before he finally pulled away from her.

It took her a few seconds to open her eyes, and when she did, she saw Michael looking over her head, smiling triumphantly at Jenn.

She couldn't breathe.

It felt like something had ignited inside of her. Her chest was burning, sending little heated sparks down through her stomach and out through her fingertips.

With an embarrassingly sharp intake of breath, she finally started breathing again, but neither Jenn nor Michael seemed to notice. Lauren was vaguely aware of the bantering going on over her head—something about how Jenn should have known better than to dare Michael to do anything—but she couldn't focus on their conversation.

Her lips felt warm and tingly, and she fought the urge to touch them with her fingertips.

She noticed Michael look down at her then, and she lifted her eyes just in time to see him smile at her; he tugged a piece of her hair and winked, and then he picked up his drink and walked away as casually as if he'd just said a passing hello to them.

Lauren stared after him, watching him walk away, still unable to form a coherent thought.

"Well, shit," Jenn said from beside her, although her voice seemed far away. "I gotta give him credit; it certainly looked like the boy has skills."

"I can't believe you did that," Lauren mumbled, staring straight ahead. Now that Michael was out of sight, she timidly brought her fingers to her lips; the second she touched them, they tingled with sensitivity, like she'd been burned.

"I know, right?" Jenn laughed. "*You're welcome,*" she sing-songed, hopping up and grabbing Lauren's wrist. "Vamos, chica. I need a refill."

And Lauren allowed her body to be towed further into the wilderness in search of the keg, although her mind was still back on the fallen tree, kissing Michael.

Oddly enough, as the night went on, Jenn seemed perfectly content to move past the little incident on the log; to Lauren's surprise, she never even brought it up again. But as the hours passed, no matter how many conversations Lauren tried to get into, no matter how many times she filled her five-dollar plastic cup at the keg, no matter how many times she scolded herself for going back to that moment, she couldn't stop thinking about it.

Maybe Jenn had been right? Lauren thought as she stood with a group of people who were laughing and talking, completely oblivious to her zombie-like state. She sipped her beer, her eyes on the floor.

She'd never been kissed like that in her life.

The gentleness, the tenderness, it had to mean something, didn't it? Suddenly it didn't seem that farfetched that Jenn could have been right in her assumption. After all, she *had* been right about one thing—one thing Lauren couldn't deny anymore if her life depended on it.

She was hopelessly in love with Michael Delaney.

By the time Lauren had finished her third beer and Jenn had disappeared somewhere, cozying up to some senior, Lauren had convinced herself she needed to find Michael. She needed to know what he thought of that kiss.

She needed to know if it changed anything for him.

It took her a while, but she finally found two of Michael's friends leaning up against a tree with a couple of girls, passing around what appeared to be a cigarette, although Lauren knew better.

"Hey," she said when she reached them. "Have you seen Michael?"

The one she knew was named Phil turned toward her, looking bored. "Michael?"

"Del," she clarified, and Phil smirked.

"What do you want with Del?"

"To talk to him," she said, folding her arms and looking up at him. For as long as she'd known Michael, she never really warmed to his friends. They embodied the persona that Michael portrayed to other people, except with these guys, there was nothing else underneath.

"Well then you're out of luck, little girl," Phil said, pausing to take a long pull of the joint at his lips. He exhaled, and most of the smoke wafted into Lauren's face. She jerked her head back and coughed, and he smiled. "I don't think Del's much in the mood for talking right now. But he's over there somewhere," he said, gesturing toward a cluster of trees.

Lauren turned from them, ignoring the giggles from the girls as she walked in the direction Phil had indicated. She found herself having to focus against the darkness as the trees became more dense.

Lauren stopped walking, allowing her sight to adjust to the deepening shadows, and for a second, she thought maybe Phil had sent her on a wild goose chase for his own amusement. Just as she was about to turn and walk back out toward the crowd, she heard a rustling and snapping of twigs, and she looked over her shoulder to see Michael walking out from behind a tree, sipping his beer.

"Hey," she said, and Michael glanced up, catching sight of her.

"Hey Red," he said with a smile. "Where's your other half?"

"She disappeared with Trevor McLaine a little while ago," Lauren said with a shrug, and Michael threw his head back and laughed.

"Well, I'm glad she took my advice, even if Dennis didn't get to reap the benefits. Hopefully this will mellow her out a bit."

Lauren half smiled. "Listen," she said, the alcohol in her system making her bold. "Can I talk to you for a minute?"

"Sure. What's up?"

"I just…," she said, faltering now that the moment was upon her. "I just…I wanted to talk about…what happened before."

"What do you mean?"

She looked up at him; his expression was completely relaxed.

"I mean," she cleared her throat. "I mean before. On the tree."

Lauren watched as his expression changed; he pulled his brow together and tilted his head, a small smile on his lips. "Oh, come on. You're not mad at me, are you? It was just a dare."

Before she could even respond, there was a crunching sound, and Lauren looked up to see a girl approaching them, coming from the same direction Michael had just appeared from only moments before.

She was giggling, one hand adjusting the straps of her tank top and bra while the other tried unsuccessfully to make her disheveled skirt presentable.

She walked right up to Michael's side, wrapping her arms around his waist, still giggling as she planted open-mouthed kisses along the side of his neck.

Lauren swallowed, her eyes pinned on the girl. For some reason, the only coherent thought she could come up with was that she was wearing too much makeup. Her eyeliner and lipstick were both heavy and dark, making her look harsh instead of feminine. Her name was Tanya. Or Tina. Something like that. But despite not knowing her name, her reputation was something Lauren knew well.

She watched her lavish Michael's throat with attention, and she couldn't help but notice how her lipstick was smudged around her mouth.

She didn't want to think about how it had gotten that way.

Lauren ripped her eyes away from the girl, looking back up at Michael. He seemed completely oblivious to the person at his side, sucking on the skin just below his ear. His eyes were on Lauren, his expression gentle.

Concerned.

"Hey," he said softly. "You're cool, right?"

It took every ounce of strength in Lauren's body to pull a smile, but she managed a shaky one. "Yeah, I'm cool," she said, hoping her voice didn't falter. "I just meant that…I wanted to ask you to take it easy with Jenn. Quit instigating her, okay?"

Michael grinned then, a combination of relief and mischief chasing the concern from his eyes. "No promises," he said. He walked the few steps over to her with Tanya/Tina in tow and planted a kiss on the top of her head.

And then he turned and walked back toward his friends with another girl's lips all over his skin.

Del sat on the floor up against the side of his bed, his head bobbing slightly to the song thumping out of his stereo.

And then he grit his teeth and took a swig from the bottle in his hand as his mind went back to that afternoon.

To the moment Tanya had smacked him across his face.

In front of the entire cafeteria.

Del shook his head, swallowing his mouthful of whiskey. That fucking bitch. He could not believe he spent the last month of his life with that girl. And he had an even harder time believing that the slap she bestowed on him wasn't just a ploy for attention.

He knew she didn't really care about him, just the way he didn't really care about her. They never even pretended to care about each other. So honestly, how upset could she have been that he had grown bored with her? After all, their entire relationship was a joke. In fact, even referring to it as a relationship was a joke in itself; anything that began with a girl on her knees in the middle of the woods could hardly be constituted as anything meaningful, at least not in his eyes.

But they had used each other to satisfy a need for the past few weeks. And then he had ended it.

And she slapped him. As if he had wronged her. As if she didn't know exactly what their situation had been about. As if she didn't basically set the terms of it herself.

Michael grit his teeth again. It took everything he had in him not to knock her on her ass. Who did she think she was? How dare she put her hands on him, in front of a room full of people, no less? He didn't take that shit from anyone.

But she was a girl, and so he had to satisfy himself by grabbing a bottle of Jack from his mother's stash downstairs and drinking the afternoon away.

A few minutes later, Del heard the faint sounds of a car pulling up outside, followed by the sound of a door closing gently, and he smiled.

Of course she'd come.

She was there in the cafeteria. She saw it all unfold.

Michael laughed humorlessly, shaking his head as he took another swig from the bottle.

By the time the track on his CD player changed to the next song, he heard the light footsteps on the stairs, and then his door cracked open slowly as she peeked her head in.

"There she is," he said with a grin, his voice tinged with alcohol. "I knew you'd come."

She opened the door with a sad smile. "And I knew you'd be drunk," she sighed, closing the door softly behind her.

"Well, I guess we're pretty predictable, aren't we, Red," he said, swirling the contents of the bottle in his hand.

"Well, we *have* done this dance a few times," she said, nudging him with her knee as she reached him. "Don't you ever get tired of dating girls like that? You know how it ends."

Del rested his head back on the bed, looking up at her as he shrugged indifferently.

She sighed, folding her arms over her chest. "So, do I officially have my friend back?"

Del pulled his brow together. "What does that mean?" he asked, and Lauren shrugged.

"It's just…this was a bad one. I hardly got to see you or talk to you when you were with her."

"Oh," Del said, looking down at the bottle and suddenly feeling like shit. He hadn't meant to neglect her at all, but now that she pointed it out, he *had* been spending most of his time with Tanya. Not that he preferred her company, but what she offered him was always enough to draw him away. "Sorry about that."

"The other girls you hung out with…they just kind of ignored me. But she really didn't like me, did she?"

Del shrugged dismissively. "Of course she didn't."

For a second, Lauren almost looked hurt. "But she doesn't even know me."

"She didn't have to. She was insecure. And a bitch," he added as an afterthought, taking another swig from the bottle.

"But you dated her."

"Yeah," Del said after he had swallowed. "I guess you can say that."

A beat of silence passed before he heard her soft voice. "Why?"

Del smiled acerbically. "Come on, Red."

Lauren rolled her eyes and shook her head. "Well, whatever," she said as she dropped down onto the floor beside him and leaned back against his bed, and Del felt himself move toward her automatically, drawn to her warmth and the familiar, soothing scent of her hair. "Let that be a lesson to you," she said. "You should start dating girls for other reasons besides the fact that they put out."

He laughed out loud as he rested his head on her shoulder and closed his eyes. This was exactly what he needed.

"Yeah, I know. Because all the nice girls are just lining up to be with a guy like me."

For a second, he thought he felt her stiffen beside him, but he couldn't be sure.

"I still don't get what I ever did to her," Lauren mumbled, and Del smiled. For some reason, he found it amusing that she would be bothered by what someone like Tanya thought of her, since Tanya wasn't even worthy of breathing the same air as Lauren.

"You didn't do anything to her. You're female, and you're the most important person in my life. Girls like her aren't used to feeling like they have competition, that's all."

This time Del was sure he felt her stiffen next to him, although he wasn't sure why. He brought the bottle to his lips, taking another sip. Did she really not understand why another girl might see her as a threat? "And I mean...look at you," he added nonchalantly, the alcohol in his system making him cavalier.

"Look at me?" she echoed with genuine confusion.

"Come on, Red. We've gone over this. You're not as invisible as you think you are. Do you think guys don't notice you? That their girls don't notice them noticing you?"

"Stop it."

"Stop what?" he asked.

"Patronizing me," she said, her voice soft.

Del lifted his head slightly, looking at her. "I'm being serious."

"You're drunk."

"And you're intimidating."

Lauren scoffed before she pushed him off her shoulder with a roll of her eyes. "Now I *know* you're drunk."

"Hey," he said, his expression taken aback. "I'm serious." He reached for her and pulled her back so he could rest his head on her shoulder again. He hated that she didn't see herself clearly, and he was suddenly overcome with the need for her to hear what he was saying, to believe it. "You're smart, you're beautiful, you're classy... that in itself is intimidating as hell, but then you're incredibly sweet on top of that. It's sort of like the 'girl next door' fantasy. But it's more than that."

Del turned his head slightly, looking up at her profile. She was staring straight ahead, blinking quickly, and he watched her throat bob as she swallowed. It was obvious that what he was saying was making her uncomfortable, but he couldn't bring himself to stop.

"Because as nice as you are, a guy still knows he'll have to work to win you over, you know? He knows he'll have to impress you…he'll have to earn your respect. It's intimidating as hell," he added with a laugh. "Even after being friends with you all this time, sometimes you still intimidate me."

She turned her head to look at him, and Del heard her breath catch at his proximity. He watched her eyes flicker back and forth between his, and then her lips parted as if she were about to speak, but seconds passed and no words came.

Before he could think about consequences, before he could even think about what he was doing, he lifted his chin, closing the small distance between them and pressing his lips to hers.

Part of him expected her to freeze up. Another part of him expected her to pull away from him in shock or disapproval. Or maybe perhaps she'd follow Tanya's example and give him his second slap of the day.

But instead she leaned into him, instantly shaping her mouth around his.

Del felt his heart quicken in his chest at her reaction, and he reached behind him, blindly putting the bottle on the floor before he brought his hand back up and slid it beneath her hair. The way she was kissing him only served to provoke him, and he cupped his hand around the back of her neck and pulled her further into the kiss.

As soon as he did, he felt her lips part as her tongue entered his mouth, and all sense of restraint or coherency left him in a rush. Somewhere in the back of his hazy mind, he knew he shouldn't be doing this, knew he had just crossed a line, yet he deepened the kiss with a sense of urgency, shifting his body closer to hers.

Suddenly he felt her leg come over his hips as she moved to straddle his lap, and Del forced himself to stifle a groan.

She brought her hands to his face then, tilting it up so she could kiss him more freely, and he allowed her to, relishing the way her tongue felt against his; gentle but determined, and mind-numbingly sensual.

His head started to spin with the taste of her, with the feeling of her weight on his lap, and he couldn't think anymore. He didn't want to. He just wanted to lose himself in what was suddenly happening.

Del brought his hands to her sides, gripping her waist, trying to keep himself grounded. She felt so tiny in his hands, and suddenly he was grazing them up her sides, stopping on her ribs before sliding them back down to her hips.

Lauren nipped his bottom lip then, igniting a visceral reaction in him, and he gripped her hips and pulled her firmly against his own.

She gasped against his mouth, followed by a soft, throaty moan that nearly caused him to lose his mind. He jerked back and stared up at her, wide-eyed and breathless.

"Jesus Christ," he exhaled before he brought his mouth back to hers, and she met him in earnest, kissing him with renewed intensity.

He hadn't expected any of this: for her to kiss him back, for her to take control the way she was, for that sexy, womanly sound to come out of her mouth.

She was determined. She was confident. She was perfect.

And he wanted her. Badly.

Del slid his hands up under her shirt, gripping her waist and feeling the heat of her skin against his palms, when the sound of a door slamming below them caught his attention. He was hoping he'd imagined it until he heard the muffled yell from downstairs.

"Yo, douchebag! How's your face?" The laughter of two other boys followed, and Del instantly pulled his hands from under Lauren's shirt and pushed her back somewhat roughly by her shoulders.

She whimpered in protest and leaned back toward him, clearly oblivious to the sounds coming from downstairs, and Del reached down again and gripped her hips, lifting her off his body and forcibly putting her down on the floor next to him.

She looked completely stunned: her eyes were darker than he'd ever seen them, her hair somewhat mussed, and her chest was heaving as she stared at him. She was pure sex in that moment, and he felt something frighteningly powerful tearing at him. Every part of his body was charged; it actually felt like his blood was vibrating in his body. He had never been this turned on in his entire life, but he knew it was so much more than that.

Lauren leaned forward on her hands, attempting to bring her mouth back to his, and for a second, he gave himself over to the raw need and met her, their lips moving together again, still hungry. He felt her hand come to the side of his face as she ran her fingertips over his cheek, feather-light and gentle despite her urgency.

In that moment, something irrevocable ignited inside him, and he knew he'd never be the same.

"Tell the truth, Delaney! Did she slap you because you can't hold your load?" a voice called, spurring another bout of raucous laughter. As the sounds of his friends coming up the stairs burst into his consciousness, Del jerked away from Lauren again.

"You should go," he said through his labored breath.

Lauren stared at him for a second before she blinked suddenly, her eyes widening as she glanced at the door, as if she'd just come back down to earth and heard them for the first time.

Del reached for his bottle as she jumped up from the floor, stumbling a bit as she composed herself, and just as his bedroom door burst open, she turned and headed toward it.

"See you tomorrow," she called casually over her shoulder, but the look in her eyes was pure fire, and Del could only swallow and nod in return as she squeezed her way through his rowdy friends and slipped out the door.

He spent the next hour in relative silence as his friends continued to take turns tormenting him for the Tanya incident. He knew they attributed his silence to being drunk, or angry, or both, and he let them.

But the entire time, all he could do was sit there reliving that moment with Lauren.

And when they finally left, having tapped themselves out of crude jokes for the evening, Del laid in bed for hours; sleep eluded him as he replayed those last few minutes with her over and over, until his heart rate sped up and his breathing became irregular.

Eventually, the heat of the memory wore off, along with the buzz of the alcohol, and was quickly replaced with an overwhelming sense of guilt.

What the hell had he been thinking?

How could he have kissed her that way? *Handled* her that way?

And what would have happened if his friends hadn't shown up when they did? If he had allowed himself to—

Del couldn't even let himself finish the thought. He would have never forgiven himself.

He would have hated himself.

And what was he supposed to do now? What was she thinking? After she had time to decompress, would she be angry? Offended? Or worse, would she expect to eventually finish what they started?

Del closed his eyes and pinched the bridge of his nose. He was such an asshole.

At around four in the morning, he fell into a restless sleep, still wondering what the hell he was going to say to Lauren the following day.

By the time he pulled into the parking lot of the school, he had decided on a plan of action.

He would avoid her.

He knew it was weak and pathetic, but he had already determined that he was an asshole. Might as well add coward to the list as well.

His inexcusable plan worked until fifth period, when he turned the corner to see her waiting at his locker. She shouldn't have been there. She had gym now, all the way on the other side of campus.

He faltered for only a second before immediately putting on a casual face and continuing toward her.

Her expression was tentative as she looked up at him.

"Hey," she said softly, stepping back to allow him access to his combination lock.

"'Sup?" he said.

There was a beat of silence before she uttered the dreaded words. "Can we talk?"

"About what?" he asked casually, spinning the lock and not even paying attention to the numbers.

"About last night," she said, and this time, there was a hint of annoyance in her voice.

"What about it?"

Del knew it was a dick thing to say as soon as it came out of his mouth, but he didn't know how else to handle the conversation. He hadn't prepared for it at all.

Out of the corner of his eye, he saw her shift as she folded her arms and cocked her head at him. "Are you going to say it was a dare again? Because it wasn't this time."

Yes, she was definitely annoyed now. Her words were clipped, her tone brazen.

Del turned his head toward her, his hand still on his combination lock. "No, I wasn't going to say it was a dare. I was going to say it was a mistake."

Lauren's brow instantly smoothed as she took the tiniest step back, the hurt apparent in her eyes.

Fuck.

He needed to fix this. He didn't want to hurt her. It was exactly the opposite.

Del's hand fell from his lock as he turned toward her fully.

"That came out wrong," he said softly. She just continued to stare up at him, that bewildered expression tearing his heart in two, and he exhaled heavily and shook his head. "Look," he continued. "Our friendship is the best thing I've got going on in my life. And…if I want it to stay that way, then we can't do that again. That shit gets too messy, okay?"

She blinked up at him, the confusion and hurt in her eyes slowly giving way to something else. Acceptance? Indifference? Concession?

"Okay," she finally said, her voice gentle again.

Del crouched slightly, bringing his eyes to her level. "You're too important to me," he said, his voice bordering on desperate. "Do you understand? I really need you to understand."

She looked at him for a second before she nodded. "I do," she whispered. And then she leaned over and kissed his cheek. "See you later," she added with a smile before she pushed away from the lockers and continued down the hall.

As he stood there, staring down at his combination lock, he knew he should have been feeling relieved that she had been so understanding, that she was so willing to put their friendship before anything else.

But that memory would haunt him for years to come, that moment when she told him she understood, when she looked up at him with that smile.

Because this time, it didn't reach her eyes.

December 2011

Lauren walked through the glass door that Adam held open for her, the wine in her system making her feel warm and tranquil, despite the cold December air that assaulted her as she exited the restaurant.

She watched as Adam approached the valet, handing him their ticket and saying something to him that made the man laugh. She never tired of watching him interact with people; there was something about him that instantly disarmed whomever he was speaking to.

The restaurant he had taken her to was extremely exclusive; in fact, Lauren felt a little out of her element when they first arrived. The staff, much like the décor, was overtly formal, maybe even a bit stuffy. But within seconds, Adam had everyone who waited on them engaged in conversation, smiling and laughing. Over and over again, she found herself completely captivated by his charisma, as if it were the first time she was witnessing it.

Lauren smiled as she walked over to him, gently taking his hand and intertwining their fingers as she rested her head on his shoulder.

He squeezed her hand gently, turning his head to look down at her. "You sleepy?" he asked, his voice a soft purr against Lauren's cheek that only added to the serenity she was feeling.

She shook her head and looked up at him, and he smiled before leaning down and planting a kiss on her forehead. "Good," he said. "I couldn't let you fall asleep before midnight on New Year's Eve. That would be blasphemous."

"Blasphemous?" Lauren echoed with a laugh.

"Absolutely," he said, releasing her hand as the valet pulled his car up in front of them. "Or at the very least, pitiful," he added with a smirk over his shoulder as he opened the passenger door for her.

Lauren laughed again, sliding into the seat as Adam tipped the valet and wished him a Happy New Year.

"So," Adam said once he was seated beside her and starting the car, "shall we begin phase two of our date?"

"What's phase two?" Lauren asked as she buckled her seatbelt.

"Depends. I have a few options. You can decide where the evening takes us."

Lauren smiled. "Kind of like those *Choose Your Own Adventure* books?"

Adam laughed, looking over at her. "Exactly like that. So, your character can either attend this party one of my neighbors is throwing—apparently he's notorious for his New Year's parties, although I've never been," he said. "Or, your character can go somewhere low-key. Lauren Monroe, choose your adventure."

She looked over at Adam's profile, the smile curving his lips, the angle of his jaw, highlighted and defined every few seconds by the flash of streetlights as they passed, and her decision was made.

"Low-key," she said.

"You got it," Adam said, glancing in his rearview as he switched lanes and took the highway entrance ramp.

They drove for a little under an hour, and Lauren was so consumed by their conversation that she paid no attention to where they were going until the terrain suddenly turned bumpy.

She glanced out the window, seeing nothing but trees and darkness.

"Are we going off-roading?" Lauren asked, reaching out to steady herself on the dash. "I didn't think we were going on an *actual* adventure."

Adam smiled, his eyes still on the road. "We'll only be off-roading for a few more minutes."

"Okay, but just so you know, hiking in the dark is definitely not my idea of low-key. And there's no way I could do it in these shoes."

"Or that dress," Adam said, glancing over to let his eyes run down her body before he brought them back to the road, and Lauren stifled a triumphant smile.

A few minutes later, they came upon a sudden break in the trees. Adam slowed the car, bringing it to a complete stop and cutting the engine and the headlights.

If she hadn't already trusted him, she would have been terrified. It was as if the car was covered with a tarp. She couldn't see anything, save for tiny little specks off in the distance that she assumed were the lights of some far-away town.

She glanced over to where Adam was sitting; as her eyes adjusted to the darkness, she could just make out his features. He was smiling at her, his eyebrow quirked.

"What are you thinking?" he asked.

"Um, that you're planning on murdering me and disposing of my dismembered body out here? Either that, or you just brought me to make-out point."

Adam burst out laughing, the hearty sound of it filling the car, and Lauren smiled as she unbuckled her seatbelt.

"Not exactly," Adam finally said through his laughter. "But good to know where your mind is."

She turned in her seat, facing him fully. "Okay, I give. Where the hell are we?"

He followed her lead, unbuckling his seatbelt and shifting in his seat so he was facing her. "I did find this place hiking once. I used to do it a lot right after I recovered from my neck injury." He turned to look out the blackened windshield. "I've never come here at night, though. I just always thought tonight would be a cool night to do it."

"Why?"

He smiled and glanced down at his watch. "You'll see in about four minutes."

"Oh my God, it's four minutes until midnight?" Lauren asked, surprised. When Adam nodded, she said, "How is that possible? It feels like the night just started."

"I know," he said. "It's always like that with you."

She smiled. "You mean the night flying by?"

Adam looked down as the corner of his mouth lifted in a smile. "Night, day, phone calls, chiropractic appointments." He took a small breath, and to Lauren's surprise, he almost looked sheepish. "I always feel like time goes too fast with you." He laughed softly as he looked up at her. "Or maybe I just never feel like it's enough."

Lauren stared at him, and he looked down again. "I know that sounds—"

She leaned forward, cutting him off as she pressed her lips to his.

He chuckled softly in surprise and amusement, kissing her back. "That wasn't a line, you know," he said against her mouth, and she nodded.

"I know," she breathed before taking his bottom lip between hers, and he made a small sound in the back of his throat, leaning forward and kissing her fully.

His hand came to her face, his thumb caressing her cheek as his fingers slid behind her ear, and she shivered, shifting her body and trying to get as close to him as the console in between them would allow.

A sudden hissing sound followed by a muted pop caused Lauren to open her eyes just in time to see a rainbow of colors explode in the sky, lighting it with a million shimmering twinkles. She broke the kiss, turning her head to look out the windshield; just as the colors fizzled away, the silence was filled with a new series of hisses and pops as fireworks shattered the darkness, some little starbursts of color, while others were tremendous explosions of glitter and light.

Lauren stared out the windshield in awe until she felt his thumb on her cheek again, and she finally pulled her eyes away from the spectacle to look at him.

"Happy New Year," he whispered.

Another pop sounded, louder than the ones before, and by the sound of it, and the way light danced over Adam's face, Lauren knew it must have been amazing.

But this time, she kept her eyes on him.

He leaned toward her, bringing his mouth back to hers, and she kissed him, the soft sounds of their lips brushing together mixing with the muted booms of the fireworks in the distance.

Lauren shifted again, trying to get closer, and when the console prevented her, she came up onto her knees and tried to maneuver around the stick shift. Adam immediately sat back against his seat, gripping her hips and helping her over the console and onto his lap.

He slid his hands into her hair, gazing up at her, and as she leaned down to kiss him again, she felt his hands slide down the sides of her neck and over her shoulders.

She shivered, and Adam pulled back slightly, their lips barely touching and their breath mingling together. He ghosted his hands over her ribs, his thumbs grazing the sides of her breasts, and Lauren gasped softly against his mouth before closing the tiny distance, kissing him more earnestly.

He had been so patient with her, always so patient. But she was pushing the boundary right now, and she knew it.

They had only been on three dates before this, so it wasn't as though it was completely unreasonable that she hadn't been intimate with him yet. And every time they'd gone out, he'd always been a perfect gentleman, never pushing, never taking it to a new level without her permission.

But she knew he was ready for more. Hell, even *she* was ready for more. At least, her body was.

But she just couldn't bring herself to sleep with him yet.

She told herself it was because she wanted to make sure this was something real, something meaningful, before she gave herself over to him.

But she knew what the real reason was.

She knew what always happened whenever she slept with someone. She knew what she would end up doing. And she wasn't ready for that to happen yet. She liked him too much.

Adam hummed in contentment against her mouth before pulling back slightly and brushing the hair out of her face. "So," he said breathlessly, "where does the character go from here?"

Lauren dropped her eyes, taking a small breath before she bit her lower lip.

"Hey," she heard him whisper, and she tentatively lifted her gaze to his. "It's okay," he said softly.

"I'm so sorry," Lauren said, moving to get off of him. "I shouldn't have—"

His hands immediately came to her hips, stilling her. "Don't be sorry. We *both* agreed to take it slow. That's what we're doing."

Lauren looked at him expecting to see the frustration behind his kind words, but all she saw in his eyes was complete sincerity.

She hated herself in that moment. Why couldn't she just give him what he wanted? What *she* wanted?

"I do want you, Adam," she whispered.

He smiled a slow smile before he trailed the backs of his knuckles up the side of her body, and Lauren's eyes fluttered closed as she instinctively arched toward him.

She quickly regained her composure before opening her eyes and looking down at him.

"I know you do," he said.

Lauren closed her eyes again, nodding softly as she took a deep breath.

"Do you want to know why my last relationship ended?" Adam asked, shifting her so she was sitting on his lap rather than straddling it.

"Why?" Lauren asked, resting her head against his shoulder as he trailed his fingertips over the skin at her wrist.

"Because she tried to fast-forward everything. She was always on to the next step, the next phase. She treated our relationship like it was a race to the finish line." He reached up and took a strand of Lauren's hair, tucking it behind her ear. "And it's not that I don't want what's at the finish line. Living together. Marriage. Babies. I see myself with all of that one day. But this," he said, gesturing between them. "This part—the beginning part—and the way it makes you feel? The newness of it all, the thrill of anticipation. That doesn't last forever. So...I don't know, I think it's kind of nice to prolong it."

Lauren closed her eyes and smiled. "So what you're saying is, you don't mind savoring things?"

"I don't mind savoring you."

She lifted her head off his shoulder and looked up at him and he smiled. "You ready to go home?"

Lauren nodded gently, too overcome to speak.

They drove home in comfortable silence—the radio humming softly between them as he gently played with her fingers, releasing her hand only to shift gears.

And when he walked her to her door, he thanked her for spending New Year's with him and kissed her in a way that made her question her sanity for not dragging him upstairs and having her way with him.

She watched his car pull away before she turned to unlock her door, and just as she turned the key, she heard her cell phone ringing. Lauren dug through her purse as she stepped into her apartment, flipping the light on as she pulled her phone out and looked at the screen.

Instantly, butterflies flooded her stomach.

Incoming Call from Michael.

Ever since that night a few weeks ago when Lauren had taken care of Erin for him, things had changed between them. They were quickly becoming friends again, and the ease with which it was happening made Lauren realize what a fool she'd been for thinking it could have been avoided. So it wasn't unusual for her to see his number now.

But every time she did, she'd react the same way, and she hated it. And tonight, on the tail end of her evening with Adam, those butterflies felt even more traitorous.

She hit the button to take the call as she removed her coat.

"Hey."

"Miss Lauren!"

The tiny bell-like voice was not the one she expected, but she grinned.

"Hi, sweetheart! What are you doing awake? It's way past your bedtime!"

"Daddy let me stay up to see the ball!"

"He did? Wow!" Lauren said with the enthusiasm she knew Erin was expecting.

"Yep! And he let me have a whole ice-cream sundae. And you know what else?"

"What else?" Lauren said, smiling to herself as she stepped out of her heels and walked back to her bedroom.

"We took out all the pans and hit them with spoons when the ball came down. We were *loud*!" Erin shouted before she squealed with laughter.

"My goodness!" Lauren laughed. "Well, it sounds like you had a lot of fun."

"We did," she said. "Oh, and I almost forgot, *Happy New Year*!"

"Happy New Year, sweetheart," Lauren said, unzipping her dress and letting it pool at her feet.

"Gotta go! Here's Daddy!" she said, and then Lauren heard the sounds of the phone changing hands.

"Okay, but we have to start being quiet now, honey. It's late and people are trying to go to sleep," she heard Michael say before he took the phone. "Hey," he finally said. "Sorry about that. I figured you'd be up, and she was insistent that we call."

Lauren smiled as she quickly pulled an oversized T-shirt over her head. "How is she not passed out yet?"

Michael sighed. "I screwed myself during the celebration process. She's riding a hardcore sugar high. I might not get to sleep until next weekend."

"Come on. This isn't your first time partying with a three-year-old. You should have matched her sugar intake with your own coffee intake. That's just a rookie mistake."

Michael laughed. "That's brilliant," he said through a yawn. "Where were you when I needed that idea two hours ago?"

She smiled as she crawled into her bed. "I can't imagine she can go for much longer. She'll crash soon. And from the sound of it, she won't be the only one."

"Pathetic, right? I was nodding before the ball dropped."

"Pathetic indeed. This from the guy who showed up completely tanked in my driveway at five in the morning one New Year's, still raring to go."

"Ah, that's right," Michael said slowly. "I believe I puked in your neighbor's rosebush that night."

"Hmm, nothing says nostalgia like vomit," Lauren sighed as she pulled the comforter up over her legs, and Michael laughed.

It was moments like this that Lauren couldn't comprehend how she had ever lived without his friendship. Jenn had asked Lauren at their monthly dinner two weeks earlier what it was worth, why she would ever want to be Michael's friend again. And although Lauren didn't give her an answer, she had done a lot of thinking since the night she spent at his house, and she knew what it was worth.

It was about redemption.

Everyone deserved the chance to be redeemed, and Michael had gone his whole life never having it. He never got to redeem himself with his father. He never got to redeem himself with his brother. And if he was trying to redeem himself now for what he'd done to her, then she was going to let him, even if it left her vulnerable.

Lauren knew she could handle herself. One of the things he'd taught her about herself was that she was much stronger than she thought. She didn't have to be foolish. She didn't have to love him again.

She knew those feelings had the potential to resurface, but wasn't being aware of that enough to prevent it? There was no way it could sneak up on her; she knew what her downfall could be, and so she could consciously remain in control of it. So far, she had done a damn good job of keeping it just friendship. Jenn should have been proud of her.

"Well," Michael sighed, "at least there was one benefit to me staying in tonight."

"What's that?"

"I was able to avoid the black ice."

"Oh…my…*God*," Lauren said, her voice breaking on the last word as she disintegrated into hysterical laughter. She was vaguely aware of Michael laughing on the other end, but she could barely hear him over her own.

Lauren curled forward, holding her stomach as she gasped for air.

"I take it you remember that," Michael said with a smile in his voice, and Lauren nodded as she wiped the tears from her eyes, still laughing too hard to answer.

After a full minute passed with Lauren still unable to get control of herself, Michael sighed.

"Alright, alright, it wasn't *that* funny."

"You're kidding, right?" Lauren said, still breathless as she wiped her eyes with her comforter. "I think I can safely say that it was, and always will be, one of the funniest things I've ever seen."

The night that Michael had shown up drunk on her driveway, he had woken her up by throwing twigs at her window. Lauren had thought it was an adorable gesture until she opened the window to find Michael barely able to stand.

"You missed New Year's," he had slurred. "Come down and party with me."

"Michael, it's five in the morning," she hissed out her window. "And I think you've done enough partying."

"Pshh," he said, waving his hand at her. "Come on, Red. Come down and hang out with me."

"I can't," she whispered, looking back into her room to make sure no one had heard the commotion and come to check on her.

Michael shrugged. "Suit yourself. Happy New Year!" he yelled, throwing his hands in the air and taking a dramatic bow before he turned and jogged sloppily down her driveway.

"Michael!" she whisper-yelled after him, noticing the precarious shine on the blacktop. "Watch out for the black ice!"

"Watch out for the black guys?" he called over his shoulder, the confusion in his voice mixed with drunken amusement. "What the hell is wrong with—" The words cut off as Michael's legs soared out from under him, and Lauren watched as he flew into the air, his arms flailing at his sides before he landed flat on his back and glided a few feet until his legs were under her mother's parked car.

Lauren hadn't thought about that night in years, but now she couldn't get the image out of her mind. Every time she thought she'd composed herself, she'd start laughing again.

"I don't know what the best part of that story is: the epic fall you took, or the fact that you thought I was trying to warn you about black guys," she said through her cackling.

Michael stifled a laugh. "You do realize I could have killed myself. It's cruel of you to laugh."

"Hey, I came running down to make sure you were okay, and double and triple-checked before I even let the first smile crack," she said. "That was no easy feat, so I've earned the right to laugh freely now."

"Yeah, yeah," Michael said.

"You were so wasted. I can't believe you even remember that."

"Remember it? How could I not? You reminded me of it every chance you got for the next year of our lives."

Lauren smiled as she laid back against her pillow, and the words were out of her mouth before she could think better of them.

"I really missed you."

There was a beat of silence, and Lauren's smile fell as her heart stopped. But before she could even curse herself for the slip-up, she heard him sigh, his words so soft that she wasn't even sure they were meant for her ears.

"God...me too."

December 2002

*L*auren pulled into Michael's driveway and cut the engine, trying to shake off the sudden sadness that had momentarily overtaken her excitement.

The entire drive to his house, she had been so eager to give him his Christmas present. Getting her hands on it had proved to be nearly impossible; she'd never tell him the lengths she went through to get it, or how much she ended up paying for it, but she could just imagine the look on his face that would make everything worth it.

But as she turned onto his road, her heart dropped slightly. Every house on the street was lit up, a myriad of blinking lights and giant blow-up Santas and twinkling artificial icicles.

Every house except his.

It was literally a blackened hole on a street full of color and festivity, its darkness somehow overpowering the brightness of all the others combined, and the thought of him coming home to this house night after night put an unpleasant heaviness in her chest.

Lauren exited her car, looking up at the dim light coming out of his window, and she smiled as the image of him opening his present made its way back into her mind. She turned and grabbed the bag, shutting the car door and jogging up the front steps to his house.

A long time ago, Michael had told her to just walk in when she came over. It had taken her forever to feel comfortable doing so, but eventually it just became routine. His mother was usually holed up in her bedroom, and on the rare occasions that she made an appearance, she would simply ignore Lauren anyway.

Lauren opened the front door, startled to see Mrs. Delaney sitting on the couch, staring straight ahead as she absently swirled a small glass of brown liquid in her hand.

There was no tree, no smell of Christmas dinner, not even a Christmas card displayed anywhere. And although Lauren had expected as much, there was the tiniest part of her that still hoped, that figured maybe decorating the outside of the house was too laborious for a woman, but the inside would be different.

She took a small, steadying breath. "Hi Mrs. Delaney," she attempted softly.

The woman stared straight ahead as if Lauren hadn't spoken.

Lauren bit her lip, dropping her eyes before she began walking past her toward the stairs.

"You seem like a smart girl."

Lauren froze. It was the first time in two years the woman had acknowledged her at all, let alone spoken to her.

"Although I'm a terrible judge of character," she added with a sardonic laugh.

Lauren turned toward her; she was staring down at the glass in her hand as she swirled it slowly.

"But if for once I'm right," she said huskily, "you should stop coming around here." She lifted her eyes then, looking at Lauren. "He'll just ruin you."

A loaded silence filled the space between them as Lauren stared at the woman before her, completely at a loss for words. She wanted so badly to be able to make sense of her, to find any ounce of humanity in those eyes that might belie the words that just left her lips.

But there was nothing.

And suddenly she felt a heat lighting in her stomach that made it hard for her to breathe.

How could a mother say that about her own son? What could he have ever possibly done to deserve that?

And why did he have to be stuck in this horrible house with her?

She could feel the heat building, spreading up through her chest and into the back of her throat, making her eyes sting.

Lauren had always prided herself on giving people the benefit of the doubt, on treating people with respect, but she couldn't find it in her heart to do either for this woman.

"Your son," she said slowly, giving due weight to every word, "is one of the best people I've ever known." She inhaled a shaking breath. "And I feel sorry for you that you don't know him."

With that she turned and headed up the stairs, refusing to look back, even when she heard her mumble something about a stupid, naive girl.

By the time she reached Michael's door, her hands were shaking. She stopped and closed her eyes, taking a steadying breath and trying to rid her expression of any remaining animosity before she opened the door.

He was lying on his bed, one hand behind his head and the other holding the remote, aimlessly flipping through the channels on his television.

When the door opened, he turned his head, smiling when he saw it was her.

"Hey Red," he said, sitting up. "What are you doing here? Don't you have family stuff going on?"

"Yeah," she said, walking in and closing the door behind her. "But I just wanted to stop by and say Merry Christmas."

Michael tossed the remote on the bed behind him. "You mean your holiday spirit wasn't sucked right out of you the second you crossed over the threshold?"

Lauren forced a sad smile, dropping her eyes to the floor.

"We don't really do Christmas here. Obviously."

Lauren looked up. "Ever?" she asked, and Michael shrugged.

"Not since my brother died."

"Oh," Lauren said faintly. A beat of silence passed before she said, "Well, do you want to come over to my house?" *Forever?* she thought. More than ever, she just wanted to take him and run with him some place far away.

"Nah, that's okay," he said. His eyes dropped to the package in her hand. "What's that?" he asked, quirking his brow as a tiny smile lifted the corner of his mouth.

At his expression, Lauren smiled her first genuine smile since she pulled into his driveway.

"Your present," she said.

Michael grinned. "Didn't I tell you not to get me anything?"

"Yes," she said, crossing the room to sit on the bed beside him, "and by the expression on your face, I can tell you're really broken up over the fact that I didn't listen."

Michael laughed, shifting to face her on the bed as she handed the bag to him.

He dug his hand in the bag like an eager child, and again, Lauren felt a heaviness in her chest as her eyes began to sting for him. She cleared her throat and pushed those feelings away, focusing on the moment.

He pulled the flat, rectangular box out of the bag, and immediately his jaw dropped.

"Get the fuck out of here," he said in complete awe, tossing the bag on the floor and holding the box in two hands.

Lauren grinned, and he lifted his eyes to her, completely shocked. "Holy shit, are you kidding me?" he said, and she laughed.

"Do you like it?"

"Jesus Christ, Red, how did you get this?" he asked, turning the box over to read the back.

Lauren had never gotten into video games. Michael had tried a few times to show her how to play, but it was never her thing. But apparently this new game, Metroid Prime, was supposed to be amazing. It was the first 3D game in that series for GameCube, and also boasted a first-person adventure premise. It had gotten all sorts of amazing reviews before it was even released in November, making it essentially impossible to find during the holiday season.

"It wasn't that big of a deal," she lied.

He smirked at her and shook his head. "You are so full of shit."

Lauren laughed. "I just had to betroth myself to some Arabian prince. Like I said, no big deal."

"Well, that's unfortunate. Totally worth it, but unfortunate," he said, and Lauren leaned over and smacked his chest, causing him to laugh.

"This is..." he looked back at the box, shaking his head before he lifted his eyes to hers. "Whatever you had to do to get this, seriously...thank you." He leaned over, pulling her into his chest as he hugged her, and Lauren closed her eyes.

"You're welcome," she said into his shirt.

Too soon, she felt him release her, and she sat back as he stood from the bed and walked to the other side of the room. She assumed he was going to put the game into his system, but he walked past the television and over to his closet, grabbing something off the top shelf.

When he turned back toward the bed, she could see it was a small square box wrapped in shiny green paper.

"Merry Christmas Red," he said, tossing the box to her before he sat back down on the bed.

"You got me something? I thought you said—"

"I know what I said. Shut up and open it."

Lauren looked up to see him motioning with his head toward the box in her hands, encouraging her.

She carefully peeled back the paper and pulled out a red, hinged box.

Inside was a necklace, made up of several tiny silver leaves connected with delicate vines, twirling and intertwining up to the clasp. The leaves were faceted so that the light shimmered off them in prisms, making them sparkle.

"Oh my gosh, this is so…*pretty*." She brought her fingertip to one of the leaves, the movement causing it to glitter. "Is this ivy?" she asked, looking up at him.

Michael smiled. "We had to do a project in art. Some crap about symbolism in nature. I couldn't come up with anything, so Miss Abramo assigned me ivy." He shrugged. "It made me think of you."

"What do you mean?" Lauren asked.

He shook his head. "Here," he said, reaching for the box and pulling the necklace out. He opened the clasp and held it out, and Lauren leaned forward as he put it around her neck, closing it behind her.

Michael sat back, and the corner of his mouth lifted in a smile. "It looks good on you, Red."

Her hand came to the necklace, holding it against her skin as she felt her cheeks get hot. "Thank you."

They sat there in silence for a moment before Lauren looked down at her watch. "I should be getting back," she said softly.

"Alright. Well, thanks for coming over. Give me a call tomorrow."

"Are you sure you don't want to come back with me?" Lauren asked.

"No, I'm good. I got this," he said, holding up the video game with a smile.

"Okay," she said, standing from the bed, not wanting to leave him even though she knew she had to. "But if you decide you want to get out of here for a bit, just come over."

"I will. Merry Christmas," he said, hugging her once more, and she gave him one last squeeze before she grabbed her purse and headed back downstairs.

Thankfully, Michael's mother was nowhere to be seen when she came back through the living room; Lauren didn't know if she'd be able to curb her tongue if they had another encounter, and the last thing she wanted to do was have it out with that woman.

She drove home in silence, one hand on the wheel and the other playing with the delicate silver vines at her throat.

As soon as she got back home, she bypassed the crowd of her family in the living room and ran upstairs, powering up her computer. And then she opened her search engine and typed in "ivy symbolism" before hitting enter.

Several sites came up as a result, and Lauren clicked on the first one and began reading.

Ever furrowing and intertwining, the ivy is an example of the twists and turns our lives often take, but because ivy has the propensity to interweave in its growth, it is also a testimony to the long-lasting connections we can form with others throughout our lives.

Lauren bit her lip, closing out of the website and clicking on the next one.

Ivy is a tribute to strong relationships because of its ability to grow and flourish, even in the most challenging environments. It seems to be virtually indestructible and will often return after it has suffered damage or has been severely cut back. Because the ivy is unbelievably durable and known to withstand harsh conditions, it represents incredibly loyal relationships and our ability to stand by those we care about, even in the toughest of situations.

Lauren's breath left her in a soft rush, and she closed out of the website and clicked on one more. This one stated simply:

Ivy is symbolic of strong, lasting relationships that are guaranteed to stand the test of time.

With a smile on her lips, she dropped her head back on the chair and closed her eyes, trailing her fingertips over the necklace once more.

"I love you, Michael Delaney," she breathed, and it felt so good to finally say it out loud, even if no one but her could hear it.

January 2012

Lauren sat at the stoplight, mentally running through the list of errands she still hoped to get done. She couldn't remember the last time she'd had a day off during the week, and when she first woke up that morning, she didn't know what to do with herself. Her new semester of classes didn't start for another couple of days, so she literally had an entire day laid out before her like a blank canvas.

That lasted all of about five minutes.

After cleaning her apartment, she finally collected the small laundry bag of dry-clean-only clothes that had been sitting in the bottom of her closet and dropped them off to be cleaned. She stopped by the post office and picked up a book of stamps. She went to the bank and transferred some money from her savings account to her checking account in preparation for those post-holiday credit card bills. And now, she was on her way to the grocery store.

As she waited for the light to turn green, the sound of grinding metal caught her attention, and she glanced to the right, noticing the crew of construction workers gathered around a large sheet of metal, some holding it in place while others methodically walked around with some type of hand-held tools that either cut it or drilled holes in it. One of the men stopped and removed the goggles from his eyes, checking over his work, and she smiled softly when she recognized him.

Lauren had completely forgotten he was working on the new medical offices going up on West Linn Street.

Just as the light turned green, she saw him cup his hands in front of his mouth and blow into them before rubbing them together. She frowned slightly as she began to pull forward, watching as his breath repeatedly left his mouth in a wispy cloud. In fact, the whole group of them looked like they were steaming, their exhales alternately providing puffs of white smoke that wafted around them.

He bounced on his toes, rubbing his hands together one more time before he pulled his goggles back down and got back to work.

Lauren glanced down at her dashboard. Eighteen degrees outside today.

She scrunched up her nose as she glanced in her rearview, catching one last glimpse of the men as they continued working over the piece of metal before they disappeared from view.

Before she had even consciously decided to do it, she made a quick left turn, putting on her blinker at the end of the street and turning into the Dunkin Donuts drive-through. Five minutes later, she was heading back toward West Linn Street with a Box O'Joe and fifty count of Munchkins in her passenger seat.

Lauren found a parking space at the end of the street and exited the car, ducking her head against a particularly sharp gust of wind; she couldn't imagine having to work outside on a day like this. She walked a little faster, the box of coffee in one hand and the donuts in the other, looking out from under her lashes as she tucked her chin into her scarf.

As she approached the small group of men, Michael removed his goggles again, bending slightly to examine something on the sheet metal. After a moment he straightened. He was about to bring his goggles back down when he spotted her.

He looked surprised, but he smiled, pulling his goggles completely off as he placed what looked like a drill on the pavement.

"Hey," Lauren said, bouncing on her toes to keep warm as he approached her.

"Hey," he said, jamming his hands in his pockets. "It's freezing out here. Why are you walking? Where's your car?"

"Down the block," she said, motioning with her head. "I just came down here to give you guys this," she added holding out the coffee and donuts.

He looked down at what she offered. "You got us all coffee?" he asked. When he looked back up, there was something behind his eyes that made her chest feel heavy with an emotion she couldn't quite place.

Lauren nodded. "It's cold," she said softly. "I just figured..." She shrugged.

Michael looked at her for a second before a smile began playing at his lips. "You would've had to fend off most of these guys with a cattle prod anyway. But now? All bets are off."

Lauren laughed nervously. "Well then, maybe *you* should give it to them."

He laughed loudly before he quirked his brow at her. "Come on now Red, I've never known you to be shy."

He turned then, calling to the guys, and Lauren froze.

It was the first time he'd used his old nickname for her.

The heaviness instantly settled back in her chest, and this time, she had no trouble identifying it.

Longing.

She should have been panicked over that revelation; she realized that. She should have been trying to find a way to remove herself from the situation so she could get composed, so she could chase that godforsaken feeling out of her body. It was a fail-safe method that had proven successful whenever she felt herself slipping with him over the past few weeks.

But for some reason, the only thing she could bring herself to do in that moment was smile.

She didn't even realize how much she had missed his pet name for her until she'd heard it again.

Michael had the men's attention now, and he turned back, gesturing to her. "This is my friend Lauren. She brought us coffee."

Immediately, she was inundated with calls of thanks, compliments, and a few whistles. She looked down and laughed, handing the boxes to the two men who walked over. "There are cups in that bag, and cream and sugar," she said.

"Well, aren't you a doll," an older gentleman with graying hair said. "Thank you, sweetheart."

"Anytime." Lauren waved at the other guys. "Stay warm," she called, and again, they shouted their thanks to her.

Michael smiled. "Well, I better go get some before those animals drain that thing," he said. "And you should get the hell out of this cold."

"Wait," Lauren said. "I have something for you in the car."

"For me?" he asked, his brow lifted, and she nodded.

"Hurry though, I'm freezing," she said as she turned and started walking quickly down the block.

She was vaguely aware of Michael following her, but she was too focused on picking up the pace. The wind had started to pick up, making it borderline unbearable to be outside.

When she reached the car, she jumped in, quickly closing the door behind her, and Michael walked around, getting into the passenger side.

"God." Lauren's teeth chattered as she started the car and blasted the heat, holding her hands in front of the vents. "How the hell do you do it?"

"You get used to it after a while." He rested his head back on the seat and turned to look at her. "This was probably a stupid move though."

"What was?"

"Getting in this car with you."

She pulled her brow together as she focused on playing with the knob for the heat. "Why?" she asked with strained casualness.

"Because I'm warming up. It's going to be that much colder when I go back out there now."

"Oh." She felt her shoulders soften in relief as she looked over at him.

"What did you think I meant?"

She shook her head. "Nothing," she said, reaching into the console and pulling the large Dunkin Donuts cup out of the holder. "Here, maybe this will make going back out there a little more bearable."

"What is this?" he asked, taking it from her.

"Hot chocolate."

A slow smile formed on his lips. "With whipped cream?"

She nodded once.

"And...?"

Lauren smiled. "And rainbow sprinkles. And a cherry, of course."

Michael's smile turned into a full-blown grin, and Lauren laughed.

When they were in high school, Michael used to order this drink all the time, claiming it was like "an ice-cream sundae you could have in the winter." Lauren always got a kick out of it, the way he'd walk through the halls with his intimidating posture and unnerving expressions while holding such an innocuous, juvenile beverage concealed in a coffee cup.

She nodded in the direction of the work site. "Tell them it's something manly," she said. "Like black coffee with a shot of whiskey."

He burst out laughing before he looked down, shaking his head with a smile. He spun the drink slowly in his hand before he looked back up at her. "How do you remember these things?"

Her expression softened. "You were my best friend, Michael."

His smile dropped. For a moment, they just stared at each other, and then he looked down. "I know," he said softly. After a few seconds, he cleared his throat. "I should probably..." He gestured with his head toward the construction site, and Lauren nodded.

"Yeah. Try to stay warm, okay?"

She turned toward the steering wheel, and suddenly his hand was on her chin, turning her face back toward him as he leaned forward and brought his lips to her cheek.

She closed her eyes as his mouth left her skin. "Thank you," he said. She felt the backs of his knuckles brush over her cheek, right where he had just kissed her, and then he was out of the car before she could even formulate a response.

Michael walked back down the block, hot chocolate in hand and a smile on his face, completely oblivious to the cold now.

When he got back to the site, most of the guys were sitting on the curb drinking coffee and eating the donuts Lauren had just dropped off. He walked over to where Dean was leaned up against a streetlight, warming his hands on his cup of coffee.

Dean glanced over at him. "Was that her?" he asked before he took a sip.

"Who?" Michael asked, taking a sip of his own and smiling as the sweet beverage hit his tongue. *Tell them it's something manly, like black coffee with a shot of whiskey.* He laughed to himself.

"Your girl," Dean said. "The one you've been after."

Michael looked up, his expression turning serious. "I'm not after her," he said. "She's a good friend of mine."

Dean looked at him for a second before he smirked. "Okay," he said, turning his attention to the other side of the street. He brought his cup to his mouth, but Michael could still see him smiling.

He looked at Dean for another second before he dropped his eyes, rolling his cup in between his palms, feeling the heat of the liquid and the icy chill of the air alternating on his skin.

"Can I ask you something?" he finally said.

Dean looked back at him. "What's up?"

"You and Melinda. How's that going?"

Only a few months ago, they had been in the middle of an ugly custody battle over their daughter. But recently, Michael knew they'd been trying to work on their relationship.

Dean inhaled deeply. "We got *a lot* of shit to work out. But we're trying. We're getting there."

Michael nodded, and for a minute, the only sound was the murmuring conversations of the guys around them mixing with the cars passing by. "How?" he finally said.

"What do you mean?"

He inhaled slowly. "I mean…how do you fix something you really fucked up?"

Dean looked at him, and after a second he nodded in understanding.

"Well," he said, "we have a kid involved. So when we put her needs in front of our own, that helps."

"Yeah," Michael agreed, running his fingers over the lid of his cup.

"But honestly? What women need?" Dean paused to take a sip of his coffee. "Actions. Not words. Sorry doesn't mean shit, begging doesn't mean shit, and promises don't mean shit."

Michael nodded and looked down. "I'm just...I'm at a loss, man. I just don't know..." He sighed, shaking his head.

Dean leaned over. "You gotta prove to her that you're never gonna do whatever messed with her in the first place ever again. You gotta show her there's no reason to be afraid of giving you another chance. And that's work, my man. That's work." He pushed off the lamppost and started to walk away, but turned at the last second. "But from what I just saw, I think she'd be willing to hear you out."

Dean clapped him on the back before he turned and walked back toward their workstation.

Michael watched him walk away for a moment before he turned and sat on a nearby bench, resting his elbows on his knees as he held his hot chocolate in front of him.

Slowly, he bowed his head.

Something had changed. Somehow, for some reason, something had changed between them over the past few weeks. Lauren seemed so much more open to him. More relaxed. More herself. Months ago, that had been all he really wanted—to have her drop that aloof charade, for her to let her guard down and just be herself with him again.

But now that he seemed to have that, he wanted more.

The taste of winning back her friendship had given him an appetite for something much bigger. And when she looked at him the way she just did in the car, there was a piece of him that believed maybe, just maybe, he could have it. That there was a chance he could fix this.

That he could have everything he wanted.

Michael dropped his head back, taking a deep breath as he blinked up at the sky.

He'd done everything except the one thing he knew he had to do.

He needed to talk to her about what happened.

And maybe if she knew the reason behind his actions all those years ago, she'd understand.

Michael sighed as he looked down at his drink, swirling it a few times before he took another sip.

He was going to talk to her. Soon. Because even if it didn't work, even if knowing the truth didn't change a single thing between them, she deserved to finally understand what had happened.

It was time for him to stop running.

May 2003

*D*el sat in the passenger seat of Lauren's car, staring out the window at the passing scenery.

"I'm not an idiot, you know."

Lauren looked at him, her expression a mixture of confusion and amusement. "Well, sometimes I'd have to disagree," she said with the hint of a laugh. "But what are you talking about?"

"I know what this is about."

Out of the corner of his eye, he could see her looking at him, and then she turned her eyes back to the road, saying nothing.

He knew he was being an asshole; she was just looking out for him. But he couldn't help it.

It was the anniversary of the night Aaron died. Lauren knew that. And what Del wanted to be doing right now—what he'd done every year on this night since he was thirteen—was to drink until he passed out. Lauren knew that too.

Which, of course, was the reason for this little road trip.

Lauren claimed she needed his help with something tonight, but Del knew better. She hated when he drank too much, especially when he used it as a coping mechanism. She had used those exact words with him once, and he'd laughed and told her not to quit her day job.

Even though he knew that's exactly what he was doing.

"Just...humor me," she said quietly before she reached to turn the radio on.

For the next twenty minutes, neither one of them spoke as Lauren drove them through the next town and pulled into the parking lot of what looked like a small warehouse.

She cut the engine and removed her seatbelt before she turned to look at him.

"Okay. Let's go."

Del squinted out the window, just making out the letters of a small neon sign hanging above the door of the building.

TRASHED.

"What the hell is this?" he asked, but she was already out of the car.

With a huff he took off his seatbelt. "Hey," he called as he exited the car, and she turned to look over her shoulder. "What the hell is this?"

"Come on," she said simply, reaching for him.

With a resigned sigh he walked over to where she was standing and took her outstretched hand.

Lauren led him to the door and pulled it open, and they walked into what looked like a small china shop. The walls were essentially floor to ceiling shelves, filled with various plates, glasses, mugs, bowls, and vases. There was a counter on the far wall, where a cash register sat above a long glass case filled with what looked like small porcelain statues and knickknacks. The man behind it appeared to be in his twenties; his hair was dyed a deep black and styled into meticulous spikes, and two piercings adorned his lower lip.

Del halted in the doorway, surveying the area with confusion, but Lauren pulled him forward as she approached the man behind the counter.

"Hi," she said. "My name is Lauren Monroe. I think we spoke on the phone?"

"Lauren, yes," he said, and Del immediately straightened his posture at the way the guy was looking at her. "Good to meet you."

She nodded with a smile. "This is my friend Michael," she said, pulling him a bit closer to the counter.

The man nodded politely at him. "Glad to have you with us. So, are you guys all set?"

"Just him," Lauren said.

"Okay then. Right this way. Your room is all ready."

The man turned and walked down a small hallway to the left of the counter, and Lauren moved to follow him.

Del yanked on her hand, and she stumbled back toward him, wide-eyed.

"I'm not going anywhere until you tell me what the hell this is."

For a second, she just stared up at him. "You don't trust me?"

He rolled his eyes. "Of course I do," he started.

"Then just come with me," she said, cutting him off. "If you don't want to do it, we'll leave."

She looked up at him for another second, reassuring him with her eyes before she turned back toward the hallway, and this time, he allowed her to pull him along.

There were two doors on either side of the hall, and Lauren followed the man into the last one on the right.

As soon as they stepped inside the room, Del released her hand and crossed his arms, looking around. One of the walls appeared to be made of plexi-glass. He could see four chairs lined up on the other side, facing the room. The other walls were painted black and had sheet metal nailed to them. Del furrowed his brow, noticing the dents, nicks, and scratches that peppered the once shiny surfaces.

But the strangest thing of all was the long table set up against the back wall; there were four large stacks of plates in varying sizes and colors, several wine glasses, a few serving bowls, and one large crystal vase right in the center.

Del turned to look at Lauren, but she was looking at the man, nodding at something he was saying.

"And that's it," he said. "Here you go." He handed her something that looked like folded cloth.

"Thank you," she said, and the man turned and walked out of the room, closing the door behind him.

She turned then, looking at him; the steadfast confidence from earlier was diluted with a hint of uncertainty now.

Before he could say anything, she walked over to him. "Here," she said softly. "You have to put this on."

Michael looked down at the gray fabric in her hand.

It was a pair of coveralls, similar to what a mechanic might wear.

"And these," she added, holding out a pair of safety goggles.

Del studied them for a second before he looked up at her, finally understanding.

"Am I...? You want me to break all this shit?"

Lauren nodded.

When Del just stared at her, she gestured toward the table. "I got you the dinner party package," she said. "Sounded like a good one, but what do I know."

Del turned and surveyed the room once more. He must have still looked confused because she said, "It's supposed to help. You know...to get rid of stress. It's much healthier than...other things."

"Red, this is ridiculous."

She shrugged. "Maybe."

He looked down at the coveralls in his hand, and for a moment, the room was completely silent.

Finally, he took a deep breath. "So I just put this on and throw shit around?"

The corner of her mouth lifted in a smile. "Pretty much."

He looked down again and nodded. "Alright," he said, reaching for the goggles.

She smiled then, the last of her uncertainty disappearing as she handed them to him. "I'll be out there," she said, gesturing toward the plexi-glass window. She went up on her toes, kissing his cheek before she turned and exited the room.

When the door clicked softly behind her, Del exhaled, turning to survey the room again.

This was stupid.

There was no way throwing a few plates against the wall was going to make him feel any better. He wanted to be home, in his room, with a bottle of Jack and his stereo blasting loud enough to make thinking impossible.

But she had looked so hopeful. And she had gone through all the trouble to set this up.

With a sigh, he pulled the coveralls on over his clothes and slid his hands into the thick, protective gloves.

Lauren came into view then, gently lowering herself into one of the chairs on the other side of the glass wall. She looked calm—peaceful, even—as she watched him.

Del walked toward the table, positioning the goggles over his eyes before he reached over and took a small blue plate off the top of the pile.

He turned then, facing one of the metal walls. He looked over to where Lauren sat, shrugging his shoulders before he threw the plate against it.

It exploded with a sharp, crunching sound.

Del flexed his hand at his side. He would've been lying if he said he didn't get the tiniest rush from it. Just the slightest flicker of adrenalin. Nothing like a shot of Jack, but decent enough.

He turned back toward the table, choosing one of the bigger plates. This time, he held it by its side, flinging it like a frisbee toward the wall.

It splintered into tiny white shards that scattered to the ground, and Del laughed, looking over at Lauren.

She was watching him, her expression even.

With a smile on his face, Del turned and grabbed one of the wine glasses. He brought his arm back, throwing it with a bit more force.

And then it happened.

As soon as it hit, as soon as the sound of glass shattering filled the tiny room, Del squeezed his eyes closed, bringing his clenched fists in front of them.

Glass shattering.

A grating shriek of metal.

His brother's shout.

This night. Eleven years ago, but it could have been yesterday. He could still see it so clearly.

And now he could hear it, too.

Del made a small noise in the back of his throat as he tried to slow his breathing, but he could already feel his hands shaking. This was why he needed to be home. This was why he needed to drink tonight. Because the alcohol blurred the memories, made them comfortably fuzzy, so that they didn't seem real anymore.

But he was seeing it now. And it was so real.

It was too real.

"Please. Please. Please," he chanted through gritted teeth. He was breathing heavily now; a slight tingling began in his spine, and his stomach churned unpleasantly.

Why did he have to call him that night? Why the hell did he have to be so pathetic? Why couldn't he have just learned to take care of himself?

And why couldn't his brother have told him no? Just once, why couldn't he have refused him?

"Goddamn it, Aaron!"

Del whirled suddenly, grabbing the first thing his hand landed on and launching it against the wall.

"I'd do anything for you. You know that, right?"

The bowl crashed against the metal as he brought his fists to his eyes again, shaking his head quickly.

"But what if you forget you love me, like Daddy did?"

"Never. I'll never forget."

Del spun wildly, not even seeing what he pulled from the table as he whirled around and heaved it, and before it even made contact with the wall, he was reaching for the next object.

"It's your fault your father is gone, and now you took your brother too."

"Fuck you!" he shouted, grabbing an entire stack of plates from the table and flinging them at the wall with the full force of his body. *"Fuck you!"*

He spun back to the table, grabbing two wine glasses and throwing them both, stifling a sob in the back of his throat.

"I'm sorry I made you come get me when you were sick."

Del groaned pathetically as he dropped onto the table, swiping his arm across it, sending half of what was there crashing to the floor.

Metal crunching.

A hideous squealing noise.

A flash of light.

He brought his fist down hard on the table, hearing the plates and glasses rattle as a few toppled over.

"No need for sorrys, Mike. You can always count on me."

He grabbed the large crystal vase from the center of the table and brought it above his head.

"You promised!" he screamed as he turned and launched it across the room, stumbling forward with the force as the vase shattered against the far wall.

And then he dropped to his knees.

His whole body shook with tremors, and his ears rang with the sudden silence. Del fell forward onto his hands, exhaling in guttural grunts.

The shards of broken glass on the floor spun in a dizzy arc before his eyes, and he squeezed them shut, trying desperately to catch his breath.

Del had no idea how long he sat there attempting to get control over his body, but eventually he felt her presence. His eyes were still closed, but he knew she was beside him.

"Tell me what you need," she said softly.

He was still trembling slightly, his breath unsteady. Slowly, he pushed off his hands and sat back on his heels. "A drink," he rasped, looking up at her for the first time.

There was no disappointment in her expression. There was no sympathy either, which would have been worse in his eyes.

There was only understanding.

"It's in the car," she said gently. "Let's get out of here."

Del nodded, taking another second to get his bearings before he stood, and Lauren stepped back, giving him his space.

They walked to the car in silence, and Del was grateful in that moment that she knew him so well. She didn't try to hold him, or talk to him, or console him in any way. She just let him be, which was exactly what he needed.

They got in the car, and Lauren reached behind her, pulling a brown paper bag out of the backseat and handing it to him.

Del reached inside and pulled out the bottle of whiskey, tossing the bag on the floor as he unscrewed the cap and took a shot of it. Lauren busied herself with putting on her seatbelt and starting the car, giving him whatever privacy she could in the confined space.

By the time they pulled out of the parking lot, Del had taken a second shot; he rested his head back against the seat and closed his eyes, feeling the warmth seep through his body as it started taking the tension out of his muscles.

His mind was deliciously empty now; behind his closed lids it was dark and serene, and he took a deep breath, exhaling slowly.

A few minutes passed before he felt her fingers on the back of his hand, tentative and gentle.

He cracked one eye and looked over at her.

"Home?" she asked softly.

He looked down to where her hand rested over the top of his, and he turned his slowly so that his palm was facing up before intertwining their fingers.

"Yeah," he said, resting his head back on the seat as he closed his eyes again. Del lifted the bottle, taking a third shot.

She continued to drive in silence, her thumb making tiny passes over the back of his hand, and suddenly Del felt like he was melting into the seat. He wasn't sure if it was the energy he'd just exerted, the trauma of reliving the accident, the third consecutive shot of whiskey, or the way she was touching him, but whatever was causing it, he just wanted to suspend time and feel this way for a while.

By the time they got back to his house, Del had taken his fourth and fifth shots, and his body was starting to succumb to the numbness he'd been craving all night.

Lauren pulled into his driveway, putting the car in park and letting the engine idle.

He remained where he was, his eyes still closed, and she sat there in silence, her hand in his, once again giving him exactly what he needed.

Finally he spoke, his husky voice rasping through the silence. "Stay with me for a while?"

When there was no answer, he opened his eyes and turned to look at her.

Her eyes were on him, gentle despite being unreadable.

"Of course."

Lauren released his hand to turn off the car, and Del unbuckled his seatbelt and got out, walking around the side of the darkened house.

When he reached the tiny backyard, the motion light came on, casting a soft glow across the grass. He inhaled deeply before he lowered himself to the ground, resting his elbows on his knees.

A moment later Lauren came into the yard, and Del brought the bottle to his mouth again as she delicately folded her legs underneath her, sitting beside him.

The night air was heavy with the dewy scent of spring and the distant sound of crickets chirping.

"How did you know about that place?" he finally asked.

"Mr. Brennan was talking about stress reducers in psych class a couple of weeks ago. He said there were places like that. I just looked it up."

Del nodded as he looked down at the bottle in his hand, a smile lifting the corner of his mouth. "Well, thanks. I think," he added with a tiny laugh.

Lauren shifted on the grass, crossing her legs in front of her. "Do you want to talk about Aaron?"

His smile fell. "No."

Out of the corner of his eye, he could see her look down. A beat of silence passed before she asked, "Will you anyway?"

He turned toward her, irritated. "What, is this part of your psych class too? I'm not an experiment, you know."

She lifted her eyes then, looking at him.

And even in the dim light, he could see the hurt there, and he had to look away.

"I just…I know he was important to you," she said, turning away from him and picking at the hem of her jeans. "I just wanted to know about him."

Something pricked in Del's chest at her tone of voice.

At the words she had spoken.

He hadn't talked about Aaron in so long. And he realized then that one of the main reasons for that was because no one ever asked him to.

He inhaled slowly. "Aaron was my brother, my mother, my father, and my best friend. He took care of me. Maybe more than he should have. I wish I hadn't needed him so much. And I miss him every day."

He closed his eyes and swallowed. Maybe it was because he'd already dulled his raw emotions, but that hadn't hurt as much as he'd expected it to.

"I bet he needed you too," she whispered. "Probably more than you realized." Lauren reached over, taking the bottle out of his hand.

Del thought she was cutting him off and he was about to protest, but then she surprised him by bringing the bottle to her lips.

She grimaced as the liquor hit her tongue, and Del watched in shock as she took two long pulls from the bottle. She was about to take a third when he reached over and yanked it away from her.

It splashed down her chin, and she brought the back of her hand to her mouth as she whipped toward him. "Hey!"

He looked at her wide-eyed. "What the hell do you think you're doing?"

"What, you're the only one who's allowed to take the edge off?" she asked, her voice thick with the burn of the alcohol.

"Just let that settle for a minute. Jesus."

She swallowed and coughed, turning away from him, and Del could only imagine how much her throat must be burning.

A few minutes passed before she spoke again. "Thank you. For telling me all that," she finally said.

He nudged her with his shoulder, and she turned back toward him. "Thank you for asking."

She smiled softly. In the dim glow of the motion light, he could see that her eyes were glazed.

It already hit her. Of course it would have.

She looked down at the bottle and then back up at him, quirking her brow.

He had no idea what this was about, but who was he to deny her?

"Slow," he said, handing her the bottle, and she nodded, bringing it to her mouth and taking a much smaller sip. She flinched again, shaking her head slightly as it went down.

"You know," she said, her voice somewhat husky before she cleared her throat. "I was kind of jealous of you in there tonight."

He smirked, looking over at her as she handed him back the bottle.

"You got a lot of built-up aggression, Red?"

She smiled, looking down as she shook her head. "No, not aggression. Frustration, maybe."

He glanced at her. She was studying her thumbnail, and there was something about her expression that didn't sit right with him.

"Come on," he said, trying to lighten the mood. "Like you could have done any real damage anyway."

She rolled her eyes. "Shut up."

"I mean seriously, look at these things," he said, reaching over to grab her bicep. He jiggled her arm, and it flapped lifelessly under his hold. "What were you gonna do?"

She whirled suddenly, attempting to grab his arm, and he pulled it out of her reach with a laugh, jumping back slightly.

She immediately followed him, lunging forward and gripping his wrist, trying to twist his arm behind his back. He laughed at her determination, but her attempt was pathetic. He let her maneuver his body for a minute, giving her the false impression of success, and then he shifted his weight, circling his wrist quickly so that he was the one gripping her arm.

Del brought his body forward suddenly, bringing her arm behind her back, and the shock combined with her fuzzy reflexes forced her backward onto the grass.

He landed on top of her, one of his hands trapped between her body and the ground and the other on the grass beside her, holding up some of his weight.

For a second, they both froze.

And then Lauren shifted her leg slightly, urging his body into the cradle of her thighs.

Instantly he pushed off of her, wrenching his hand out from underneath her as he sat up. Del looked down, brushing the grass from his pants before he reached for the bottle that was now lying in the grass between them.

As he righted the bottle, he could see her sit up slowly. Her eyes were forward, but there was a firm set to her jaw.

She said nothing.

Del focused his attention on wiping off the mouth of the bottle with his shirt, and then he looked straight ahead, taking another shot.

"You pick girls for sex."

He closed his eyes, resting his elbows back on his knees as he swirled the bottle.

"You pick girls for sex, but they're not good for you. They're not nice girls."

"Thanks for the news flash. I had been so confused as to what keeps going wrong."

"I have a point, you know," she said, matching his tone.

"Well then why don't you stop stating the obvious and get to it?"

He heard her take a small breath, and when she spoke, her voice had softened significantly. "Did you ever think about a friends with benefits situation?"

Del froze with the bottle at his lips. He sat that way for a second before he resumed his movements, taking a long, slow sip.

Had he ever thought about it?

Jesus. Ever since they'd kissed a few months ago, all he'd been doing was fantasizing about her.

Sure, he'd fantasized about her before that a few times; after all, he was a guy, and she was a beautiful girl, and he was only human. But he never had any intentions of acting on it.

Then they'd made out on his bedroom floor.

And once he'd kissed her, *really* kissed her, felt the weight of her body moving against him, it was all he could do not to push her into the janitor's closet every time he passed her in the halls.

And nights like this, nights they spent alone together, were always the hardest.

But he knew better than to sully her. So he continued to throw his efforts into other girls. Meaningless girls. Girls that were all wrong, of course, like she had said.

On the surface, their friendship had gone back to normal after his little slip-up. But underneath it all, he knew he wanted her. He had crossed a line, and now the craving he had for her was a living thing, gnawing at him all the time.

But the absolute worst part was that he knew it was more than just a physical desire. He didn't just want her body. But he had been burying his emotions for most of his life, and emotional feelings were so much easier for him to ignore than physical ones.

That night in his room, he could see in her eyes that she wanted him too. And now the alcohol was making her brave enough to ask for it.

Del was aware that she was looking at him, that she was waiting for an answer, so he did the only thing he could think of to do.

He laughed it off.

"Enough of the sauce, Red."

"I'm not drunk," she snapped.

"Well, you're not sober."

She looked at him for a second before she rolled her eyes. "I was just asking, Michael," she said, taking the bottle from his hands and turning forward again.

She took another slow sip, and for a second, Del thought she was going to drop it, but then she turned back toward him.

"You said it gets messy, but why does it have to?"

He closed his eyes and shook his head.

"If you're friends with someone," she continued, "if you care about them and trust them, it shouldn't get messy."

"If you're friends with someone, that's *the reason* it gets messy," he said tiredly, passing a hand over his eyes.

"Are you kidding me?" she asked. "You don't think it would be so much more enjoyable if you cared about the person? Trusted the person?"

She turned further toward him, hopping up on her knees, growing more earnest as she argued her point. "Look, you told me once that I should use better judgment when it comes to guys, right? And *clearly* you need help in that area. We both care about each other, so why can't we just be something a little more to each other instead of going to the wrong people for that kind of thing?"

She was making sense. Perfect sense. But his mind was already made up.

"*Relationships* get messy," she continued. "But this?" she said, gesturing between them. "This could be great."

She was quiet then, and Del knew he needed to respond. He was racking his brain, trying to think of a valid argument, but he couldn't come up with anything. And not just because she had presented such a strong argument, but because deep down, he wanted exactly what she did.

He ran his hand down his face and made a desperate attempt at a defense. "You're a virgin."

"*So?*" she nearly yelled, her voice indignant as she whipped her head toward him. "What the *hell* does that have to do with anything?"

"I'm not making fun of you," he said quickly, trying to mollify her. "I think it's great that you are."

Her shoulders softened slightly, but her expression was still defensive.

"But...I'm not taking your virginity. That should be something special."

"What's more special than my best fr—"

"It's out of the question, Lauren," he said firmly, cutting her off.

Del saw her shoulders drop as she turned forward, the set returning to her jaw.

He'd used her real name, and she knew that meant he was serious.

Lauren closed her eyes, and he turned away from her, looking down at the grass as he picked at it with his fingers. There was a reason he went for the girls he did: because the good girls were too good for him.

And she was the best of them all.

He had to remember that he had a knack for ruining people's lives. She'd regret him being the one, he reminded himself. It should be another guy.

Although the thought of another guy getting to touch her that way, getting to be that for her, was enough to make him want to put his fist through a wall.

"You know," she said softly, pulling his attention back to the present, "for someone who's supposed to be a tough guy, you're a real chicken shit."

He whipped his head toward her, his eyes wide with surprise before he laughed.

"We'll talk about this when you're sober," he said through a smile, shaking his head as he reached over to take the bottle from her.

And even though Lauren never brought it up again, he thought about it all the time.

January 2012

*I*t felt oddly comfortable to be back on the mats again.

Lauren looked around the gymnasium as she sat on the floor, stretching her legs. She hadn't been inside a gymnastics studio in years, and yet she felt immediately at home. The smell of the mats, the sound of the vault springs clanging roughly, the repetitive patter and thuds of hands and feet hitting the mats as someone made a run.

She couldn't believe she'd lived here all this time and didn't know about this place. Then again, she'd never looked for one. When she'd first moved to Bellefonte and started teaching, there was hardly free time for anything, much less an old hobby.

Lauren stood and began stretching her quads, glancing at the door before she looked to the clock on the far wall. Five minutes to six. They should be here any minute now.

She smiled, realizing then just how excited she was about the evening.

Michael had called her earlier in the week, starting the conversation with, "I have a favor to ask you," and immediately following it up with, "You can totally say no."

He explained to her that Erin's birthday was that weekend, and when he'd asked her what she wanted to do, she'd said, "I want Miss Lauren to teach me flips." Lauren had told the class a few stories from her time as a gymnast, and apparently Erin was enthralled.

Michael assured Lauren that he'd made Erin no promises, so if she said no, it would be no big deal—she wouldn't be letting anyone down. He would just find something else for them to do, and she'd be okay with it.

And in the middle of his rant, pardoning her for something she hadn't yet declined, she laughed.

"Of course I will, Michael," she'd interrupted, putting him out of his misery. "I'd love to, actually."

And she meant it. She had grown so fond of Erin over the past few months; plus, teaching her gymnastics would be combining two of Lauren's favorite things to do.

Apparently, in the hopes of her saying yes, Michael had already done his homework. As soon as she agreed, he told her about this place, a mere fifteen minutes from where Lauren lived, and said they held "open gym" on Sunday nights from six to eight: for a small fee, gymnasts could come and use the facility to practice routines or fine-tune their skills.

So they'd agreed to meet at six, and when Michael cupped the phone and told Erin that Miss Lauren was going to teach her, she could hear the enthusiastic squeal through Michael's hand.

A few minutes later, as Lauren was using the wall to get a good stretch on her ankles, she heard the door open, and that same excited peal echoed through the gym.

"Is she here yet, Daddy?"

"I'm not sure. Let me just talk to this man for a minute and then we'll go look for her, okay?"

Lauren turned to see Michael approach the man at the front desk while Erin hopped from foot to foot, taking a few seconds to balance on each one. She glanced up, catching sight of Lauren, and grinned as she broke into a dead run.

Michael turned abruptly, reaching out for her, but he immediately relaxed when he saw where she was running. Lauren dropped to her knees and caught Erin in a hug, smiling over her tiny shoulder at Michael. He held up his finger and mouthed "*one minute*" to her, and she nodded, releasing Erin and leaning back to see her face.

"Happy birthday!"

Erin smiled broadly and danced in a circle, waving her hands over her head.

"Can we flip now?" she sang.

"Almost," Lauren said. "First, let's take off your jacket and shoes."

Erin stopped her dance long enough to let Lauren help her remove her coat and sneakers as Michael approached them.

"Hey," he said, reaching down to take Erin's things out of Lauren's hands. "Thanks again for doing this."

"It's no problem," she said, looking down at Erin. "We're gonna have fun, right?"

"Right!"

Michael smiled at his daughter's enthusiasm. "I'm just gonna go put her stuff in one of the lockers."

"Yep. We'll be over on the mats," said Lauren, reaching out for Erin's hand.

While Michael put away her things, Lauren stretched Erin out a bit. She knew they wouldn't be doing anything too intense tonight, but still, she wanted to show her the proper way to approach the sport.

Erin was an obedient student, just as she was at Learn and Grow, listening in earnest, picking up the stretching techniques Lauren showed her immediately.

By the time Michael made it back to them, they were about to start, and he took a seat up against the wall a few feet away.

"Okay, so we're going to start with a cartwheel. I'm going to show you what it looks like, and then I'll teach you how to do it, okay?"

Erin nodded, taking a step back, and Lauren took a few steps away from her before she lifted her arms gracefully. In one quick, fluid movement, she executed a perfect cartwheel, legs extended, toes pointed, coming up on the other side and finishing with her hands raised above her head, the same way she started.

"Ooooh," Erin cooed, wide-eyed. "You're good at that."

"It looks fancy, but it's easy. You ready to try?"

Erin nodded, and Lauren knelt down in front of her. "Okay, so what I want you to do is lunge forward a little bit. Bend this knee and put your weight on it, and leave this leg straight behind you."

Lauren placed her hands on Erin's waist, adjusting her weight distribution, and she smiled, casting a sly glance at Michael. "You know," she said just loud enough for him to hear, "I tried to teach your daddy how to do this once."

Michael looked over at her and smirked, shaking his head slowly.

"You did?" Erin asked, looking over at her father.

"Mm-hm." Lauren cupped her hand in front of her mouth, feigning a whisper. "But he wasn't very good."

Michael looked down, and she could see his shoulders bounce with laughter.

Erin raised her eyebrows in surprise before she turned to Michael sympathetically. "Don't worry, Daddy. I'll teach you after I learn how."

"Thank you, baby girl," he called before he stuck his tongue out at Lauren, and she chuckled at his juvenile behavior before turning her attention back to Erin.

"Okay, now I want you to put your arms over your head, the way I did before. Good. Now you're going to lean over and put your hands side by side on this line, right here, and when they touch the floor, I want your straight leg to come up behind you. Let's just practice that a few times so you get the feel of it. I'm gonna hold on to you, okay?"

"'Kay." Erin nodded, determination taking over her little features.

They practiced the motion a few times until Erin was able to do it smoothly. At one point Lauren glanced at Michael, and when he winked at her, she felt heat instantly blooming on her cheeks. She heard him laugh shortly after that, but she had no way of knowing if it was in response to her silly, girlish reaction to such an innocent gesture.

"Can I try going over?" Erin asked, pulling Lauren's attention back.

She cleared her throat. "Um, sure. If you're ready. I'll keep my hands on your waist to help you balance. Once your straight leg goes up like we practiced, you're going to push off with your bent leg to send yourself over. Try to keep your toes pointed and your legs straight."

Erin got in position, and Lauren knelt parallel to her, keeping her hands on Erin's waist to give her a little extra support. The first few were shaky, her legs falling forward or back or bending awkwardly. But the more they did it, the sturdier she became, until finally Lauren was barely touching her waist at all.

"You want to try one on your own?" Lauren asked, and Erin looked up, somewhat hesitant. "It's okay, sweetheart. I'm right here. I won't let you fall. Promise."

With a tiny breath to steel her resolve, Erin nodded and turned, raising her arms above her head. Lauren stood by, ready to grab her at the slightest signal, but she didn't need to. Erin went over smoothly, landing on the other side with her arms extended like a pro. She whipped her head toward Lauren, grinning from ear to ear before she turned and ran toward her father.

"I did it! Daddy, I did it! Did you see me? Did you see me?"

"I saw!" he said, scooping her up. "You were awesome!"

Lauren watched them with a smile until suddenly, without warning, she was struck with a thought that caused a sharp pang in her chest.

Michael had been just one year older than Erin was right now when his father left. When his mother pretty much checked out on him.

So young.

She looked at Erin, her adoration for her father beaming from her eyes as she looked up at him. She was so vulnerable. So needy. And then she thought of Michael at that age, just as vulnerable, twice as needy, and completely forsaken.

And suddenly, she felt like crying.

Lauren wanted to cross the mats and hug him. Just wrap her arms around him and rock him side to side, even though it was years too late to give that little boy the comfort he deserved.

"Show me a fancy flip!" Erin called as she ran back toward Lauren, and with a quick intake of breath, she shook off the ache in her heart.

"A fancy flip?" she asked uneasily. "I haven't done those in a long time."

"You can still do it I bet," Michael said as he followed Erin onto the mat. "Muscle memory."

Lauren scrunched her nose at him, and he laughed. "Try something easy. I bet you anything you can still do it."

She looked down at Erin, who was staring up at her expectantly, and she took a deep breath. "Okay. Something easy."

Erin clapped her hands before taking a step back, pulling her father with her to give Lauren some room.

Lauren rolled her neck and took another deep breath before she brought her weight forward on her toes. With a little hop, she was off running, bringing her hands to the mat as her legs flipped up behind her, coming together in a perfect line above her head before she whipped them around together toward the mat. As she landed, she rebounded several inches off the floor before extending her hands.

She definitely had enough power to go over again.

"Wow!" Erin breathed. "What's that called?"

"That's called a round-off," she said as she walked back toward them. "I think I'm gonna try one that's a little fancier."

Erin leaned into her father, her eyes pinned on Lauren in awe as she set herself up once more. She tightened her body, put her weight on her toes, and then she was off running again. This time, as her legs whipped around on the round-off, she threw her arms back over her head, executing a perfect back-handspring.

And because it felt so good, she immediately followed it with another before she hit her landing, arching her back slightly as she extended her arms overhead.

Erin's gasp echoed off the walls of the gym. Her face was priceless, some combination of shock and complete worship as she watched Lauren walk back to them.

Michael was grinning at her. "See? What did I tell you? Muscle memory. That never fails to amaze me, by the way. Watching you do that."

"What's muscle memory?" Erin asked before Lauren could react to his comment.

He pursed his lips, thinking of a way to explain it. "Well, sometimes if something is *really* important to you, it gets stuck in your body," he said, poking her ribs and making her laugh. "So even if your mind thinks that it's gone, it's still in there, kind of hiding inside of you, just waiting for you to remember. It never goes away."

Lauren stared at him.

She knew he was talking about her flip, but his words hit much deeper than that.

He was smiling down at Erin, but when he looked up and saw her expression, his smile fell, his face turning serious.

For a second, they just stared at each other, and Lauren found that she was struggling to keep her breathing even.

"What else can we do?" Erin asked excitedly, gripping Lauren's hand, and she pulled her gaze from his, looking down at Erin.

"Um," she said, blinking quickly.

She could still feel his eyes on her.

Lauren swallowed hard and lifted her eyes, scanning the gym for a second, and then she saw it.

The corner of her mouth lifted in a smile. "I have an idea. Come with me," she said, pulling Erin toward the back corner of the gym.

They walked across the mats and up the padded incline that dropped off suddenly into an enormous pit of colorful foam blocks. Lauren remembered this being one of her favorite exercises when she just started out.

Michael walked up the incline behind them, and she glanced over at him. He smiled at her, but his eyes were uneasy. Cautious, even.

And there he was; she could see him clearly in the expression on Michael's face. The abandoned little boy.

This time she couldn't help it.

She walked the few steps over to him, wrapping both arms around his waist as she rested her head on his shoulder.

Instantly she felt the tension drain from his body as he exhaled, wrapping his arms around her shoulders.

"Are those blocks?" Erin asked. "Is this a pool? Why are there blocks in the pool? Are we gonna swim in here? *Daddy!* Let Miss Lauren go so she can swim with me!"

Michael laughed softly, planting a kiss on the top of Lauren's head before he released her. "I was given strict orders not to steal you away from her tonight," he said. "I'm breaking the rules right now."

Lauren laughed. "I think we have to let the birthday girl call the shots tonight," she said before she unwrapped her arms from around his waist.

She looked up at him and he smiled, tucking a lock of hair that had fallen free from her ponytail behind her ear at the same time that two tiny hands clasped hers.

"Let's swim, Miss Lauren!" Erin said, tugging her away from Michael.

He took a step back, holding his hands up in surrender, and Lauren couldn't help but laugh before she turned toward Erin. "It's not a pool, sweetheart. It's something called a foam pit. You want to do something cool?"

Erin smiled broadly as she nodded, and Lauren walked her to the edge of the incline. "Okay, turn around and face Daddy. Put your back to the pit."

As Erin did what she was told, Lauren knelt beside her, putting one hand on her lower back and the other behind her knees. "Okay, on the count of three, I want you to jump as high as you can. Ready?"

"Ready!"

"Here we go. One…two…*three*!"

As Erin jumped, Lauren supported her lower back as her other hand flipped Erin's legs up over her head, sending her off the platform in a backflip. She sailed into the foam pit, bouncing into the multicolored cushions.

Erin squealed with hysterical laughter. "Again!" she called from the pit. "Do it to me again, Miss Lauren!"

Lauren laughed. "Okay, get over to that ladder and climb out. Come back around."

Michael approached the edge of the incline, looking into the pit beside Lauren. They watched Erin struggle through the large foam blocks, stumbling and giggling.

"So what do you think? You want to try taking lessons again?" Lauren asked as she bumped him with her shoulder.

"Nah. You can't improve upon perfection," he said, brushing his fingers over the top of his shoulder.

Lauren pursed her lips to hide her smile. "Come on. Give it a shot. At least this time you'll land in the foam instead of on your ass."

Before she could even process what had happened, Michael whirled and scooped her up bridal style, causing her to gasp.

He spun once and tossed her over the side and into the foam pit, and she flailed sloppily, her squealing laughter rivaling Erin's as she bounced into the foam.

She looked up to see Michael standing at the edge of the incline, looking down at her. "Well, that wasn't very graceful. And you call yourself a gymnast?"

She picked up one of the foam blocks and threw it at him, but he sidestepped it easily. Then he took a step back and did one of the worst cartwheels Lauren had ever seen off the edge of the incline, his legs splayed apart and bent like broken hangers.

When he plopped into the cushions next to her, she was laughing so hard she couldn't breathe.

"See?" he said, somewhat winded. "Perfection."

"Hey!" a little voice called.

They both whipped their heads up to see Erin standing at the edge of the incline above them, hands on her hips, her expression stern.

"Sorry! We're coming!" Lauren called up before she turned to Michael. "Stop distracting me. You're getting me in trouble," she scolded, and she could hear his laughter behind her as she made her way toward the ladder.

They spent the next hour playing in the foam pit and practicing cartwheels. When it was time to leave, Michael knelt in front of Erin, helping her on with her coat.

"So what do you think? Do you want to do this? You can take classes here."

"Yes, please. Can Miss Lauren be my teacher?"

"Well, you'll have a different teacher," Lauren said. "But I'll come here and practice with you some days if you want."

"Okay!" Erin exclaimed, stepping into her shoes.

As they exited the lobby, Michael grabbed a pamphlet with class information and folded it into his jacket.

Once outside, he turned toward Lauren, stuffing both hands in his pockets. "So…"

"Can we get hotdogs, Daddy?" Erin asked, pointing to a vendor on the corner. "I'm hungry."

Michael glanced at his watch before looking at Lauren. "We didn't eat dinner yet. I didn't think filling her up with food and then bringing her here to turn upside down was the best order of operations."

Lauren laughed. "Probably a good call."

"You want to grab a bite with us?"

"Sure."

Michael smiled as he reached down to take Erin's hand. "Okay, birthday hotdogs it is."

They walked down the street toward the vendor, and Lauren zipped her jacket all the way up to her chin, crossing her arms in front of herself against the cold.

By the time they ordered their hotdogs, Lauren's teeth were chattering. She could barely uncross her arms long enough to reach for the hotdog Michael handed her.

She looked down at Erin, standing next to her father, taking small, unhurried bites of her hotdog, and then back up to Michael, whose casual posture mirrored his daughter's. His jacket wasn't even zippered.

"My God, aren't you freezing?" Lauren said through her tight jaw, curling her hands around the warmth of the bun.

Michael smiled. "I work outside, remember? I'm kind of immune to it."

"Right," Lauren said, a shudder ripping through her shoulders as she took a bite of her hotdog.

She heard Michael laugh, and then suddenly he was behind her, wrapping his arms around the front of her body.

For the slightest second, Lauren felt herself hesitate. But his body was shielding her from the cold wind, his chest broad and comfortable behind her, and when he began rubbing his hands up and down her arms, she lost the battle.

She dropped her head back onto his shoulder, pressing herself farther back against his chest.

Damn muscle memory.

"Better?" he asked softly, and she nodded.

"Much."

He wrapped one arm tightly around her waist, holding her against him while he ate his hotdog with the other, and Lauren allowed herself to be enveloped by him as Erin skipped around them, singing to herself while she finished her dinner.

Eventually, Michael released her to throw his napkin in the trash can, and she immediately mourned the loss of his warmth behind her.

"Okay baby," he said, glancing down at his watch again. "We have to get home and get you in the tub. Say thank you to Lauren."

"Hold on," Lauren said. "I have her present in the car."

"I get a present?" Erin asked excitedly. "I thought my present was the flips!"

"Well, there's a little something else."

"Daddy, can I go get my present? Please?"

Michael was looking at Lauren. "You know you didn't have to do that."

"I know. I wanted to. Is it okay?" She realized too late that maybe she should have run it by Michael first.

He smiled as Erin grabbed his hand and started towing him toward Lauren. "Yes, it's okay. Where are you parked?"

"Right at the end of the street," she said, starting to walk in the direction she indicated, and she felt Erin take one of her hands. She looked down at Erin, walking in between her and Michael with one of their hands clasped in each of hers, and then she looked up at Michael.

He was smiling down at his daughter with the same level of adoration that Erin had looked at him with earlier, and Lauren swallowed hard against the lump in her throat.

When they reached her car, Lauren started it and blasted the heat before pulling Erin's present out of the backseat and shutting the door.

She walked around the front of the car to where Erin was standing on the sidewalk and handed her the pink bag with purple and silver ribbon curling from the handle.

"I believe you said you needed one of these. Every princess should have one," she added with a wink.

Erin reached in and pulled out the crown, a silver, sparkling tiara complete with purple and pink jewels.

She gasped and looked up at Lauren before she threw her little body forward, wrapping her arms around Lauren's neck with a strength Lauren didn't think a four-year-old was capable of.

Lauren smiled, hugging her back, and as soon as she released her, Erin put the crown on her head. "Daddy, can I wear this in the bath?"

Michael laughed. "We'll see." He turned to Lauren. "Thank you for that. For everything. Really."

"You're welcome," Lauren said as she stood. When he held his arms out to her, she didn't hesitate stepping into them this time. Her arms came up around his neck, and he slid his around her waist, holding her securely against his body.

Michael's hand came to her head, stroking down the back of her hair, and she closed her eyes and inhaled slowly. His familiar scent filled her nose, and without thinking, she turned her head slightly, nuzzling into the side of his neck.

She felt his breath catch before he tightened his hold on her, turning his face into her hair.

Butterflies exploded in her stomach, and the surface of her skin began tingling.

She could feel the heat of his breath shivering along the side of her neck with every exhale, and she slid her arms down from around his shoulders, knowing she needed to end the contact. But even as her mind sent the warning, she fisted her hands in the front of his jacket, refusing to let him go.

He turned his head a little further, and Lauren felt the fullness of his lips brush against the shell of her ear. Her heart felt like it was going to crash through her chest, and she tightened her fists in his jacket as she warred with herself over what she wanted to do and what she needed to do.

She turned her face away from his neck, taking a deep breath of cold, unscented air, and it was just enough to clear her head.

Lauren released his jacket and took a step back, breaking his hold on her. "Good night, Michael," she said.

And before he could even respond, she was walking around the back of her car. "Good night, Erin," she called.

"Good night, Miss Lauren. I love my crown," she said, holding it on her head with both hands while she spun in a circle, and Lauren smiled as she slid in the car and shut the door.

She drove off without looking back.

She could not allow herself to look back.

Her heart was still racing, and the faint tingling continued to dance over her skin.

Tonight had been about Erin. Tonight, she wanted to make Erin happy. All her focus had gone into that, and not so much into watching her interactions with Michael. Too many times tonight, the line had gotten blurred.

But the scariest thing was, she hadn't cared enough to pull back.

She needed to submerge herself in something that would occupy her mind, something that would prevent her from thinking too closely about what had just happened.

She had a case study coming up in one of her classes. It wasn't due for several weeks, but as she drove home, she began planning how to start it. Lauren knew from experience that the tedious research would be just what she needed to lose herself for a little while.

As soon as she walked through the door, she powered up her laptop and made herself a cup of tea. Then she sat on her bed with her laptop beside her and a textbook sprawled over her thighs, burying herself in her work.

About an hour into her research, the soft chime of a bell sounded from the computer, notifying her she had a new e-mail message.

She pulled her eyes from the textbook and leaned over, clicking on her mail icon, and her heart leapt into her throat when she saw it was from Michael.

Lauren knew opening the message would be unwise, not to mention counterproductive, but she clicked on it anyway.

Lauren,

Thank you again for tonight. And just so you know, Erin did wear the crown in the tub. In fact, as I type this, it's lying on the pillow next to her head as she's sleeping. Figured you'd get a kick out of that. I just wanted to tell you how much I appreciate everything you've done for her. And for me. You're still the same in the best ways, but you're different in the best ways too, if that makes sense. Anyway, I attached a song to this message. It makes me think of you. Actually, it makes me think of us.

Lauren stopped reading and glanced at the attachment. She could only see that it was by Coldplay before she quickly closed out of the message.

And then she fell back onto her bed and covered her face with both hands.

She couldn't finish reading that e-mail. And she definitely couldn't listen to whatever song he'd sent. She was on the verge of doing something stupid. Something she absolutely could not allow herself to do.

She could feel the inclination building. Like a caged animal clawing at her insides, fighting to get out.

Lauren took a deep breath and did the only thing she knew could prevent that from happening; she allowed her mind to go back to the place she'd been avoiding since she was eighteen.

August 2003

*L*auren didn't like his room like this. It made everything seem too final. Too real.

She sat on Michael's bed, looking around at the bare walls, at the clutter of boxes scattered around his floor, at his half-empty closet.

She'd had the entire summer to come to terms with the fact that he was leaving. After all, that's what people did when they graduated; they went off to college.

Except he wasn't going off to college. He was moving to New York. His friend Jay's cousin lived out there, about a half hour north of New York City, and he'd offered both of them a place to stay until they decided what they wanted to do with themselves after graduating.

Maybe that was what made it so difficult to accept. The uncertainty of it all. The fact that he didn't have a plan. Or maybe it was the fact that he was leaving without a reason. He wasn't going to school. He wasn't offered a job. He had nothing out there to call his own. So why did he have to go? Why couldn't he decide what he wanted to do with his life right here? Why couldn't he figure it all out in the house that was a mere seven minutes away from Lauren's, where she could still see him whenever she wanted?

Lauren chewed her lip as she picked at her nail polish. She knew that was an incredibly selfish way of looking at it, but she couldn't help it.

She glanced up at him. He was still looking down at the picture she'd just given him, the one she took of them at his graduation a few weeks earlier. There was something behind his eyes that made her feel sad, even though his lips were curved into a smile.

"Thanks Red," he said, holding up the picture before he turned and placed it between two folded articles of clothing in the box in front of him.

Lauren shrugged. "Something to remember me by."

Michael rolled his eyes. "Don't get dramatic," he said with a laugh, tossing a crumpled T-shirt at her.

She tried to smile as she dodged it, but it was forced. There was an ache in her chest that fluttered every time she looked at him.

Michael reached into his closet, pulling a handful of shirts off their hangers and dropping them on the dresser in front of him, and then he began folding them and putting them in the box by his feet.

"So…what are you gonna do out there?" Lauren asked.

He lifted one shoulder in a shrug. "Dunno. Maybe I'll work. Maybe I'll go to school. Maybe I'll make it as a gigolo."

Lauren laughed and threw the T-shirt back at him, and it landed over the back of his head. He reached up and pulled it off, casting a smile over his shoulder before he tossed it to the pile on his dresser.

"Will you come home?" she asked, and when he didn't answer right away, her smile fell. "You know, for holidays and stuff?"

She watched him put another shirt in the box before he shook his head.

"You won't come back at all?" she asked, a touch of panic seeping into her voice.

Michael turned toward her. "We'll still see each other, Red. You can come visit me whenever you want. But…I can't come back here." He turned back toward the box and pulled a shirt from the top of the dresser. "I need to erase this place. Get away from the fucking disaster I've created here."

Disaster? She would have laughed if he didn't sound so upset. He couldn't be serious, could he?

"Come on, Michael. No one cares about what happens in high school. So you got in a few fights. Getting suspended doesn't really count as major life errors."

"That's not what I meant."

His words were clipped, and Lauren looked up at him. His back was still to her, but he had tensed visibly.

She pulled her brow together. "Well then, what are you talking about?"

He stood like that for a minute, saying nothing. Then he dropped his head, shaking it slowly.

"What is it?" she asked softly. "Tell me."

He turned and looked at her, laughing humorlessly. "Well, I guess I got nothing to lose now, right?"

A strange feeling settled in the pit of her stomach at his words. "I don't understand what you're talking about."

Michael leaned back against his dresser, his eyes on her. "You know my dad left when I was five. But do you want to know why?"

Lauren blinked at him. She had never broached this subject with him, and she had no idea why he would be bringing it up now.

"If you want to tell me."

"Because he found out I was someone else's kid. Turns out my mom cheated on him, and I was the souvenir."

A heavy lump settled in Lauren's stomach as she tried to keep her face composed. She had no idea what to say to that.

"He wanted nothing to do with my mother, and nothing to do with me," Michael continued. "He packed his shit that night, and the next morning he was gone."

"Michael," she said softly, the word sounding somewhat strangled despite her best effort.

He shrugged nonchalantly. "He came back for my brother a few times. But seeing me and my mom made him so miserable that eventually he moved to California. So because of the bastard child he couldn't stand looking at, Aaron ended up losing his real dad."

Her shoulders dropped as she shook her head, opening her mouth to protest, but he cut her off.

"Oh, but that's not all. Because you also know that Aaron died three years later." He paused, almost like he was assessing her. "Do you know how?"

Yet another thing they'd never talked about. Why was he doing this now? His tone of voice was casual as he spoke to her, overly so, but his eyes were intense, almost wild.

It made her uneasy.

She wrapped her arms around herself, and when she spoke, it was barely above a whisper. "I heard it was a car accident."

He nodded. "Yep. He got behind the wheel of a car completely shitfaced and flipped it. Wrapped it around a tree." He turned back to his shirts before he looked over his shoulder with a wry smile. "So now you know why I almost beat that kid's ass the first day of Health."

She looked up at him.

"For talking shit about the stupidity of drunk drivers," he clarified. He laughed, but it was empty. "I still can't believe you never asked me to explain that. It was one of my favorite things about you in the beginning."

Lauren dropped her eyes and swallowed hard, trying to process what he'd just told her.

"Do you want to know why he did it?" he asked, tossing a folded shirt haphazardly into the box.

"Who?"

"My brother. You want to know why he was driving drunk?"

Lauren lifted her eyes, looking at him cautiously.

He turned back to face her. "Because I made him. My mom dumped me off at some stranger's house to get rid of me for the night, and I called him bitching and moaning because I was scared. And so he got in that car, even though he shouldn't have, because I begged him to come get me. And he did." Michael shrugged again. "And we never made it home."

Lauren was blinking quickly against the growing sting behind her eyes, and she wrapped her arms a little tighter around herself as she looked away from him. She had always known the pieces of the story, that his dad and brother were gone, but filling in the blanks, learning the specifics, felt like getting punched in the stomach.

"So that's the story of Michael Delaney," he said, resuming his folding. "The delinquent kid who tore his family apart and needs to get the hell out of here."

She couldn't speak. She could barely even process what he'd just told her. The circumstances of the losses he suffered were so awful, and he had to deal with the aftermath completely alone. *My God, what would it feel like to have no family? Especially when you needed one the most?*

"Do you know who your real dad is?" she asked softly.

"No. My mom wouldn't talk about it, so I just stopped asking."

She bit her lip. "You could find him, you know."

"I don't want to find him."

After a second, Michael looked over his shoulder. She must have looked surprised, because he tilted his head at her.

"Come on, Red. Can't you just see it? An eighteen-year-old idiot showing up on some guy's doorstep." He smiled a huge fake smile as he spoke with overdone enthusiasm. "*Hey, remember that married woman you screwed all those years ago? Well, here I am! How's it goin', Pop?*"

His face turned serious as the insincere excitement drained away. "I just don't have a dad. I've accepted that." He turned back around and grabbed another shirt. "I don't want to have to prove myself to anyone."

Too much. It was just too much. Lauren felt like she was pinned to his bed as she watched him.

"Why didn't you ever tell me this?"

"I don't talk about this with anyone."

"But it's *me*."

He looked over his shoulder. "Exactly. You didn't see me as the asshole everyone else did. And after hearing all this, how can you not?"

"Because it's not your fault."

Michael rolled his eyes and turned back to his shirts. "Here we go," he said under his breath as he resumed packing.

"It isn't."

"You know, maybe I didn't tell you because I didn't want to hear this exoneration bullshit."

"It's not bullshit," she said, her voice gaining strength. "Your mother was the one who was unfaithful. Your mother made the choice. You were innocent."

He slammed a folded shirt into the box, causing Lauren to jump. "My brother?" he nearly growled, his back still to her.

"Michael, you were *eight years old*. You were scared. Your brother was always your protector. How could you have known? And it was your brother's decision to—"

"Look," he said, whirling on her. "I've lived with this all my life. I've come to terms with my role, so stop trying to blow smoke up my ass!"

He whipped back around, resuming his folding in rough, choppy movements, and suddenly whatever was pinning her to the bed reversed its hold, catapulting her away from it.

She was off the bed before she'd even made the decision to move, ripping the shirt out of his hands and slamming it down on the dresser.

He looked down at her, stunned.

"I'm not blowing smoke up your ass! Don't you *dare* say that to me! When have I ever lied to you? I give it to you straight all the time, even when you don't want to hear it!"

He stared at her for a second before he dropped his eyes. "You're right. I'm sorry."

She placed her hand on his chest, and he lifted his eyes again. "You're blaming yourself for other people's decisions," she said firmly. "It's *not* your fault, and I'm saying it because it's the truth."

He looked at her before he shook his head gently. She could see it in his eyes, that he genuinely didn't believe what she was saying. And suddenly, it struck her why.

In that moment, she was overcome with such a rush of anger that it startled her.

"You've been conditioned this way because of *her*," she said through a clenched jaw as she gestured angrily downstairs. "Because she made you feel guilty for it all. And it's *disgusting*." She was trying so hard to remain calm, but her voice was shaking with the effort.

"When your dad left, you lost a father because of *her* bad choices. She should have owned that! And you wouldn't have had to call Aaron that night if she didn't dump you off instead of being a mother!"

She was yelling now, but she couldn't help it. She hated that woman. She physically hated her, with the full force of her entire body and soul. "When Aaron died, you lost someone too! She should have made right what she wronged! She was the adult! You were just a kid, for Christ's sake!"

Michael was staring off over her head; his throat bobbed as he swallowed, and Lauren felt her anger waver.

She hated her.

But she loved him.

And he didn't need to be yelled at over this. He'd suffered enough because of what his mother had done.

She reached for his hand, clasping it gently. "And the fact that she shut you out?" she said, her voice much softer but still shaking. "That was yet another awful decision that *she* made. She was wrong. Not you. You were the victim of all this, not the cause. Can't you see that?"

He was still staring off over her head, but Lauren saw a muscle flex in the side of his jaw.

He shook his head in response.

That's when she noticed it. The glassy shine of tears in his eyes, threatening to fall.

She threw herself forward, wrapping her arms around his waist as she dropped her forehead against his chest. Instantly, his arms came around her as he pressed his face into the crown of her head. She could feel his breath in her hair, somewhat unsteady as he fought to regain control over his emotions, and she tightened her hold on him.

She wanted to consume him, just hug him so tightly that he disappeared somewhere within her body, where she could protect him.

Where she could keep him forever.

She squeezed him tighter, planting a kiss on his chest, and suddenly the trembling breath in her hair became something else. She felt it hitch again, but it was different this time.

Lauren could feel his heartbeat against her cheek, the way it started thumping irregularly, and she knew it was a different feeling he was struggling to contain now.

This was it. Her last chance. He had told her once, "*If you really want something, you shouldn't stop until you get it, no matter what you have to do.*"

And there was nothing in her life she'd ever wanted more than him.

She raised her head so that her chin was resting on his chest, and he tilted his, looking down at her, his eyes still shining with unshed tears.

Then she went up on her toes and kissed him.

The last time they had kissed all those months ago, it had been frantic. Urgent.

This was soft. Tender. Almost reverent.

All at once, his hands were on her face, her fingertips were trailing over his back, and his taste was on her lips, just as she remembered it.

"Lauren," he said between kisses, the word both a plea and a warning.

"Just kiss me, Michael," she breathed. "Just kiss."

And he brought his mouth back to hers.

Lauren removed her hands from under his shirt and slid them up around his neck, pulling him further down into the kiss. She felt his arms tighten around her waist, and suddenly she was off the floor.

With their faces at the same level, the kiss intensified, and for a second, they were as needy as they'd been that night on his floor before his friends interrupted them.

But then he pulled back, lowering her back to the floor as he slowly released his hold around her waist.

Lauren shook her head slightly, using her hands on his neck to keep his mouth on hers once she reached the floor again. He obliged, but his kiss was gentle. Too gentle.

It felt like he was ending it.

She wasn't going to give in that easily. Not this time.

Lauren took a step back, bringing him with her, and when the backs of her knees hit his bed, she lay back onto it. He went with her, catching himself on his hands and immediately positioning himself on his side, leaving several inches in between their bodies. He was still kissing her, but what had started out as worshipful and progressed to frenzied now seemed almost cautious.

Lauren slid her hand over his waist and gripped his shirt, pulling him on top of her.

He made a small noise, but Lauren couldn't tell if it was in pleasure or protest.

When she leaned up to kiss him, he pulled back slightly, his eyes darting back and forth between hers.

"I want to," she whispered.

He swallowed, shaking his head imperceptibly. "I told you, I can't."

"I'm not a virgin," she blurted out.

Michael's expression changed as he pushed himself up, supporting his weight in his arms as he stared down at her with equal parts confusion and disapproval.

"I was with Dale Arcamone."

Michael pulled his brow together and shook his head. "What? When?" He started to get off of her, but she grabbed the sides of his shirt, stopping him.

"It was after the junior barbecue. We hung out together all day, and then we went back to his house, and one thing kind of led to another."

She saw his eyes darken. "Did you do this because of what I said?"

Lauren looked up at him and shook her head, pressing her hips up into his body, and she watched his eyes flutter closed as his jaw flexed.

She knew in her heart this would be her last chance. It was now or never.

"It doesn't matter why I did it. I'm not a virgin anymore, and you're leaving tomorrow." She took a small breath. "I've never asked you for anything but this."

He still hadn't moved, and when she gently stroked the back of his neck and pulled him down into a kiss, he kissed her back, but it was with obvious restraint. She could feel the set of his jaw, that he was still upset over this turn of events.

She didn't want him to be upset. She wanted him to be as lost as she was.

Lauren slid her hands back under his shirt, digging her fingertips into his back as she kissed him more passionately. And when she lifted her hips again, pressing up into his body, he seemed to forget he was supposed to be upset.

The tension left his jaw as he lowered his body back onto hers, gripping her hip as he kissed her with something Lauren thought felt a lot like possessiveness.

As soon as she felt him give in, she was instantly overcome with both triumph and guilt.

It had only been a few minutes ago that she reminded him she'd never lied to him.

And now, she'd no longer be able to claim that.

Michael broke the kiss, reaching behind his head and pulling his shirt off in one swift movement. Lauren barely had time to admire him before his mouth was back on hers, and his hands were tugging at the sides of her shorts.

She brought her hands to the button, fumbling with it as she kissed him, and once she had them opened, he lifted off of her, pulling them quickly down her legs. She took the opportunity to pull her tank top over her head, flinging it somewhere on the other side of the room.

His eyes ran over her body once, and then they flashed to hers as he exhaled heavily, lowering his mouth back onto hers. Without hesitation, she reached between them and started working on the button of his jeans.

She was rushing. She knew she should be savoring it, but she couldn't bring herself to slow down. She was so afraid he was going to change his mind, and she briefly wondered if he was rushing for the same reason.

In a matter of minutes, they were both stripped bare, and Michael was leaning over the side of his bed and reaching into his nightstand.

Lauren kept her hands on his waist and her eyes closed, trying to keep her breathing even.

This was going to happen. This was actually going to happen. She bit her lip at the sudden ridiculous urge to laugh.

But when he came back and positioned himself over her, laughing was the furthest thing from her mind.

Then he entered her, stopping when he met resistance.

Stopping when he heard the quiet whimper.

She tried to stifle the sound, she really did, but she had no idea it would be that intense.

He was completely frozen above her, and when she finally opened her eyes and looked up at him, she knew that he knew. His eyes were wide with some combination of shock and horror.

"I'm sorry," she whispered.

His eyes fell closed as he dropped his head. He still hadn't moved.

"It's already done, Michael," she said, her voice suddenly sounding small. "Don't stop now. Please."

He opened his eyes and looked at her. There were so many emotions flashing behind his eyes that she didn't know which one to appeal to.

She knew she only had seconds.

Lauren brought both hands up to his face, forcing him to look at her. "For as long as I've known you, you've given me a part of you that you haven't given anyone else. And now I'm finally getting to do the same."

His eyes fell closed again, and this time, he almost looked pained.

"Please don't be mad at me," she whispered. "I'll never regret that it was you."

Michael exhaled slowly as Lauren looked up at him, studying his face: his full lips, his cheeks flushed with emotion, his eyelashes fanned out beneath his closed eyes. He looked so young in that moment. So vulnerable.

And right then, her heart broke for the little boy who wasn't taken care of, but it swelled for the person who, despite everything, was able to maintain such kindness inside him, regardless of what everyone else thought they knew about him.

And she realized right then, even if she never felt it again for the rest of her life, she knew what true, unadulterated love felt like.

She ran her thumb softly over his cheek, and he opened his eyes.

This time, when he looked at her, there wasn't a trace of fear behind them. It was replaced with something so intense, so real, she felt goose bumps prickle over her skin.

After what seemed like a lifetime, Michael lowered his head as he pressed his lips to hers.

She knew this was his surrender, and her heart raced in her chest with the realization.

"If you want me to stop, just tell me and I will," he whispered against her mouth.

She nodded quickly, kissing him back, and then he was moving again.

Lauren hadn't prepared herself for what it would feel like. For the first few minutes, all she could do was concentrate on trying not to give away how much she was hurting. She kept reminding herself that it was Michael. That he was holding her. And inside of her. And they were as close as two people could possibly be.

And even if it was nothing like she expected, it was still everything she wanted.

She gripped him tighter and he answered in kind. Every inch of their bodies was touching, and Michael buried his face in the side of her neck as he exhaled her name.

At the tenderness of the gesture, Lauren closed her eyes. Her hand immediately came to the back of his head, holding him there as she felt tears welling behind her closed lids. And when he gently kissed her neck, she couldn't stop them from spilling out over her temples. Michael lifted his head slowly, his face brushing the side of hers.

He must have felt the moisture there because he whipped his head up and froze, his expression alarmed.

"Am I hurting you?"

"No no," she assured him, rubbing her hand over his back. "You're perfect. This is perfect."

He looked down at her, gauging her honesty, and she smiled softly, a tiny laugh falling from her lips as two more tears slid over her temples.

Michael smiled sadly, brushing one of the tears away before he leaned down and pressed his lips to the salty trail.

He began moving again, but it was so slow, so careful, she could tell it was with tremendous effort. She could feel the muscles of his back trembling beneath her hands.

Michael pressed his forehead to hers, and Lauren slid her hands up to the backs of his shoulders and closed her eyes, trying to take in every second. Trying to memorize it. The feel of his weight on top of her, the sound of his labored breathing, the scent of his skin. And while she was concentrating on that, something incredible happened. The burning, the throbbing ache between her legs gradually subsided, and in its wake came a pleasant stretching. A warm friction.

Lauren could feel the rigidity slowly leave her thighs as she gave herself up to the new feeling, and she found that the more she relaxed, the better it felt.

As soon as the last bit of tension left her body, Michael exhaled heavily in what seemed like relief, dropping his head onto her shoulder.

"Lauren?"

"Oh...wow," she breathed in response, and she felt his lips curve into a smile against her skin. "This is...I didn't know. Now you feel..." She closed her eyes and shook her head before she sighed. "I can't think. Just keep going."

He chuckled softly before he dropped his weight to his elbows, cradling her face in his hands as he kissed her. He was still incredibly gentle, but the tension had left his body too. He moved freely now, and his breath grew ragged, washing across her face every time he exhaled. Lauren lifted her chin, savoring the feel of it.

They began moving in unison, Lauren raising her hips to meet him, and it drew the most incredible sounds from his lips.

She could feel the smooth skin of his stomach brushing against hers, the tautness of his muscles as his arms flexed around her, pulling her closer, the silky friction between her legs, the warm rush of his breath on her skin.

It was sensory overload.

And when she felt his body go tense again, this time he fell forward, groaning into her hair, and she smiled.

There were no bells and whistles for her. No explosions. No seeing stars. But she wouldn't have changed a thing.

It was the single most incredible experience of her life.

When Michael finally caught his breath, he slowly rolled off of her, immediately pulling her back against his chest. Lauren closed her eyes, and for a few minutes they just lay there in silence as Michael held her, running his fingertips up and down her arm.

"I feel like I should say thank you, but that doesn't seem right," she said lazily.

Michael laughed softly behind her. "Thank you? Are you gonna leave some money on the dresser on your way out?"

She probably should have been embarrassed, but all she could do was laugh. She was completely drunk with him; her body felt deliciously warm and heavy. "You know what I mean," she sighed.

He pulled her further against his chest. "I know." He pressed his lips into her hair and whispered, "And if anyone should be saying thank you, it's me."

She turned her head and looked up at him, but there was no laughter behind his eyes.

She lifted her chin and kissed him gently before snuggling back against him.

They laid there in comfortable silence, Michael continuing to trail his fingertips over her skin, and Lauren wished there was a way to stop time. She just wanted to stay where she was.

And she desperately wished he could stay where he was.

"What time are you leaving tomorrow?" she asked, hating the words as they left her mouth.

"Early. Probably sun up."

Lauren glanced over at the clock on his nightstand. It was almost midnight.

She swallowed, trying to keep her voice even. "Should I go then?"

Michael shook his head behind her. "I'm not ready for you to go."

Lauren closed her eyes. "Me either," she sighed.

And she fell asleep right there in his arms, with him planting feather-light kisses in her hair.

She was half asleep and the sun hadn't fully risen when she felt a hand brushing the hair away from her face.

She was too tired to open her eyes, but all at once, the memory of where she was and what had happened came back to her.

"Are you mad at me?" she murmured sleepily.

"No. I could never be mad at you." His voice seemed far away, even though he was right next to her.

Maybe she was dreaming.

She felt him press his forehead to hers. Her eyes were still closed, but she smiled.

"Call me when you get there."

For a second, there was only silence.

And just as she lost the battle with sleep, she heard his faint whisper. "Good-bye, Lauren."

A few hours later, the sun was shining through his window, bathing her in warmth and light, and she finally opened her eyes. Lauren vaguely remembered having a conversation with him earlier that morning, but she wasn't sure if she had dreamed it or not.

But she knew what had happened between them the night before wasn't a dream, and she recalled every detail with perfect clarity, grinning like a fool as she buried her face in his pillow.

She stood up, grabbed her things, got dressed, and straightened his sheets, smiling the entire time.

And when she slid into the driver's seat of her car, she closed the door, dropped her head back, covered her face with her hands, and screamed.

She had never done drugs before, but she could imagine being high felt this way, and she could understand why people got addicted to it. Her body tingled, she couldn't stop smiling, and as she drove home, she alternated between wanting to close her eyes and melt back into the seat, or slam on the brakes, jump out of the car, and run squealing in circles around it.

On her way home she called Jenn to corroborate stories about where she'd been the night before, and when she told her what had happened, Jenn shrieked with excitement, ever the good friend, and offered to come over later to celebrate.

Lauren made it home, existing somewhere in a vacuum and functioning on autopilot. She cleaned her room. She baked cookies. She took a nap. She rehashed every detail with Jenn several times over. And that night, she called Michael.

But there was no answer. Nor did he answer her call the following morning.

Or that afternoon.

By the following night, she started to panic, thinking maybe he'd gotten into an accident, that something had gone wrong.

And just as she was planning her last resort, calling Jay to see if she could get a hold of him, she got his e-mail.

How he guessed he hadn't made himself clear the last time they had spoken. That if he was really going to start over, he'd need some time away from *everything* in his past to do it—and that included her. He pointed out how busy she'd be with her senior year coming up, and he assured her she'd hardly miss him. He reminded her that he'd moved to New York to get some distance, and she needed to respect that. He ended the short note by saying that when he finally had everything figured out, he'd be the one to contact her.

But she never heard from Michael Delaney again.

January 2012

Lauren had just finished chopping the vegetables for a stir-fry when her cell phone rang. She quickly wiped her hands on the dish towel over her shoulder before she reached across the counter and grabbed it.

Then she froze, watching Adam's number flashing on the screen.

She stood that way, trying to ignore the unpleasant feeling in her stomach. She just needed a minute to get her bearings. Just a few more seconds to pull it together. Then she'd answer.

That's what she told herself as she stood there, watching the number flash to the beat of her ringtone until finally he was redirected to her voice mail.

It was a spineless move. She knew that. Avoiding him wouldn't solve anything. But she just needed a little more time to sort out her feelings.

Lauren closed her eyes and exhaled heavily as she put the phone back on the counter. Who was she kidding? There was nothing for her to sort out. She just wasn't ready to say the words she knew she would have to say to him now.

Adam had invited her over for dinner the night before, and their date started off like all the others. Fun. Romantic. Comfortable. Essentially perfect.

Throughout dinner, as they'd talked and laughed, Lauren kept reminding herself that they'd been dating for almost two months. That he'd been more than patient. That he was a great guy and she was attracted to him and there was no reason to put it off any longer.

She held on to those thoughts for the entire evening, trying to convince herself she wasn't about to sleep with Adam because she was desperate to distance herself from Michael.

But at the end of the evening, as they headed back to his bedroom, she knew that's exactly what she was doing. When she weighed the fear of what would happen when she slept with Adam against what would happen if she didn't put a stop to her growing feelings for Michael, her choice was clear, even if it was reprehensible.

As Adam touched her, kissed her, whispered the sweetest things in her ear, she clung desperately to the hope that once she gave herself over to him, it would become about Adam, about how much she liked him, about how perfect she knew they were for each other.

He did everything right. He was slow, and skilled, and so incredibly attentive.

And she'd felt absolutely nothing.

But that was how it always happened. She would meet a man. She would flirt and laugh and feel attracted to him.

It would all feel so normal.

They'd get to know each other. She'd start to like him. Everything would progress exactly the way it was supposed to, and she'd start to believe that maybe this time things would be different.

Then they'd sleep together, and she'd feel completely hollow.

And everything would fall apart.

Lauren was always upset when it happened, but with Adam, she was devastated. She'd managed to convince herself that he would be the exception; that he was going to be everything she'd been waiting for.

That with him, she wouldn't feel so broken.

And as she drove home the following morning, all she could think about was how she wished she had put it off just a little longer, because she wasn't ready to let go of Adam yet.

But now that she'd felt it, the palpable emptiness as she gave herself to him, she knew it was over. She couldn't bring herself to do it again. Lauren had tried that method in the past: giving it time, trying to push past it, to work around it, attempting to make herself feel something other than the void that sex created for her. But it was almost degrading, going through the motions, letting a man do things to her body while her mind and her heart felt completely detached.

Maybe she just needed to accept the fact that she was one of those people who couldn't become emotionally invested in sex. Maybe she was incapable of bridging the gap between her heart and her body. Maybe this was as good as it was going to get for her.

Lauren might have been able to believe that about herself if she couldn't still remember what it was like to be with Michael. But she could still call to mind the indescribable feeling: something far beyond just physical sensation. Something that had been so powerful, so completely consuming, it moved her to tears.

And somehow, realizing she might never feel that way again was more painful than believing she was incapable of feeling it to begin with.

With a deep breath, Lauren walked back to the stove. She shouldn't be thinking about that night with Michael.

She shouldn't be thinking about Michael at all, for that matter.

And with that, she picked up the cutting board and slid the chopped vegetables into the pan, letting the subsequent sizzle temporarily wash away the two men who were battling for control of her thoughts.

She ate her dinner on the couch, distracting herself with an old sitcom rerun, and afterward, as she was loading the dishwasher, her phone rang again.

With a little lump of dread in her stomach, Lauren leaned over and checked the display. When she saw that it was Jenn, she felt only marginally relieved.

She didn't feel like having this conversation either, but there was no avoiding it. If she sent Jenn to voice mail, she'd just keep calling back.

With a tiny sigh, Lauren hit the button to take the call, holding the phone between her shoulder and her ear as she continued rinsing dishes.

"Hey," she said.

"Hey, what are you doing?"

"Just cleaning up from dinner. You?"

"Driving home from a late meeting. Total pain in my ass," Jenn sighed. "How was your date last night? Did you finally put out?"

Lauren took a breath. Might as well get it over with. "Yes."

"You *did!*" Jenn laughed. "Oh my God, I was only kidding! Well, it's about time. Adam's probably skipping through the streets whistling zip-a-dee-doo-dah as we speak."

A tiny laugh escaped Lauren's lips.

"Sooo, how was it? Worth the wait?"

She knew what Jenn was going to accuse her of: trying to get out before things got too serious. She wouldn't understand, but then again, how could she?

"I don't think it's going to work out," Lauren said as she closed the door to the dishwasher.

"*No!*" Jenn whined. "Lauren, don't do this! Come on, are you telling me the sex was *that* bad?"

"No, it wasn't bad. It was just...not what I expected."

"*So?* It was your first time with him! You need a little time to learn each other. Give the poor guy a break."

"It's not about the sex," Lauren said. "It's more about...I don't know. The connection."

"The connection," Jenn deadpanned.

"I just, I don't feel it. I can't keep sleeping with a guy I don't feel connected to."

There was silence on the other end of the phone, and for a second, Lauren thought maybe Jenn was sympathizing with her this time. But then her voice came through the phone, tinged with anger.

"I can't believe you."

"What?" Lauren said, confused.

"You're doing it again. Only this time it's worse. You're not doing it because of him. You're doing it *for* him."

Lauren shook her head. "What are you talking about?"

This was not how this conversation usually went. Jenn was supposed to be reprimanding her for her commitment issues, complaining about her fear of settling down. And while Jenn would usually sound disappointed during these rants, she never once sounded angry the way she did right now.

"Really? You're gonna make me say it?" she challenged. "*Michael*, Lauren. You're doing it for Michael."

Lauren opened her mouth to respond, but nothing would come out.

"You're falling in love with him again, aren't you."

It was more of a statement than a question, like she didn't need Lauren's answer to confirm it.

"I *knew* this was going to happen!" Jenn cried at Lauren's extended silence. "*Goddamn it*, Lauren!"

"So what if I am?" Lauren blurted out. She didn't even know if there was any truth to what Jenn said, but she suddenly felt extremely defensive.

"You're really asking me that?" Jenn said, her voice incredulous. "After what he did to you? I can't *believe* you'd be this stupid!"

Lauren ripped the phone from her ear and ended the call, slamming it down onto the counter. She didn't want to hear anymore. The absolute last thing she needed right now was to be scolded like a child.

The phone rang again, and she lunged forward, swiping it from the counter.

"*What?*" she shouted.

"Whoa. Is this a bad time?"

Lauren dropped her head and exhaled heavily.

"Sorry," she said, bringing her hand to her forehead. "I thought you were someone else."

"Well shit," Michael said with a laugh. "I'm glad I'm not whoever you were expecting."

Lauren sighed, trying to regain her composure.

"Hey," he said, his voice turning serious. "You okay?"

"I'm fine."

"No you're not."

When Lauren didn't respond, Michael asked, "Are you home?"

"Mm-hm."

"I'll be there in twenty."

Lauren whipped her head up. "No, no, don't do that."

But he'd already hung up.

She stared at the phone for a second before she dropped her head back, her arms falling limply to her sides. "Fantastic," she exhaled at the ceiling.

She tossed her phone onto the counter, vowing to never answer it again for as long as she lived, and then she padded across the kitchen and opened her refrigerator, pulling out a bottle of Kendall Jackson.

She poured herself a glass, holding it up in a one-sided toast. "To complete and utter dysfunction," she said, taking almost half of it down.

By the time there was a knock on her door, Lauren was already on her second glass.

"Come in," she called from where she sat on the living room floor.

She heard the door open, and she turned her head to see him standing in the entryway.

"You didn't have to come here."

"I know that," he said, removing his jacket.

Lauren nodded, looking down to run her finger along the top of her wine glass. "Where's Erin?"

"She ditched me tonight," he said, laying his jacket over a chair before he walked into the living room. "She's having a girls' night with our neighbor."

"That's sweet," Lauren said. "I didn't know you had a little girl next door."

Michael laughed. "Little girl? Mrs. Brigante is sixty years old. Apparently girls' nights have no age restrictions. But still, no boys allowed."

Lauren laughed, taking another sip of wine.

"So, whatever it is, it must be pretty bad if you're drinking alone."

Lauren shrugged. "Well then go get a glass and make me a little less pathetic."

He smiled down at her sympathetically, and then he turned and made his way into the kitchen. She heard him opening cabinets until he found the right one, and then he walked back into the living room and sat on the floor next to her with his back up against the couch.

Lauren leaned over and grabbed the bottle, pouring some into his glass. For a minute, they just sat next to each other in silence.

Then Lauren said, "This is oddly familiar. Only it used to be whiskey."

Michael smiled. "And it used to be straight out of the bottle. We've classed it up a bit, apparently."

Lauren laughed. "And it used to be *you* that was being consoled."

"Yeah, well. That's because I was always the fuck-up."

"No, it was because you always dated whores."

Michael smiled half-heartedly, looking down at his glass. "Not all of them were."

She turned her head to look at him, realizing how offensive that last comment must have been. One of those women had been the mother of his child.

"Will you tell me about Erin's mom?" she asked softly.

Michael licked his lips, his eyes still on his glass. "There's not that much to tell. Her name's Samantha. I met her at a party. She was a friend of a friend and we just…clicked," he said, lifting his glass and taking a long sip.

When he didn't continue, Lauren said, "So what happened?"

He turned toward her with his brow quirked. "Aren't we supposed to be talking about you?"

When Lauren just looked at him expectantly, he sighed.

"We were dating for about six months before she got pregnant. She was twenty-one at the time, and she didn't want to keep it." Michael raked his teeth over his bottom lip before he said, "But I convinced her to. I didn't need something else to regret. I was twenty-four years old. Definitely old enough to face the consequences of my actions instead of taking the easy way out."

Lauren kept her eyes on him as she took another sip of her wine.

"Obviously, she agreed to keep the baby," he said, playing with the stem of his glass. "But that was the beginning of the end for us. I think she resented me for convincing her."

He took another long sip before he said, "A few months later, she tells me that she's getting back with her ex. I guess they'd rekindled their relationship while ours was going down the shitter."

Lauren frowned, and Michael looked over at her.

"He didn't want another man's baby. Of course he didn't," he said with a hollow laugh. "I know all too well how that story ends."

Lauren dropped her eyes, chewing on the inside of her lip.

"She tried to get an abortion, but no doctor would do it that far along in her pregnancy. So she had the baby, and she gave her to me. Signed over her rights in the hospital."

Then he tilted his head back, draining the last of his wine before he reached for the bottle and filled his glass again.

Lauren stared at him, her throat suddenly feeling tight. She pictured him at twenty-four years old, coming home with a newborn, completely alone. No wife, no girlfriend, not even his mother to turn to for guidance. Going strictly by doctors' advice and parenting books.

Her heart felt like it was breaking in her chest.

Then suddenly, out of nowhere, she felt it harden.

"Did you love her?"

Michael looked up at her. "Samantha?"

Lauren nodded.

He sighed. "Yeah. In my own way, I did. Or at least I thought I did. But after she left Erin, I couldn't even if I wanted to."

Lauren pursed her lips, nodding slowly as she looked down. He loved Samantha. He gave himself to girls like that all the time.

But he'd walked away from her.

And suddenly, it was as raw as if it had happened yesterday.

Without warning, everything she'd been bottling for years came rushing to the surface.

She was furious.

Furious that she couldn't have a real relationship because of him. Furious that she'd gotten in a fight with her best friend because of him. Furious that Jenn was right, that she probably just ruined another good thing because of her goddamn feelings for him.

And it wasn't about closure. It wasn't about answers. It wasn't about getting her friend back.

It was about finally getting to stand up for herself, after all this time.

"You loved her," she said. "She was a shitty person, and you loved her."

He kept his eyes straight ahead, but Lauren watched his shoulders rise as he inhaled a deep breath.

"You did it over and over," she said with paper-thin restraint. "Gave your heart to these worthless girls." She took a breath before she said the words she'd been waiting almost nine years to say. "So what was wrong with me?"

Michael closed his eyes and dropped his head, nodding slowly. "You know, for the past few months, I've been going back and forth between wishing we could just have this conversation and praying we never would."

"What was wrong with me, Michael? Why did you walk away from me like that?"

She watched him put his glass of wine on the floor before pressing the heels of his hands into his eyes and rubbing roughly.

"Tell me why."

He slid his hands down his face. "We were *friends*, Lauren—"

"Oh, don't give me that bullshit," she snapped, cutting him off. He turned his head and looked up at her, startled. "We're both adults now. You knew it was more than friendship for me. You knew I was in love with you. Anyone with eyes could see that I was."

He looked away from her, and she could feel herself losing the hold on what little composure she had as she pushed off the floor and stood over him.

"That last day? When we were together?" she said, her voice shaking. "It was more than friendship for you too then. Even if it was just for that moment. Don't even try to tell me it wasn't."

She saw a tiny muscle flex in the side of his jaw, but he still wouldn't look at her.

"How could you just walk away like that?" she demanded. "After everything we were to each other? Why would you do that to me?"

She thought of them together in that bed. Her first time.

"I mean, was I *that* bad?"

"*No,*" he answered firmly before she'd even finished the question, whipping his head up to look at her. "Stop it. Don't go there."

She threw her hands in the air. "Well then give me an answer!" she shouted. "I deserve to know why you abandoned me!"

"Don't you get it?" he said, jumping up to face her. "Don't you get that it wasn't about *you?*"

Lauren shook her head in disbelief. "Don't give me that. I know you've been hurt. I know you've lost people in your life. But if you're gonna stand here and tell me this was about your fear of that happening again, that's complete bullshit," she spat. "It's not fair that you applied that fear to me. I never gave you a reason to."

"Don't you think I know that? Don't psychoanalyze me," he said with disgust. "You think I'm gonna say it was all subconscious? That it was me trying to protect myself because I was afraid to love someone and have them leave me again? This wasn't some subliminal self-preservation crap. It was intentional. I *wanted* you out of my life!"

Lauren swooped down and grabbed her wine glass as she pushed past him. "Well, you got what you wanted Michael, so now I wish you'd just leave me the hell alone!"

She stormed into the kitchen and slammed the glass down in the sink, causing it to shatter. Before she could even check to see if she'd cut herself, she felt him grip her arm and spin her back around.

"Let me finish!" he shouted. "I wasn't protecting myself! I was protecting *you!*"

Lauren was completely frozen, as much at his tone as she was at his words.

He took a breath, and although he kept his hold on her arm, when he spoke, his voice had softened significantly.

"Because if I didn't leave, it would have ended in disaster. It always did with me. I didn't know how to have healthy relationships. Shit, I still don't know if I do. And I couldn't put you through that."

She ripped out of his grip and took a step back, completely appalled. "So what you're saying is you tried to avoid hurting me by *hurting me?*" she cried.

"I had to, Lauren! I've been fucking up people's lives since the *day I was born.* You *know* that. My very existence ruined every life it touched."

She took another small step back, folding her arms as she stood her ground. "You know I never believed that."

"Of course you do!" he exclaimed. "You're just another example of it!"

"*But it didn't have to be that way!*" she yelled, silencing him. "You made that decision! You could have taken a chance! Maybe it wouldn't have worked out. But maybe it would have been the best thing to happen to both of us. Did you ever think about that?"

He stared at her, saying nothing.

"And now where are we?" she said, her voice breaking. "You had a child with a woman who was a horrible excuse for a person and a mother, and I ruin every goddamn relationship I start. How was that the best decision for anybody?"

"Christ, Lauren," he groaned, shaking his head in frustration. "You're speaking in hindsight. Can't you see it from my point of view? I didn't trust myself not to screw up with you, so I had to walk away. But if I left, I'd be hurting you. It was a lose-lose for me."

He took a step toward her, his eyes almost frantic. "I was a scared fucking kid, and I picked what I thought was the lesser of two evils. I did what I thought was right, because in my mind, the alternative would have been so much worse. I thought it would be better to leave you angry but intact than to drag you down with me. You were too good for that. You were too good for *me*. You always were."

Lauren stood there, digging her nails into her palms beneath her folded arms. Anger, confusion, regret, and frustration swirled in her gut, making her body feel like a live wire.

Michael turned away from her, dropping his head back and fisting his hair before he whirled back around. "Do you know what the messed up thing is? Your freshman year, right after we met, I remember standing in the hall when you were leaving class, and Mr. Benton questioned you about hanging out with me. He said something about being careful of the company you keep. And you told him you'd expect better from a teacher."

Lauren felt her shoulders soften as her defenses momentarily faltered. "I don't remember that," she murmured.

"Well, I do. I'll never forget that. The way you stood up for me. And I remember swearing then and there that if anyone ever caused you pain, I'd kill them." His eyes were desperate now. "Do you think I wanted to be the one? Do you think it didn't rip me to shreds to do it? That I haven't thought about you constantly since the day I left?"

He took another step toward her. "I'm so sorry, Lauren. There aren't even words for how sorry I am. I made a horrible decision, and I wish I could take it back."

Michael's eyes darted back and forth between hers, waiting for her to speak, but she couldn't think beyond the surfeit of emotions churning through her body. She could barely breathe.

He looked down, shaking his head. "I just…I didn't know what to do with us, you know? I never planned on crossing that line with you. It wasn't supposed to go that way. We were supposed to be friends. I was supposed to look out for you, to keep you away from idiots like me. You were never supposed to love me. I wasn't prepared for it."

She exhaled slowly, unfolding her arms as she felt the tiny fissures forming in her resistance.

"I always knew I would fall in love with you," he said softly, "but you were never supposed to love me back."

Lauren's expression fell. "What did you just say?"

Michael looked confused by her shock. "I loved you," he said, like it should have been obvious. "So much. My God, more than anything."

All at once, Lauren's vision tilted, and she reached behind her and gripped the edge of the sink to steady herself.

He loved her?

No. That's not how it happened. She'd already determined long ago what went wrong. She fell in love with her best friend who didn't love her back, who slept with her out of pity because she begged and then ran away to get rid of his mistake. And she had come to terms with his cruelness, with her stupidity, as best she could.

But now everything she knew, everything she thought she had a handle on, was completely upturned.

Lauren closed her eyes as she shook her head, and she heard Michael take a step toward her.

"No," she said, holding her hand up to stop him.

He hesitated for just a second, but then he took another step toward her, and she took a quick step back and shook her head frantically.

"No. That makes it so much worse," she nearly sobbed. "It's so much worse now."

"Lauren—"

"I can't do this right now. You need to go," she said, her voice breaking.

"Lauren, just—"

"You need to go."

"Please don't do this—"

"I said get out!" she shouted suddenly.

His shoulders dropped as he stared at her, and she turned away from the expression on his face.

The look of utter defeat in his eyes.

She heard the sounds of him exiting the kitchen, the shuffling noises as he put on his jacket, and then the front door closed softly, and there was silence.

Lauren let her knees give out as she slowly slid down the front of the cabinets until she was sitting on the kitchen floor.

She hugged her knees into her chest as a feeling of panic began to envelope her.

She closed her eyes, remembering the incapacitating pain. The double loss. Not only was her love unrequited, that in itself would have been painful enough to deal with, but in the same shot, she also lost her best friend in the world.

And she never could figure out which one hurt more.

It never healed. She could openly admit that now as she sat up against the kitchen sink with tears pooling in her eyes. It had been more like living with a disability. She had learned to work around it, to accommodate it, but it had never gone away.

All these years, she thought it had been so simple. The boy she loved didn't love her back. He had handled it callously, and she had been a fool.

But now? He left because he *loved* her? That whole time, he had been in love with her?

She exhaled heavily and dropped her forehead to her knees as the first tears fell.

She meant what she said to Michael. This made it so much worse than thinking he just didn't want her.

He loved her, but he still left her. And he never came back. Not even a second glance.

How could they ever move past this and start again now? How could she trust him? If he'd been able to crush her when he was in love with her before, what would stop him from doing it again?

And how badly would it hurt the second time around?

February 2012

Lauren sat cross-legged on the floor, stringing multicolored beads onto a thread of yarn.

"I found another sparkle one!" Erin declared proudly, holding up the tiny gold bead embedded with glitter.

"Lucky girl," Lauren smiled. "There aren't that many in there."

Erin studied it closely before she held it out to Lauren. "Do you want it? Your necklace doesn't have any sparkly ones."

"That's okay, sweetheart. You keep it. I'm almost done."

"'Kay," Erin said, furrowing her brow in concentration as she attempted to get the tiny bead on her string.

As Lauren secured the last bead on her own necklace, she glanced up at the clock and then quickly threw a look over her shoulder toward the vestibule.

There was no way her luck would hold out much longer.

It had been two weeks since Lauren asked Michael to leave her apartment, and in that time, she'd had no contact with him whatsoever. She hadn't called or texted, which was well within her control, but she'd also managed to avoid him at Learn and Grow, something she figured would be virtually impossible.

Most days now when Lauren's shift ended, Erin would remain at the center playing with the late pick-up group. And she had started arriving in the mornings before Lauren, or else she would suddenly appear in the pre-K room out of nowhere on the days that Lauren happened to beat her there.

Granted, Lauren avoided the vestibule at all costs, so maybe they would have run into each other by now if she hadn't been taking such precautions to prevent it.

Or maybe he was taking the same precautions she was.

Lauren felt like she had exhausted all of her courage in the past two weeks. First, there had been the argument with Michael. Then, the morning after Michael left her apartment, she had called Jenn. Lauren apologized to her friend for the outburst and admitted that Jenn had been right about everything, and that it *was* incredibly stupid of her to even entertain the idea of rekindling anything with Michael. She ended the conversation by assuring Jenn she had a handle on whatever it was she was feeling and that nothing would come of it.

Three days after that, she called Adam and told him she had some personal issues she needed to deal with, and because of that, she wasn't in the right place to continue a relationship with him. He had been upset, but extremely understanding, which ironically only made it harder on her. Truth be told, a little piece of her wanted him to yell at her for leading him on for two months. She wanted him to tell her to go to hell. But instead he told her he still cared about her, and if she ever changed her mind, he would love to try again with her someday.

It made her feel wretched.

After that, she just didn't have it in her for another confrontation with Michael. And even if she did, there was nothing left to say.

"Is this long enough?" Erin asked, holding up her string of beads.

"Perfect," Lauren said. "Tie off the end like I showed you and then you can wear it."

Erin looked down as she worked her little fingers around the yarn, trying to make a knot. After a minute, she said, "I wanted to ask you to come over, but Daddy said I shouldn't."

Lauren stilled for a second before she gently cleared her throat. "That's sweet of you Erin, and I would love to, but I've been very busy lately."

"That's what Daddy said." She finished her knot as she sighed. "Maybe one day."

Her normally bubbly voice sounded completely deflated.

"Hey," Lauren said, forcing a smile as she ran her hand over Erin's hair. "I still see you everyday."

"But you don't see Daddy."

Lauren's smile fell, and she turned toward the supply basket, trying to hide her expression.

What could she possibly say to that?

She took a small breath before she grabbed the scissors and turned back to Erin, cutting the excess yarn from her necklace.

"Are you mad at Daddy?"

Lauren lifted her eyes to see Erin looking at her intently.

Like she already knew the answer.

Even at four, she was too smart to be lied to. "I'm not mad. I'm…" She took a breath. "I don't know what I am." Lauren fastened the beads around Erin's neck. "But it's nothing you need to be sad about," she added with a reassuring smile.

When she had finished securing the necklace, Lauren sat back, watching as Erin looked down at her creation and rolled it between her thumb and forefinger. "Daddy never gets mad at me, you know."

"Oh no?" Lauren asked, beginning to scoop the unused beads into a pile.

"Nope. He only gets disappointed."

Lauren smiled softly as she took the lid off the bead canister.

"So are you disappointed then?" Erin asked.

Lauren sighed. "Yeah, I guess I'm disappointed. Hey, you wanna have a race?" she asked, trying to change the subject. "Let's see who can clean up the most beads."

Erin leaned over and scooped up a heap with both hands. "Daddy said even when he's disappointed in me, he never stops loving me."

Lauren forced another smile. "That's true, sweetheart. Your daddy will always love you, no matter what."

"Well then do you still love Daddy?"

Lauren whipped her head up. "What?" she choked.

Completely oblivious, Erin dumped two fistfuls of beads into the container. "Even though you're disappointed. You didn't forget to still love him, did you?"

Lauren was completely frozen as she stared at her.

"*You're losing*," Erin sing-songed as she dumped another handful of beads into the container.

She had to swallow twice before responding. "That's because you're such a good cleaner," she said weakly. She attempted to scoop up a handful of beads, but she realized her hands were trembling.

"Keep cleaning, sweetheart," she murmured, dropping her meager fistful into the container as she stood from her place on the floor.

"Where are you going?"

"Just...to the bathroom," Lauren managed as she turned and exited as quickly as she could without drawing attention to herself.

As soon as she was inside, she shut the door, falling back against it as she reached behind her body to turn the lock. And when her chin started to tremble, she rushed forward and turned on the faucet, gathering the cold water in her hands and splashing it on her face.

She gripped the sides of the sink and lifted her head, staring at her own reflection.

Almost instantly, her eyes welled with tears.

Lauren had always wished Michael could learn how to let go of his past, to absolve himself of everything he'd taken the blame for.

But how could he ever forgive himself for this if *she* wouldn't forgive him?

It was true he had absolutely crushed her all those years ago. But she knew now it wasn't a selfish move on his part. It had actually been selfless. He had done what he thought was in *her* best interest. He was young, and he was wrong, and it was a huge mistake. But he owned that. So how could she keep condemning him?

Lauren may have been disappointed by his actions, but that didn't change the fact that she loved him.

It had taken a four-year-old to make her see that.

She stared at her reflection as a breathy laugh fell from her lips.

And then she turned off the faucet and bolted out of the bathroom.

Lauren rushed past the chaos in the pre-K room and out to the vestibule, rummaging in the front desk until she found her cell phone, and before she had even made it outside, she had already dialed the number.

She paced in front of the day care center, her heart rate increasing with each subsequent ring.

Then she was directed to his voice mail.

She hung up, staring down at the phone for a second before she hit the button to redial his number.

When she was redirected to his voice mail again, this time she took a breath and waited for the beep.

"Michael," she said. "It's me."

She paused, realizing she hadn't thought through what she was going to say.

"I need you to call me," she finally managed, adding quickly, "Erin is fine. I just…I really need to talk to you."

She stood there for a second before she closed her eyes and exhaled, hitting the button to end the call.

The ball is in his court now, she told herself as she walked back into the building. *It's out of your hands.*

And while that should have provided her with some level of relief, it only made her more anxious.

Lauren went back inside and helped the children clean up, and then she stood in the vestibule for the first time in two weeks to help with dismissal.

In a matter of fifteen minutes, all the regular students had been picked up, but Erin remained once again.

Lauren lingered for as long as she could, finding a shelf to straighten here, a toy to put away there, hoping he would show up before she had to leave for class.

"What are you still doing here?" Deb asked as she walked past Lauren to the file cabinet. "Delia has the late pick-ups tonight."

"Oh, I know…I was just," she looked around. "I couldn't find my phone. But I got it now." She held it up with a tiny smile as she walked toward the exit. "See you tomorrow."

"Good night," Deb called cheerily as she rooted through one of the filing drawers.

Thirty minutes later, Lauren was sitting in a lecture hall staring through the professor in the front of the room. She realized within the first five minutes of class that attending had been a pointless endeavor. She couldn't focus on a single word of the lecture.

She had her phone on the desk, set to silent, and every minute or so she would glance down at the display, even though she hadn't felt it vibrate.

She spent the entire class running through different scenarios in her mind. What would happen if he called and he was angry. What would happen if he called and he was reluctant. What would happen if he called and was just as anxious to put this behind them as she was.

She planned what she would say in each situation, rehearsing it in her mind, until suddenly the professor was dismissing them.

By the time Lauren was pulling onto her street, a feeling of despondency was beginning to overshadow her anxiety.

It was almost seven o'clock. Erin had already been picked up. He would have seen her missed call by now. He should have already listened to her message.

As Lauren walked into her apartment, she realized there was one scenario she hadn't accounted for.

What would happen if he didn't call her back at all?

She had been so concerned with making sure she'd say everything right when the time came that she hadn't even thought about the possibility that she might not get the chance.

Lauren walked into her apartment, stripping off her jacket and throwing it over a chair before she sank down onto the couch, staring at the screen of her cell phone.

After five minutes of silence, she tossed the phone to the other side of the couch and stood up.

She couldn't keep torturing herself all night. Either he was going to call her, or he wasn't, but staring at the phone for hours wasn't going to change anything.

She was going to make herself dinner. Then she was going to take a bubble bath, something she hadn't done in years. And maybe after that, she'd finally start watching some of the shows that had been sitting in her DVR for weeks.

But first, she needed to e-mail one of her classmates and ask for a copy of the notes from tonight's class.

Lauren powered up her laptop, signed into her professor's website, and found the list of students from her class. She scrolled down, clicking on the e-mail address of one of the girls she sat next to and asked for a copy of the notes she'd missed.

Then she closed out and clicked on her inbox, deleting a few spam messages and reading a hilarious forward from Jenn. Just as she was about to log out, her eye landed on the e-mail from Michael, the one he'd sent a few weeks ago on Erin's birthday.

Lauren bit her bottom lip, slowly running her finger over the track pad, and she clicked on it, rereading the words that had originally sent her into a panic.

But tonight, they made her ache.

She scrolled down to the bottom of the message and clicked on the song attachment she had refused to open that night.

The first chord broke through the silence of her apartment, giving her goose bumps.

When you try your best, but you don't succeed
When you get what you want, but not what you need
When you feel so tired, but you can't sleep
Stuck in reverse.

And the tears come streaming down your face
When you lose something you can't replace
When you love someone but it goes to waste,
Could it be worse?

Lauren closed her eyes and pressed her lips together, trying to stop them from trembling.

And high up above or down below
When you're too in love to let it go
But if you never try, you'll never know
Just what you're worth.

Lights will guide you home
And ignite your bones
And I will try to fix you.

The sob that ripped through her throat momentarily drowned out the music, and she covered her face with her hands, trying to catch her breath. But the more she gasped, the faster the tears came until she was only hearing bits and pieces of the song intermingled with her stifled sobs.

…when you lose something you cannot replace…
…I promise you I will learn from my mistakes…
…Lights will guide you home…
and I will try to fix you.

With the music still playing, Lauren leapt from the chair and scrambled out of her room, grabbing her keys from the entryway table on her way out the door.

And then she was running down the walkway.

She hadn't even thought to grab a jacket; the freezing February air bit at her skin, and a cold drizzle had dampened her hair by the time she got to her car.

Swiping at the tears that wouldn't stop, Lauren sped down the road that would take her to him. They had wasted almost nine years, and she refused to waste any more time. She had to apologize. To tell him she finally understood.

She needed to tell him she had forgiven him.

By the time she had gotten to Michael's apartment, it was pouring. Lauren jumped out of the car and ran up to his front door, ducking her head against the freezing, needle-like rain that was stinging her skin.

She rang the doorbell before wrapping her arms around herself; the cold air was becoming unbearable as her clothes quickly became soaked through.

"Michael?" she called, knocking on the door.

When a few seconds passed and he hadn't answered, she knocked again, a little harder this time. "*Michael?*"

"Hello?"

Lauren whipped her head in the direction the voice came from, squinting against the downpour. The door of the apartment next to Michael's was open, and a small elderly woman was standing in the entryway, silhouetted with light from inside.

"Are you okay, dear?" she asked, pulling a knit cardigan a little tighter around herself.

Lauren opened her mouth to respond just as a little voice cut through the darkness.

"Miss Lauren! You came over!"

From behind the old woman, a tiny head popped out, completely throwing Lauren off guard.

But then it clicked. Michael's neighbor. The girls' nights.

Lauren waved sheepishly at Erin, swiping at the strands of hair that were plastered to her face.

"Are you looking for Michael?" the old woman asked.

Lauren nodded. "I didn't mean to disturb you, I just—"

"We're playing Go Fish! Wanna come play?" Erin called from the doorway.

The old woman smiled and placed her hand on the top of Erin's head. "He's out, honey. Why don't you come in and dry off while you wait for him?"

The icy rain spilled over her cheeks and down the sides of her neck as she stood there, taking in Erin's tiny, hopeful expression and the look of sympathy the old woman was giving her.

And suddenly her answer was clear.

"No, no thank you," she said softly, hoping the woman could hear her over the din of the downpour. She forced a smile and waved a good-bye to Erin as she turned and quickly made her way back to her car.

Lauren started it up, clenching her jaw against the violent chattering of her teeth as well as the emotion she felt swelling up in her throat.

Michael had left work, picked up Erin, come home, dropped her off with the neighbor, and gone out. And she knew there was no way he hadn't checked his voice mail somewhere in there.

He obviously didn't want to talk to her. And there was no way she could bring herself to be waiting for him in his neighbor's house, sopping wet and pathetic, knowing that was the case.

If he was angry now, Lauren thought as she drove mindlessly down the rain-soaked roads, she deserved it. After all, he had apologized, had owned fault, had essentially poured his heart out to her, only to be coldly turned away and ignored for the past two weeks.

By the time she pulled into her parking space, her tears had stopped, although she could distinctly feel the sting they left behind. Lauren exited the car and ducked her head against the unrelenting rain, watching as her feet spattered the puddles up over her shoes. She was completely soaked, but she couldn't feel the cold anymore.

"Hey."

Lauren whipped her head up as she sucked in a startled breath, coming to an immediate halt when she saw him. She blinked quickly against the raindrops that were assaulting her vision, but she knew she was seeing clearly.

He had his hood up, his head slightly ducked against the rain as he looked up at her. She watched his eyes drop to take in her appearance before making their way back to her face, and she realized how ridiculous she must have looked, drenched from head to toe with swollen bloodshot eyes and mascara running down her face.

Michael stuffed his hands in his pockets, his expression confused. "Where were you?"

Lauren swallowed. "I...," she began, and then she exhaled heavily, wiping the saturated hair away from her face. "I was at your apartment. Looking for you."

The confusion on his face was quickly replaced with concern. "I was taking a test. I got your message when I got out, and I called you a few times, but you weren't picking up."

Lauren pulled her brow together and shook her head, but then she realized that in her haste leaving the house, she'd not only left her jacket behind, but her purse and her phone as well. A tiny ember of relief lit in her belly, sending little sparks of warmth up through her chest.

"It made me nervous. That message, and then you not answering," he said. "So...I came here."

She knew she should say something, but her throat was growing tighter by the second. All she could do was stand there like an idiot, blinking against the rain and her impending tears.

His eyes were darting back and forth between hers. "Are you okay?" he finally asked.

She forced her body to work, nodding her head slightly. "Yes," she managed. But then her breath caught on a sob, and she choked out, "No."

"*No?*" he said, removing his hands from his pockets as he instinctively stepped toward her. But then he stopped abruptly, almost as if he realized he would be breaking a rule, and he stepped back, bringing his hands to his sides.

The look in his eyes was so heartbreaking that Lauren's restraint instantly crumbled. She threw herself forward, wrapping her arms around him as she buried her face in his chest and burst into tears.

Immediately his arms came around her, pulling her into his body. "Hey," he cooed softly as he ran his hand over the back of her head. "Hey, it's okay. I'm here."

She nodded against his chest, but she couldn't manage anything beyond the sobs that kept bursting from her lips.

Suddenly her feet were off the floor, and then she was moving. Lauren curled up against him, tightening her hold around his neck as he carried her toward her front door. He reached behind his head, taking the keys out of her hand and opening her door, and then he placed her gently on the couch. Lauren brought her hands to her face, gulping for air as she tried to get her bearings, and she could hear the sounds of him in the bathroom, opening and closing cabinets.

When she heard him turn the light off, she looked up to see him walking toward her with one of the large, plush towels from her linen closet. He removed his jacket and tossed it on the floor in the entryway before he leaned over and wrapped the towel around her shoulders, rubbing the tops of her arms vigorously.

Lauren brought the ends of the towel up to her face, wiping away the rain and the tears, and she felt the couch dip as he sat next to her.

She turned then, crawling into his lap as she buried her face in the crook of his neck.

Michael sat back as he tucked her against his body, running his hand up and down her back as she continued to hiccup pathetically in the aftermath of her breakdown.

When she finally achieved some semblance of control, she lifted her head and looked up at him. "I'm so sorry. For everything," she whispered.

"Don't," Michael said softly. "You have nothing to be sorry for."

"Yes, I do," she said. "My reaction, the way I treated you that night, the way I've been treating you for the past two weeks. None of that was okay."

"Lauren," he said, pulling the towel a little tighter around her, "you've been much nicer to me in these past few months than I ever deserved. Your reaction was mild, and long overdue, if we're being honest."

She shook her head. "I understand why you left now. I need you to know that I forgive you."

Michael closed his eyes as he exhaled slowly, his shoulders softening in relief before he nodded. "Just know that it killed me," he murmured as he lifted the corner of the towel and wiped underneath one of her eyes. "Every day. I kept wanting to call you, to come back home to you, to ask you to come out to me. You have no idea how much."

He swallowed, and Lauren gently placed her hand on his chest. "But the more I battled myself," he continued, "the more time passed. And the longer I stayed away, the easier it was to convince myself that you'd gotten over me by then. And I thought it would be so unfair to you, to worm my way back into your life after you'd already moved on, especially since I didn't think I could be what you needed. I painted myself into a corner, and I didn't know how to fix it, or even if I could."

Michael looked down at her hand, and he lifted it to his mouth, kissing her palm before he placed it back on his chest and looked up at her. "But I never stopped loving you. Not for one second."

And then Lauren did something her heart had wanted her to do from the second she saw him standing in the vestibule of Learn and Grow holding his little girl.

She kissed him.

She felt his hand curl into a fist behind her back, gripping the towel, but his lips remained gentle as he lifted his chin and kissed her back.

The second their lips touched, every hair on her body stood on end. It felt like an electric current was running through her, from the crown of her head to the bottom of her feet, and she pressed her body against him, bringing her hands to the side of his face.

"I should have pushed," she said. "I should have pursued you." As she spoke, her lips ghosted over his. "But I thought that you didn't want me," she whispered. "And I was too hurt and too proud and too stupid."

She brought her mouth back to his, and he made a small noise in the back of his throat as he kissed her again, this time with a hint of the urgency she could feel in the fist that was still clenching the towel tightly behind her back.

Lauren pulled back slightly. "So it was my fault too," she said softly, and Michael shook his head, shifting his weight as he released his hand from the towel. He slid it up under her hair, gently winding it around his hand before he pulled lightly, forcing her to tilt her head back. When she felt the heat of his mouth on her throat, her eyes fluttered closed.

"It doesn't matter anymore," he whispered against her skin. "We're right where we're supposed to be now."

And when Lauren brought her head back down, their mouths met in a searing kiss that confirmed what he had just reassured her of.

This was exactly where she belonged. Because the way he was holding her, the way his mouth felt on hers, made everything else she'd ever known of contentment feel like a sham.

She felt his fingertips curl under the hem of her shirt, and when he slowly slid it up her abdomen, she broke contact and lifted her arms, allowing him to peel the soaking garment from her body.

"Michael," she breathed as she came back to him, and he exhaled heavily as his hands came to the sides of her waist.

"Should we...?" he asked, glancing down the hall.

"No," she sighed, kissing him again. "Here. I don't want to wait anymore."

Michael wrapped one arm securely around her back and supported her head with the other before shifting his weight from the couch and lowering them onto the floor.

"That night with you," he said, kissing across her collarbone. "Nothing compared to it. Nothing ever came close."

"I know," she breathed. And she did. Because they hadn't done anything but kiss, and she could already feel it. The thing that was missing with every other man. The thing that made her heart come alive in her chest and her body thrum with emotion and her soul feel like it was home.

Michael kissed a slow path across her chest and down the line of her stomach, and by the time he was unfastening the button to her jeans, she could feel the rapid beat of her heart pulsing throughout every part of her body.

He slowly peeled away her sodden jeans before bringing his hands back to her body. He was touching her like she was porcelain, looking at her as if she were sacred, and she laid there, trembling beneath his hands while he reacquainted himself with her body.

When she couldn't stand it any longer, she sat up and began removing his clothing. She tried to be as gentle as he had been, but her need for him had taken over entirely, and she found herself jerking the garments from his body in rushed, clumsy movements.

He grinned at her, helping her remove the last of his clothes before he lowered her back to the floor.

Lauren brought her hands to his waist, looking up at him. "This is real?" she asked.

It seemed like such a silly thing to say, but having everything she wanted fall into place, especially after so long, felt too good to be true. She wasn't even sure what she was asking him: Were they really about to do this? Was he feeling what she was feeling? Was everything about to change?

He rested his weight on his elbows as he cradled her head in his hands. "Yes," he whispered, as if in answer to all three.

She closed her eyes and tightened her hold on him.

"Open your eyes. Look at me," he whispered.

She did as he asked, and in one slow, smooth movement, their bodies were connected.

"God," he breathed, dropping his head to her shoulder, and she tightened her legs around his hips, urging him forward.

As soon as he began moving, Lauren was completely overcome. On the one hand, she had waited so long to be with him again, but at the same time, it seemed like they had never been apart, like there had never been anyone else but him.

She was instantly spellbound, completely lost. Everything else in her world fell away, and the only thing that existed or even remotely mattered was Michael, finally there with her, his hands traveling over her body and the brush of his lips everywhere he could reach.

She felt like she was being worshipped.

The last time they had been together, he had been so careful. This time, there was a confidence in his movements and determination behind his actions. He could read her so easily; he understood exactly what she needed and when, and he knew just how to prolong the intense sensations he was giving her, drawing out every feeling until it was almost unbearable. And when he knew she couldn't take anymore, he doubled his efforts until he drove her over the edge, kissing her passionately and swallowing every moan she offered up to him.

There were no words for what Lauren felt in that moment. It was far beyond just physical pleasure, encompassing every square inch of her body until she felt like she might burst out laughing and crying simultaneously in its aftermath. But instead she focused all of her remaining energy on making him feel the way he had just made her feel.

It wasn't long before she felt his body begin to tense, and when the slow, steady rasp of his breath grew rapid, she pulled him down to her, bringing her lips to his ear.

"I love you," she whispered.

Then he was gone, pulling her against his body as he gave himself over to the release. Michael fell forward, his overworked muscles trembling with the effort of keeping his weight off of her until finally he rolled onto his back, pulling her against his side.

Lauren placed her hand on his stomach, her breath fast and heavy, and she could feel his heart racing against her cheek.

"Jesus Christ," he finally said, and Lauren laughed softly as she closed her eyes.

"I know."

"I thought I built it up in my head," he said through labored breath. "What it felt like to be with you."

She shook her head. "To think we could have been doing this for years."

Michael groaned softly. "Don't remind me what an idiot I am."

Lauren smiled. "You're not an idiot. I kind of like you."

He burst out laughing. "You *kind of like me?*"

"Little bit."

He laughed again, pulling her further into his side as he pressed his lips against the top of her head. After a minute, he said, "What made you approach me that day?"

"Hmm?" she asked as she lazily trailed her fingertips over his chest.

Michael shifted as he placed his hand behind his head and looked down at her. "In high school. I've always wondered about that. Why did you give me those notes?"

Lauren smiled as she realized what he was talking about. "Because you looked so sad the day before."

"*Sad?* How do you figure?"

"Not when you were flinging desks across the room," she clarified, and she felt his chest bounce with laughter beneath her. "I meant after that, when you were sitting in the parking lot."

"Ahh, that's right," Michael said slowly, nodding his head. "I forgot about the part where you stalked me."

Lauren reached up and pinched the inside of his arm, and he yelped out a laugh as he ripped it out of her reach. She went up on her elbow, laying partially on his chest as she looked down at him. "You didn't look so scary then. You looked like you needed a friend. So I wanted to do something nice for you."

Michael reached up to touch her face just as she added, "I had no idea you would turn out to be such an asshole."

He raised his eyebrows as she looked down at him fighting a smile, and then suddenly both of his hands were on her waist as he tickled her. She squealed loudly as she tried to push off of him, but he shifted his weight so he was on top of her, pinning her down and continuing the torturous movement of his fingers up and down her sides as she screeched with laughter and gasped for air.

When he saw the tears at the corners of her eyes, he finally stopped, rolling off of her as he pulled her back on top of him with a laugh.

Lauren pushed herself up on her hands as she attempted to catch her breath, and he smiled up at her, swiping the hair out of her face as he leaned up and kissed her.

When his mouth transitioned from tender to insistent, Lauren pulled back slightly.

"Okay, this isn't helping me catch my breath," she exhaled, and he chuckled softly, shifting their weight so she could rest her head on his chest. Michael slowly pulled his fingers through her hair, and Lauren sighed and closed her eyes.

"So," Michael said as his fingers lulled Lauren closer and closer to sleep. "What happens now?"

"What do you mean?" Lauren murmured softly, and she felt his chest rise beneath her as he inhaled deeply.

"I mean, with us. What happens now?"

Lauren lifted her head, resting her chin on his chest as she looked at him.

She did her best to keep a straight face as she said, "Oh, come on. You're not going to get all clingy on me, are you?" She bit the inside of her cheek as she watched the shock register on his face before she said, "I don't know what you were looking for, but I just needed a little stress relief."

He stared up at her for a second before the corners of his mouth twitched, and then he rolled them so he was on top of her again.

"Stress relief?" he asked as he settled his hips between her thighs. "That's all this was?"

"'Fraid so," Lauren said, fighting every urge in her body to press up against him.

He smiled. "Well," he said, lowering his head as he gently dragged his teeth over the skin beneath her ear, "I heard that going for a master's degree can be pretty stressful."

"It's torture," she breathed, her eyes fluttering closed.

She felt his lips curve into a smile against the skin of her throat. "Could be that you might need stress relief on a regular basis then," he said as he kissed his way up the column of her neck.

Lauren dropped her head back. "I couldn't agree more," she said. "It's a good thing batteries are on sale at Target this week."

His head snapped up as he looked at her, and she burst out laughing as she hooked her hand behind his neck and pulled him down to her. "I love you," she said against his lips.

She felt him smile before he kissed her softly, and with a gentle shift of his hips, he reconnected their bodies.

"I love you too," he whispered. "Always have."

And when his mouth found hers again, slow and reverent in the darkness, there wasn't a doubt in her mind it was true.

Epilogue —
May 2015

"Hey, Mom. Happy Mother's Day!"

"Thank you, sweetheart," Lauren's mom said. "I just got your card. Daddy and I are still laughing."

Lauren smiled as she slid a little further beneath her comforter, shifting the phone to her other ear. "I cracked up in the middle of the store. In fact, I made such a scene that two people came over to pick the card from the shelf and read it themselves."

Lauren's mother laughed. "I'm putting it up on the fridge. Your brother will get a kick out of it later."

"Hey, Laur?" Michael called from just outside the bedroom door. "You want coffee?"

"Is that my son-in-law?" her mother asked.

"No, it's some random guy I picked up at the grocery store last night. He looked kind of cute, so I figured why not?"

"Very funny," her mother drawled, and Lauren laughed.

"Well, who else would it be?"

"Put him on," she said. "Daddy wants to get central air this summer, and he's set on doing it himself. I'm hoping I can get Michael to talk him out of it."

Lauren rolled her eyes. "Michael?" she called.

A second later, he popped his head into the bedroom. "Yeah?"

"My mom wants to talk to you so she can get you in the middle of an argument between her and my dad regarding central air installation."

He laughed as he walked farther into the room and reached for the phone she outstretched to him. "Hey, Ma," he said before he mouthed "*Coffee?*" to Lauren. She nodded and he smiled before saying, "I refuse to take sides before I hear all the facts."

Lauren smiled, and he winked at her before he left the room with the phone tucked between his shoulder and his ear.

She closed her eyes and reached her arms over her head as she pointed her toes, stretching her body before letting it fall limp with a contented sigh. Her eyes were still closed when she heard a tiny knock on the door, and she cracked one eye and lifted her head to see Erin standing in the doorway.

"Hey," Lauren said, pushing up on her elbows. "Good morning, sleepyhead."

Erin smiled and walked into the room. "I've been up for a while. I just didn't know if you were awake," she said as she climbed up onto the bed. "I have something for you."

"You do?" Lauren asked, sitting up, and Erin nodded, handing her a tiny folded square of pink tissue paper.

"How sweet of you," she said, genuinely touched by the gesture. "What did I do to deserve this?"

Erin shrugged sheepishly, and Lauren leaned over and ran her hand over the top of Erin's hair before unraveling the filmy paper. Neatly folded inside was a small crystal heart dangling from a thin black cord. Lauren held it up, and the pendant twirled from side to side, refracting little rainbows of light from the window.

"Do you like it?"

"It's beautiful! I love it," Lauren said, smiling at Erin before she held it up a little higher to admire it in the light. "In fact," she said, sitting up straight, "I'm going to put it on right now."

Erin watched with a smile as Lauren fastened it behind her neck. "How does it look?"

Erin reached into the neck of her T-shirt and pulled out the exact same necklace, holding it out for Lauren to see. "It's perfect. Now we match."

"Well, now I like it even more," Lauren said with a smile.

Erin grinned, but then her smile faltered as she looked down. "I have something else too."

"*Two* presents?" Lauren asked, surprised.

"Well, no. It's just this," Erin said, holding out a card in a lavender envelope. Lauren hadn't even noticed her holding it when she walked in.

The look on Erin's face had changed; the excitement from earlier had transformed into something that looked to Lauren almost like anxiety.

She couldn't help but feel somewhat apprehensive in response as she slid her finger beneath the edge of the envelope and pulled out the card.

On the front was a large sun overlooking a meadow full of flowers, and inside the sun was written:

Hundreds of stars in the pretty sky,
Hundreds of shells on the shore together,
Hundreds of birds that go singing by,

Hundreds of lambs in the sunny weather,
Hundreds of dewdrops to greet the dawn,
Hundreds of bees in the purple clover,
Hundreds of butterflies on the lawn,

Lauren opened the card and read the final line:
But only one mother the world-wide over.

She cupped her hand to her mouth as her eyes flooded with tears. Because underneath that, in her careful, rounded hand, Erin had written: *Can I call you Mom?*

Lauren looked up to see Erin watching her carefully. And when she dropped the card and held out her arms, Erin flew into them, wrapping her little arms around Lauren's body and squeezing.

"Of course you can," Lauren squeaked out, planting a kiss on top of her head. "Of course you can, sweetheart."

Erin laughed softly against her shoulder, and Lauren smiled as she closed her eyes, forcing the tears down her cheeks.

"Well, then, Happy Mother's Day," Erin whispered.

Lauren pressed her lips together as her chin trembled. "Thank you," she finally managed before she kissed her head again.

"*Erin,*" Michael called from the kitchen. "Get in here and clean up this mess!"

"Okay!" she called before she pulled back and smiled up at Lauren. Then she hopped off the bed and ran from the room.

Lauren looked down at the card on the bed, and she lifted it, reading it one more time as a fresh round of tears spilled from her eyes.

"So I think I managed to get out of that unscathed—"

Lauren looked up as Michael entered the room with two cups of coffee, his words cutting off when he saw her face.

"What happened?" he asked.

Lauren held up the card, and Michael pulled his brow together as he placed the mugs down on the dresser and crawled onto the bed, lying on his side next to her as he took the card from her.

She watched his expression soften as he read it, and then he slowly lifted his eyes to hers.

"You didn't know about this?" she asked.

Michael shook his head. "A few days ago, she asked for her allowance early. But it was when Mrs. Brigante was coming by to take her on one of their lunch dates. I just figured she wanted to try to pay." Michael trailed off, looking back down at the card before he lifted his eyes back to Lauren.

She smiled softly. "I said yes, by the way."

Michael placed the card on the bed as he scooted toward her, wrapping his arm around her lower back and pulling her further against him. He ran his hand softly over her cheek before he smiled. "Did you stare at her blankly for ten minutes before answering, like you did when I proposed?"

She smirked. "Of course not. It's only entertaining watching *you* squirm."

He grinned before he leaned in and kissed her softly. "Thank you."

"You don't have to thank me," Lauren said as she snuggled into his side. "You know how much I love her. I'm beyond honored."

Michael laid back with a sigh, blinking up at the ceiling as he intertwined their fingers. "You know, I never believed in the idea of maternal instincts."

Lauren lifted her chin and looked up at him, and he smiled down at her sadly. "I mean, between my mother, and Erin's mother," he looked back to the ceiling and shook his head. "I just thought that all the crap on television, the mom who bakes cookies with you and kisses your boo-boos, the one who is always there to talk about your problems...I just never believed it."

Michael turned his head and looked at her. "But watching you with her? I know it's a real thing now. Even before this," he said, holding up the card. "Even before the words. You were already an amazing mother to her." He leaned down and kissed her temple. "Now it's just official."

Lauren played with the end of his T-shirt. "You think I'm an amazing mom?" she asked softly.

"I really do," he answered without hesitation.

She chewed the side of her lip as she took their clasped hands and rested them on her lower abdomen. "Amazing enough to be the mother of two?"

For a second there was only silence. Then she felt him shift beside her, and she lifted her eyes to see him staring down at her.

"What does…are you…?" he fumbled.

Lauren sat up slowly. "I took the test this morning."

She kept her eyes carefully on him as he stared at her in shock.

And then a breathy laugh fell from his lips, and Lauren smiled.

He lunged forward, taking her face in his hands as he pulled her mouth to his. "Oh my God," he said between kisses. "Are you serious? You're not kidding, are you?"

Lauren laughed. "I'm not kidding."

He kissed her again before he pulled back, still looking at her in awe, and she laughed again.

Then he lowered his head and planted a soft kiss on her belly.

She smiled down at him as she laid back onto the pillows, and when he gently rested his head on her abdomen, she closed her eyes and brought her hand to his hair, running her fingers through it.

"So, do you think you're ready for this?"

"Without a doubt," he said softly.

"All of it?" she asked. "The swollen ankles, the mood swings, the middle-of-the-night trips to get me some impossible-to-find flavor of ice cream?"

He laughed softly. "I'll get you everything you could ever want. I promise."

And Lauren smiled, because lying there beside him, with his child growing in her belly, she already had it.

CPSIA information can be obtained
at www.ICGtesting.com
Printed in the USA
BVOW06s2234280118
506573BV00001B/53/P